Quiet Mafia
BOOK TWO

Quiet SECRETS

J.L. DRAKE

QUIET SECRETS

QUIET MAFIA SERIES

Cover Design by Spellbinding Design
Editing by Lori Whitwam
Formatting by RedDoor Author Services

Dedication

To my girls,
Elizabeth Clark, Jamie Johnson, Kim Kelchner, and Veronica Nelson for being there for me when I really needed you during this difficult year.

Pronunciation of Main Cast

Elio Capri
Ell-e-o Ca-pre

Sienna Giovanna
See-enna Gio-vanna

Francesco
Fran-cesco

Piero
P-ero

Mariano
Mari-ano

Niccola
Nee-cola

List of Main Cast

Capri Family
Piero - Don
Andrea
Elio – Underboss
Francesco – Consigliere
Niccola – Caporegime
Vinni – Caporegime
Donatello – Solider
Gain – Solider
Ernesto – Solider
Harris – Solider
Bosco – Uncle (brother to Piero)
Noemi – Aunt (married to Bosco)

DeSimone Family
Roberto DeSimone – Don
Bria DeSimone
Mariano DeSimone – Underboss

Sides
Wyatt Burn – Sienna's best friend
Gail Burn – Wyatt's sister
Aldo – Elio's trainer
Cara Di Vaio – Sicily house friend
Anna – Capri family friend
Aurora – Capri family friend
Georgio – Sienna's boss
Donte – Capri cook
Jacob Raine – NYC mobster

Chapter ONE

Certi segreti è meglio che restino tale

Elio

"Drop your guns!" Francesco yelled. "Stop!"

Nothing registered as I pulled back the hammer and my finger twitched on the trigger. I kept it pointed at the man holding Sienna. A dark storm swarmed my head and filtered out all rational thoughts.

"For the love of God, stop!" Francesco was now in my face, and I struggled to see around him. "Elio, put the gun down."

"Why?" I shouted, annoyed he was interfering. "Get out of my way!"

"Elio," he pleaded as he studied my face. When he

realized I wasn't going to lower my gun first, he whirled around and faced the woman. "Elenora, lower your gun."

"Him first!"

"I didn't start this," I shouted, not moving my eyes off Sienna's terrified expression. She was mouthing something, but I couldn't follow.

"Don't test him, Elenora. You have no idea what he'll do for her," Francesco pleaded.

"Let me go!" Sienna tried to rip her arm out of the man's hold, but he yanked her back, and she fell to her knees with a cry. "Elio, stop." Her scream burst through my murderous state. "She's my mother."

Mother? What the hell is happening here?

My gun wavered slightly, and the man holding her pulled her around behind him. To what, shield her from me?

A cloak of red filled my vision, and I blinked back my rage. Sounds came and went in waves while my head calculated the wind speed versus my bullet finding its way into the main artery running through his neck.

"Stop!" The desperation in Francesco's voice as he held his arms out straight between us began to seep into my consciousness, but I was a hair of a second from staining the road with blood. "Hey," he directed his attention to the man who held Sienna, "let her go, or I can promise you he will drill a bullet into your head."

He's right. I will.

The man looked at Elenora for direction.

"Sienna, do you know them?" Elenora snapped.

"Yes!" Sienna tried to find her footing.

After a moment's hesitation, Elenora gave him a nod to let go. Sienna shoved his shoulders, making him step backward on the uneven ground.

"Get off me!" She raced over to me and flung herself into my arms. I wrapped my free hand around her back and held her close, but kept my gun pointed at him.

"What did you do?" Elenora glared at Francesco, but she lowered her weapon and ordered her men to do the same.

"What I had to." He looked back at us, and I could see the pain of whatever was happening wash over his face. "Elio, this is Sienna's mother."

"Hey," Sienna put her hand on my arm, "it's true, she is. Please stop."

I tried to make sense of what was happening. My brain seemed to be struggling with just how we got to guns being pulled, and Francesco suddenly being here, and knowing Sienna's mother.

I waited a beat more, then lowered my weapon with a growl. It took all my strength not to pull the trigger. I never lowered my weapon until I knew the entirety of any situation, but when Sienna was involved, I broke all my rules.

"Oh, thank God." Francesco heaved forward, resting his hands on his knees.

"What the hell is happening here?" I barked at everyone.

"We need to talk," Francesco, my father's loyal *consigliere* and second father to me, said quietly, "but not here in the open."

"I'm not leaving." Sienna madly brushed her tears away. "I've waited a long time for this."

"And I understand that," Francesco moved closer to her so he could lower his voice, "but not here, not like this. We need to get somewhere private, not here on the side of the road. Remember everything else that's going on right now."

She blinked and studied him, knowing he was right, then stepped around to address our visitors. "Will you come and talk?" Elenora gave a nod. "No guns." Elenora nodded again.

"All right." Sienna turned her gaze to me, and I took a moment before I finally nodded. "All right," she repeated and turned to take my arm. We walked back to my car. It was still running and was parked in the middle of the road. Her hand shook as she gripped her purse, no doubt reeling from what the hell just happened.

"Vinni, take Wyatt with you," I ordered over my shoulder for him to take Sienna's best friend, who still seemed to be stuck in a trance.

"Yeah, boss."

"Are you okay, Sienna?" She nodded but didn't speak. "Don't check out on me." I kissed the top of her head. "I have a feeling another storm is about to hit us." I opened the car door and helped her inside.

Francesco came up next to me.

"What the hell is going on here?" My rage still idled at the surface, ready to blow at any moment.

"Let's take this to your uncle's." He glanced over at Elenora, who was getting into her car. "Mariano is at the

Hill HHHouse."

"Are you insane?" My jaw nearly dropped to the ground.

"Trust me on this."

Normally, I wouldn't ever question Francesco, but taking strangers to my uncle's home to hold an unplanned meeting was just not how we operated. Especially without background checks on any of them.

I cleared my throat and rubbed my jaw as I stepped closer to him and spoke quietly. "I have always trusted you, my friend, but this makes me very nervous."

"I know." His eyes pleaded with mine.

"Fine." I nodded once, unsure what else to say to him at this point. The whiplash from the last fifteen minutes had done a number on my head.

I eased behind the wheel and left Sienna to her thoughts while I slipped into a memory of my own.

"Ah!" I sent the ceramic sculpture across the room, bursting into a billion pieces as it hit the marble floor.

"Elio!" Aunt Noemi came racing in the room with her hands on her mouth. I saw my Nonna in the doorway behind her saying a silent prayer and grasping her rosary beads.

"It's okay, Mama." Niccola directed her out of the room before turning to face me.

A fierce storm whirled inside my chest. My heart fought to contain itself as hot blood coursed through it like the blast from a stick of dynamite.

"Cousin," Niccola stepped further into the room, "I know you're suffering, and I won't even pretend to know

what you're going through, but this isn't good for you. Your heart can only take so much."

"I know that!" I shouted and whirled to face him. My fingers itched with the need to hurt someone as my anger raged. "I know my heart can't take it." I used my fist to bang on my chest, and tears stung my eyes, "I know this isn't good for me. I never asked for any of this!"

"You didn't, but sometimes it's just not in the stars."

"What about the moon?" I shouted louder. "What about the gods? Do they have no sympathy for love? No sympathy for the souls that walk this Earth?"

"Niccola." Francesco had appeared and motioned for my cousin to leave. He approached my Nonna, who still stood near the door, and assured her everything would be all right. He quietly closed the door and turned to me.

"No." I held up my hand, not needing anyone else inside my head. I breathed heavily and tugged at the top button of my dress shirt, needing more air. There wasn't any.

I kept picturing what her face must have looked like when she discovered the house was empty and we had left her.

"Son," he stood in place, knowing better than to approach me, "what happened that has you this upset?"

The room tilted, and I felt a sharp hit to the stomach as my anger surged again.

"Ah!" I swept the glass knickknacks off the table next to me. The sound was deafening. "I left her with those wolves! I left the only person I truly loved behind

because I didn't want to subject her to this life. What's so bad about this life?"

"You were being selfless, Elio. It was noble of you."

"Noble?" I gripped the edge of the table. I needed something to hang on to before I caved inward. "Tell me something, Francesco. Is it noble to knowingly rip the heart from the one you love and then leave her all alone to pick up the pieces, without even an explanation?"

"Love is a tricky thing."

"Love is the root of all pain." I felt my expression darken as I looked over at him, exposing my soul. "It embeds itself in you and lays dormant like cancer, and when you think everything is wonderful and just how it should be, it squeezes its tentacles around your heart and lets you bleed out a slow, miserable death."

I closed my eyes and gave in to the anger, letting it smother me in a toxic cloud.

"What can I do for you, Elio?"

"Go get her for me," I whispered.

"You know I can't do that."

"Can't or won't?" I slowly opened my eyes to see a pained expression on his face.

"The last I heard, she left the Di Vaio house, but then I lost track of her after a few days. I'm not sure if she went back or not."

I stood at his news, shocked that he had not told me this yet.

"So, she could still be there?" I marched toward the door, but he stepped in my way and placed a hand on my shoulder.

"Leave if you must, Elio, but maybe get some rest and wait until morning. Take a breath and search your heart again. You made the decision against having her live in this kind of family, remember? Yes, we love all of those around us, but we also shed blood and take lives. All I ask is that you really think, once again, about what's best for her. Your father just survived a hit. Who is next? It isn't safe for any of us right now."

I shifted my jacket on my hot skin and headed for the door. He was right. I should take the night to think.

With a glass of scotch in my hand, I sat in the dark in my new home just below my parents' Hill House. The place still smelled of fresh paint. No matter how many times I went back and forth, I knew I couldn't walk this Earth without Sienna by my side.

By six a.m. I had my bag packed and a flight to Sicily booked for nine. I tossed my belongings in the back of my car, and as I went to ease behind the wheel, I spotted a square envelope tucked under the windshield wiper. Plucking the contents free, I found a photo printed on a piece of card stock of Sienna in the city. The photo looked to be taken from a bit of a distance. The words at the bottom had my hand on my weapon while I scanned the property's perimeter.

"If you go after her, we'll kill her before you can ever reach her."

At that moment, Francesco arrived and caught wind of my mood.

"What is it?"

I handed him the photo and watched his facial cues

to see if he knew anything about it.

"I'll make some calls." He pulled his phone out, and I sank to the hood of my car while a sick realization hit me. She could get hurt because of me.

When we parked at my uncle's, I shook my head to clear the memory and focus on the now. I glanced over at Sienna, who looked more annoyed than anything. Her fists had her skirt bunched up between her white knuckles.

"Hey," I turned to face her and gently broke her hold on the fabric of her suffering skirt and twisted her to look at me, "whatever is going through your head right now, stop your thoughts. Don't go there, at least until we know more, okay?"

She swallowed and took a deep breath and seemed to shake herself out of it. "I'm okay." She flexed her fingers. "I'm just trying to follow what happened back there."

"Me too." I kissed her freezing hands and looked out the windshield at the greenery that covered about half of the stone manor in front of us. "Let's go inside and wait for the others."

"Okay." She reached for the doorhandle.

Buttoning my jacket, I held out my hand and took hers, then we started up the huge marble staircase. I didn't have to worry about hiding who we were to each other here; this was our safe place. A place to conduct business. Anyone who might be a threat to us wouldn't be leaving the property in one piece, anyway.

"Where are we?" She eyed the electric fences and the

giant maze I had recently used with Stefano Coppola's men. That reminded me, I should pay my new informant, Samuele, a visit soon.

"A place of business," was all I offered.

She raised a skeptical eyebrow but didn't press the issue.

"Elio," my aunt caught us in the doorway, "what are you doing here?"

"Aunt Noemi, this is Sienna Giovanna, a friend of mine." My aunt glanced quickly at me. I could see she was wondering if Sienna really was just a friend, or perhaps something more. The mere fact that I had brought her here would have raised her curiosity. I just smiled warmly and let the topic be.

"It's lovely to meet you." She held out her hand and welcomed Sienna to the house. My aunt had never met Sienna and knew nothing about our past. I tended to be very private, and I knew Aunt Noemi would welcome anyone I brought to meet her with open arms. If only because it didn't happen often.

"We're meeting some people here."

"Oh? I didn't get a call." That would be strange to her; we always called in our visits. My Nonna, Greta, lived here full-time, and my aunt and uncle would often come and go between our two properties. It was our number one rule to call ahead. I filled her in as best as I could as we drew further inside.

"Will Vinni be joining you?" She motioned for us to follow her out to the patio as she asked about her youngest son. I loved it here. The view over the stables and their vineyard went on for miles. Turned out, funneling money through wineries was easier than we expected. We now owned six.

"Yes, he should be arriving any moment."

"Good, I need to speak with him." She handed Sienna a bubbly water, and I shook my head, opting for a plain bottle of water instead. "So," she took a seat across from us, "do you ride, Sienna? We have a stable just over there."

"I have, a bit. Yes."

"Wonderful. Maybe we could ride sometime."

"I'd like that."

My aunt smiled at me. She seemed excited to find someone who was interested in riding too. "Tell me more about yourself, Sienna."

Sienna blinked a few times and cleared her throat, looking up at me for help.

"Aunt Noemi." I pointed to the door, thankful Vinni had just walked in at the perfect time.

Vinni looked fit to kill, with Wyatt trailing behind him, his face as white as a ghost. As soon as Wyatt spotted Sienna, he rushed to her side and began to sputter an apology. She just nodded at him and stroked his arm.

"Haven't they arrived yet?" Vinni looked around.

"Not yet."

"What the hell?" Vinni pulled out his phone, and I did the same. I dialed Francesco.

"I'm here." Francesco rushed inside holding up his ringing phone. Sienna jumped to her feet. "Just," he held up his hands as we both took a step forward, "give me a second to take a breath."

"Where are they?" I looked past him, not liking the idea of them being unsupervised in the house.

"They're not coming."

"What?" Sienna called out at the same time Vinni did.

"They're not comfortable meeting here." Francesco shrugged.

I squinted at him, catching his lie. I knew his every expression.

"A word?" I motioned for him to follow me into the hallway, out of earshot of the others.

"So, coming here was just a way for you to be alone with her and to draw us away from them?" He closed his eyes for a moment, and I knew I was right. "You've known me since I was born, and yet you lie to my face."

We both turned our attention to the girl we had saved from the dockyard. She mindlessly roamed from room to room. She reminded me of one of those vacuum robots that bumped into pieces of furniture or walls with no real purpose but to move the dust around. I needed to figure out what to do with her. I shook my head and got my thoughts back on track.

"Elio," he placed a hand on my shoulder, "there's much that needs to be revealed, but it has to be done delicately. The time was not right then, nor is it now."

"You can't expect Sienna to accept that. She just met her mother after years of searching for her, and her reunion was met with guns drawn and hateful words spoken."

"I know." He closed his eyes as though my words hurt him. "I'm not expecting her to."

"Where are they now?"

"Staying at a hotel."

"All right, now what?" I tossed my hands in the air.

"Elenora wants to meet with Sienna, alone."

"No way." *He must be out of his mind.* "Over my dead body."

"Elio, I promise you she'll be fine."

"How?" I nearly shouted but stopped myself. "How do you even know her mother?"

He covered his mouth and let out a long sigh, and I knew I wasn't going to like the answer.

"That's a long story, and there are many layers to it."

"Meaning?" I was getting tired of these cryptic conversations.

"Meaning this whole thing has roots that date back well beyond your years, that can *and* will affect us all if not treated carefully. I can't just come out with it. It's as if Pandora's Box is about to explode and reveal all its secrets at once. Secrets as important as these need to be revealed in a much more controlled setting. Elio, please, I beg you to be patient and trust me."

I cursed and paced, unsure how to navigate something so obviously big without knowing what the hell it was all about. I was used to being in control, but I was out of my depth.

"So, what am I supposed to do? Let you take her there?"

"Yes."

"No." My jaw nearly hit the ground with what he was asking of me. "I won't allow it."

"There's no other choice here. Elenora won't step foot on Capri land!" he shouted. "You must let Sienna go to her, because once this unravels, Elio, you better hang on because it's going to get messy."

A sound sent both of us spinning around to find Sienna staring at us. Her face looked white, but her stance told me she was not going to back down.

"Which hotel?"

Dammit.

"No." I shook my head.

She looked from me to Francesco. "What hotel?"

"Il Giglio."

"Will you take me?" She tugged on the bag that hung from her shoulder.

"Yes."

She gave a tight nod before addressing my fuming anger.

"Piero trusts Francesco, you trust him, and so do I." Her voice was barely a whisper. "I don't know what's going on here, but if going there alone is how I will get some answers on my past, then so be it."

"Not without me, you're not."

She reached up and placed her hand on my chest but paused when the sound of clinking stones reached our ears. It was a very familiar sound to me, so I shook my head and waved at her to continue.

"Elio," she went on, "I've faced a lot of things without you. I can handle this." She waited a beat before she let her hand slip away then headed down the hallway.

When the door closed, I took a deep breath and felt him behind me.

"We're not really letting her go there without us, right?" Vinni half laughed.

"Of course not." I motioned for him to get Wyatt, and we headed out.

TWO

Sienna

Francesco parked the car but didn't move when I started to get out. He hadn't spoken one word the entire drive. He just kept checking the rearview mirror, which put me even more on edge.

"Are you coming?"

"Sienna," his hands squeaked as they ran over the leather steering wheel, "whatever happens from here on, I need you to know one thing."

"Okay." My hand fell away from the doorhandle.

He turned, and his haunted look said volumes about what might be ahead.

"I need you to know you can trust me."

"I do know that."

"No," he shook his head and reached for my hand, "you're going to hear a lot of things, and you're going to be led down many paths, but no matter what, you must remember that I will be the one person you can always trust to tell you the truth."

I pressed my lips together as a cold prickle shot up my spine and made my scalp tingle. A hundred questions blew through my mind at that moment, but one lingered there the longest. "Do you know my mother?" Clearly, he did. He had known her name, but then everything had happened so quickly. I wasn't exactly sure of anything.

His gaze fell, but he quickly recovered, and he swallowed hard.

"Yes."

"Wow." A strangled laugh choked out of me, more from shock than anything else. "Well, tell me this. Did you always know she was my mother?"

"Yes."

"Right," I whispered, once again feeling like I was caught in an alternate universe. How…how could he keep this from me? How had he let me go all those years without so much as a whisper of the truth?

"Sienna—"

"Trust you?" I pushed open the door and didn't look back. An icy chill spread through my veins as I took the steps to the Il Giglio hotel. I made a beeline for the lobby and saw the men who had been with my mother earlier. Oscar, who looked to be around my mother's age, and the one who had manhandled me stepped forward and blocked my path.

"Ms. Sienna, Elenora would like you to join her in the dining room." He stepped aside to let me pass, but at the last second, he blocked it again. "My apologies for earlier. Sometimes I forget my own strength."

I glanced up at him and saw his eyes had softened, so I gave him a little nod and waited for him to move again. I wanted to lash out and put him in his place, but I was in uncharted territory here, and I knew I would need to stay calm. No matter how hard it was.

To my surprise, the dining room was empty. The staff was serving Elenora while the rest of her men were standing guard. She sat perfectly straight, ankles crossed, with only her wrist resting on the table. Large windows lined the balcony which overlooked the gardens and driveway below. Soft music played, and some pretty, pink flowers popped against the stone interior. When she spotted me, she gracefully rose and pointed to a seat across from her.

"Thank you for coming." She moved as though to hug me but hesitated, then decided against it. "Please take a seat. I took the liberty of ordering you something. I hope you enjoy fresh pineapple and oranges."

I ignored the food that was placed in front of me and kept my purse on my lap for something to hold on to. I studied her features and mannerisms, trying to catch things we might have in common. She sat, adjusted her linen napkin, and began to eat as if we met up every Sunday for brunch. No hurry to jump in and explain where she had been my entire life.

"You remind me a lot of my mother," she finally

said, dabbing gently at the corners of her mouth, "the way you watch me and observe those around you." When I didn't comment, she went on. "It's a good trait. It's important to be aware, especially with the company you're surrounding yourself with."

"Don't," I warned, feeling my back go up. "No one will speak badly of the Capri family in front of me."

"We will be circling back to that later." She once again ignored my tone. "But first I have some questions for you, as I'm sure you do for me."

"Just a few." I found it hard to curb my sarcasm. She glanced over at me and pushed her plate away, waving at the waitress to remove it. Her deep navy-blue eyes stared into mine, and I pushed down the hurt. This was not how this was supposed to go. We were supposed to hug and cry and say a billion and one things at the same time. *I can't believe you're here* and *I can't believe we're hugging*. Not this cold reunion where apparently many secrets lay just under the surface.

"When did you first meet Francesco?" I jumped in, wanting some kind of control of the situation.

"A long time ago." She glanced over at Francesco, who stood in the doorway, then brought her eyes back to me. "How was your life growing up?"

"Seriously?" I scrunched up my face, disgusted with her question.

"Yes, seriously. I'm trying to understand how on God's green Earth you got tangled up with the Capri syndicate."

"Let me get this straight." I stood, tipping my chair

backward. "You abandoned me when I was young. You left me with a stranger, who later dropped me off at another stranger's house to live. I grew up being physically abused and emotionally wrecked. I ended up on the streets and somehow managed to survive it all to get where I am today, and all that you want to know is how I got tangled up with the Capri family?"

"Sienna," she took a long breath then tossed her napkin on the table and stood, "as overwhelming as this is for you, it is for me too. I apologize for my lack of warmth and empathy. I tend to hide it at the worst of times. Leaving you was the hardest and worst decision of my life, but I had to do it. Though I thought things were going to turn out differently, they didn't, and I'm still trying to understand it all. Please," she pointed to the chair that was upright again, thanks to Oscar, "take a seat, and let's try this again."

Francesco had moved a bit farther into the room when I overturned my chair. He gave me a pleading look to do as she said. I eased down into the seat and nodded for her to begin.

"Let's start slow and work our way to the bigger questions as we get to know one another." She poured some ice water into a glass that held cucumber slices. "I read in the article that you're a journalist. What led you into that profession?"

"You," I answered simply. "I figured I could find you if I dug hard enough. I needed a job that would let me do that."

"I didn't want to be found."

"Apparently." I couldn't help but feel a sting from her answer.

"There were reasons for it."

"I bet." I sipped some water. "Why do you need an entourage of men?" I swept my hand about to indicate the obvious muscle around her.

"Protection."

"From whom?"

"From the ones who want to hurt me." She leaned back and motioned for one of them to come over. "However, Ugo here is your first cousin."

I blinked up at the man who looked nothing like me, and more like Elio, and tried to digest that I did have family.

"Nice to meet you, Ugo," I said softly.

"You as well."

"Can you tell me a little about—"

"Back to your post." Elenora cut me off as her curt voice directed Ugo. Taken back, I threw her a look. "We'll get there," she said as she turned back to me, her voice lowered.

Well, that was a warm way to discover my cousin.

"Do I have any other family?"

"A little, yes."

"Are any of them on my father's side?"

"Yes, there are some there, too. Where are you living now?"

"Somewhere safe." I kept my answers as vague as she did. After all, why should I give her any detail when she was the one who held all the cards? "Why now, why here?" I blurted, feeling drained with the dance we were in. At this rate, I realized I might have to take notes in a journal just to remember the tiny bits of information she was giving me.

"Because of this." She pulled a copy of *Fab Magazine* out of her purse and dropped it in front of her. "Why did you do it?"

"It's the same answer as why I chose the profession I did—to find you." I shrugged, not understanding what she wasn't getting. "I did it in hopes that after all these years, it might lead you to me. And it did."

"It also will lead others to you." Her face morphed into a serious expression.

"Others?"

"I left you because our lives were in danger, and we still are in danger, Sienna."

"I guess I missed the family newsletter, because this is the first I've heard of this." I folded my arms, mad as hell that, for the second time in my life, I was being told that someone may want to hurt me. What did I ever do to make all these people angry with me?

"Why didn't you stay in Sicily?" She changed direction again.

"Because I was done with that chapter of my life and deserved a new one."

"Why are you with the Capri family?"

She was relentless, and it was growing old. I threaded my purse over my arm and slowly stood. I watched as her body language showed her annoyance that I wasn't staying put.

"You haven't earned the right to ask that question yet, Elenora." I wanted to be able to call her Mama, but the hurt that she was causing me was too much. "And in case you weren't aware, your old friend Francesco is the *consigliere* of the Capri syndicate." With that, I left, hurrying out into the lobby where I came face to face with Elio and Vinni. Elio reached for me as Oscar and another man caught up to me.

"Ms. Sienna, you must stay." But as he reached for my arm, Elio blocked it.

"Today was the one and only time you will ever touch her," Elio growled, and his stance made him appear to grow to almost double his normal size.

"If she has questions," I stepped in and spoke directly to Oscar, "she can ask Francesco."

"Sienna," Elenora called as she approached us. She glared at Elio, which only fueled my fire more. "I think that's enough for today, but I want you to meet me here tomorrow, after we've cooled off. We need to talk more. Please, we must try this again."

I thought for a moment, fighting my need to lash out at her. I had waited too damn long for answers. I wasn't about to brush off this opportunity, but now it would be on my terms.

"All right."

"Good, meet me here—"

"No," I shook my head and heard Elio shift, "if we are doing this again, it's my way. You had your chance." I folded my arms and raised my chin to show I was serious.

"Where?" She didn't argue.

"My parents' place," Elio said over my head, "Hill House, The Sunflowers Fields Vineyard, five p.m. Take the south entrance. It will lead you to where we'll be."

"Don't," Elenora stuck a finger in his face, "get in my way."

"Enough." I stepped forward. "If you want to meet me, that's where you'll find me. But let me be very clear here." I moved closer. "If you want any kind of relationship, you better drop the twenty questions act and start looking at me like the daughter you left behind."

"Fair enough." Her eyes softened when she finally looked at me. "I'll be there at five." She turned on her heel, and her men followed her.

"You okay?" Elio's hands fell to my shoulders.

"No," I headed for the door, making his hands fall away, more annoyed than when I arrived, "not even close."

Chapter
THREE

Elenora

My fingers curled around the railing of the balcony as I watched them head to their cars.

"Madam." Oscar handed me a cup of tea before leaving me alone with Francesco. I stirred the sugar cube in a figure eight with the tiny silver spoon and narrowed in on my daughter as she slipped inside the front seat of Piero's son's car.

"Who is he to her?"

Francesco moved into my view and took out his phone to decline a call.

"I asked you a question, Cesco."

Francesco's jaw flexed as he looked at me. I couldn't see his eyes behind his sunglasses, but I could tell my showing up unannounced had been a shock to him. "He's her friend."

"You promised—"

"And you promised me, too." He looked back to the car as it disappeared down the hillside. "I think it's safe to say a lot has happened, and a lot didn't go as planned."

"He's reckless," I snapped. "Let's not forget what he got into when he was younger."

"He needed an outlet. There was nothing wrong with what he was doing."

"It was illegal."

Francesco chuckled darkly as he rubbed his face. "Right, because what we both do isn't?" He shook his head. "Besides, having allies in different countries is smart."

"Right," I scoffed, wondering how a gang could possibly be an asset to an Italian mafia syndicate.

I turned away, feeling a wave of emotion wash over me. I was used to dismissing the pain of leaving my child to fend for herself all these years, because it was the only choice I had. However, the strain of the day and how it had unfolded had left me exhausted. Francesco's hand fell on my shoulder, and I flinched at his touch.

I closed my eyes, hating what I'd become, cold and unattached. "I wanted this day to go differently, but when I saw a younger version of Piero look at my daughter the way he did, I let my own issues cloud my judgement."

"Elio is a good man, in spite of what you believe." He leaned against the railing and folded his arms. "You don't get to judge someone you don't know, Elenora."

My armor shot straight back up. Slowly, I leaned back to use the chair for support as the words leapt from my lips. "How long has my daughter known Elio Capri?"

"Here's how this will work, Elenora." He pushed off the railing, and as he towered over me, my men immediately tensed. I had to hold up a hand to stop them. "When I feel you're ready for the answers, I will give them to you."

"How is that fair?"

"Nothing about this has been fair." A moment later, he was gone, leaving me to gnaw on his words.

Elio

The pipe above me dripped steadily, forming a muddy puddle by my feet. Rainwater rushed through the grooves of the cobblestone street where I huddled in the protective covering of the alcove. My fingers were still stained with blood from a necessary morning kill, and I noticed little drops of bleach had left their marks on my leather shoes. I grimaced at that, but it reminded me of my small victory. We had a long road to take down the Coppola syndicate, and every death meant we were that much closer to ruling Italy all on our own.

I waited impatiently for Samuele, my informant, to meet me. Both Vinni and Niccola were watching from a safe distance in case he decided to bring company. I checked the time. He was fifteen minutes late, and my anger grew with each passing minute.

We couldn't afford to lose much more time chasing down where Val was being held. My head still hurt at the thought that Antonio, her uncle, had once been loyal. He was a part of the syndicate. The day he admitted to me that he had flipped on our family because Stefano had taken his niece, I knew the chances of getting her back were slim to none.

Heavy footsteps drew my attention across the street to a window, and I spotted him coming toward me. We had arranged to meet one street over, but because I didn't trust him, I choose to intercept.

"Whoa!" he shouted as I grabbed him by the jacket and pushed him up against the wall with my arm to his throat. Samuele's eyes were just as fearful as they were on that day in the maze when I had given him two options. Continue to live as a Coppola soldier and be my informant inside Stefano's organization…or die.

"You're late!"

"Our meeting ran late." He tried to shove me off, but I outweighed him by fifty pounds.

"What did you find out?" I stepped closer, daring him to lie to me, then stepped back and brought my phone to my ear. "Vin," I said quickly and hung up. A little red laser beam appeared on Samuele's chest, and he jumped and tried to tuck himself farther into the alcove. "Samuele," I held my hand up to tell Vinni to back off, "I don't have much more time or patience for you. Tell me what I want to know or…" I let my words trail off.

"Shit." He rubbed his head madly, knowing there was no way out. "Fine! She hasn't been sent out of Tuscany yet—"

"Why is she still being held here?" I had assumed she would be shipped off fairly quickly.

"Stefano knows you'll come looking for her, so he's using her as bait to lure you out."

"Where are they holding her?"

"At the Grand Hotel, where we're all staying."

"How many men?"

He hesitated, but when I went to make a move, he sputtered. "Stefano is like you. He appears to be alone, but there are always several watching."

I loathed that he compared Stefano to me, but I wouldn't give him the satisfaction of knowing it bothered me.

"When is the next shipment of girls going out?"

"There isn't one yet." He held up a hand when I started to attack him for lying. "Stefano's changed. Like a shift in his mood, almost like something is preoccupying him."

"What is so big that would stop him from doing his shipments?"

"Probably it's from above."

"Meaning?"

"Stefano isn't the one pulling *all* the strings."

My phone rang. "Yeah?"

"You've got company, two guys." Niccola spoke fast. "Head south. We'll meet you at the food vendor at the end of the street."

I tossed my hood over my head and said, "Wait for my call."

"We're done here. I won't do this again!"

I pointed my gun at his temple then wrapped a hand around his neck, squeezing his vocal cords.

"I wonder how your wife will feel when your oldest son doesn't come home from his next soccer practice. Or when your youngest mysteriously vanishes on her way to school. Or, God forbid, something goes tragically wrong when your sister undergoes her surgery next month."

"Don't you—"

I held a pamphlet to his daughter's private school and watched his pupils contract.

"If you want your family to live, you'll come when you're called and do as I say." I removed his gun from his belt and shoved it in his hand, pushing the barrel toward his mouth.

"I'm not part of any trafficking." He shook. "I never even knew about it, until they took Val!" He paused and blinked a few times. "They're going to kill her." His hands wrapped around the cold steel of his gun. "If not Stefano, someone above him will."

Don't react. Another reference to someone above Stefano? Who could be above Stefano?

My phone rang again, and I knew my time was up. I stepped out into the pouring rain, and just as I rounded the corner, I heard a gunshot.

Without breaking stride, I wove my way through the dinner rush on the street, through the kitchen of a family friend and out the back door where I slipped into the waiting car. Niccola checked his mirror to ensure no one was following us.

"Well?" Niccola asked as he studied my face. I closed my eyes for a moment as I digested what I had heard.

"Something either spooked Stefano or he's preoccupied with something else, because he isn't sending out a shipment of girls right now. Val is being held at the Grand Hotel, so, Vinni, get your people on that."

"Sure thing." He nodded as he turned up the street, beeping at some cattle that had moved onto the road.

"He did say someone else might be pulling the strings."

Niccola glanced at me, confused. Stefano was the head of the Coppola syndicate, so no one else should be calling the shots. "Could it be his *consigliere*?"

"I don't think so, and I can't beat it out of our informant because he just killed himself."

"No, he didn't." He handed me his phone to show a video he had taken. The two men I was warned were coming my way could be seen. One shot him in the head, then they tossed his body in the back of an unmarked truck.

"What are the chances he was fed true information before he came to you?"

"Only one way to find out." I nodded at Vinni to get eyes on Stefano's hotel.

I removed my jacket and spent the twenty-minute car ride home mulling any and all possibilities on how to get Val back and wondering just what the hell Stefano was up to.

Vinni handed me an umbrella, and I raced up the steps of my parents' house and hurried inside. Mama was the first to greet me with a worried expression.

Immediately, I knew something was up. "What's wrong?"

She pointed over her shoulder and whispered, "There's only so much a person can take in one day, and I think she might be maxed out."

I hung my coat up and followed the voices then peered around the corner and spotted Mariano and his mother with Sienna, who looked more than finished. As I moved farther down the hallway, I spotted Wyatt hunched over the bar in the back, looking fit to kill. When he spotted me, his face dropped in relief as I joined him at the bar.

"Everything okay?" I asked quietly as I loosened my tie with one hand and poured a stiff drink with the other. They still hadn't spotted me, so I took the opportunity to eavesdrop.

"Mariano is trying to convince her to spend the night out with him." His gaze moved to my bloodstained hands.

"That won't be happening," I muttered as I sipped my drink and held the bottle up to him, but he shook his head. I took that opportunity to wash my hands clean in the bar sink.

"Yeah, well, they've had her pinned here for over an hour and haven't once listened to her protest about being busy with work. Even your mother came to her rescue, but…" He shook his head, exhausted. "Not to mention that he dragged her all over town while he did errands because he said he wanted to spend time with her. She might actually kill the guy, Elio."

"I wouldn't be opposed to it." I smirked. I stood and casually began to walk toward them with a hand in my pocket. It wasn't the first time I'd been in a room with a bunch of snakes, and it surely wouldn't be the last.

"Good evening, Elio," Bria greeted me in the fake way she always did. We never spoke much. Not since I peeled her from my bed, years back, after she came into my room looking to cheat on her husband. I thought she was a gold-digging tramp, and she thought I was too much like my father, loyal.

"Bria." I nodded then glanced at Mariano, who now had his hand wrapped around Sienna's wrist as he tugged her up from the chair.

"Sienna, a package arrived from your boss. Mama has it in the kitchen for you." I offered the escape.

"Thank you." She started to pull away from Mariano, but he moved with her.

"Mariano," I called after him, "a word."

He cut his eyes at me with a heavy sigh, and I barely contained my patience. It was wearing dangerously thin with his disrespect toward me. Not to mention he wanted what was mine.

Once Bria disappeared out back and I knew my mother had Sienna elsewhere, I relaxed.

"I want you to spend the next few days at the docks."

He started to speak, but I lifted my hand in a warning and made a further effort to throw him off. "I need a person I know I can trust to watch over our men."

"Why can't Vinni or Niccola do it?"

I leaned into him and lowered my voice. "I got word that Stefano's been spending a lot of time downtown, so I sent them there. We need to watch to see what he's up to." I caught his eyebrows crease for a quick moment before he subconsciously snapped the rubber band on his wrist. My teeth ground together as murderous thoughts clouded my judgement. I still couldn't believe this man I once thought was my best friend was involved with Stefano and trafficking girls through my dockyard. "It's only a few nights until I can figure out what happened to the cameras, why they keep flickering on and off." My hands in my pocket fisted tightly, and the urge to slam him into the wall and watch the blood trickle from his nose from the impact was consuming.

"All right." He dropped his hand heavily and disappeared out back, no doubt to complain to his mother.

Something caught my eye. It was my father in the doorway. He nodded for me to follow him. We entered his office where we would be out of the DeSimones' hearing range. Francesco was there ahead of us. Papa sat and waved at me to join them. Then he turned to Francesco.

"I've known you since we were in college, and up until today I've always thought we knew everything about one another, but it seems I was wrong about that. I understand that we're grown men and are entitled to our own lives, but when it directly affects my family, I have the right to know what's happening."

"Of course, you're right." Francesco nodded and settled back in the chair, his eyes closed as if collecting his thoughts.

"I've known Elenora since I was nineteen." He stopped speaking.

"Is that it?" I hated all the vague answers we seemed to be getting. "You've known her for years. So, she and her, what, *mini syndicate,*" I tossed my hands in the air, "are heading this way tomorrow morning, crossing into our homeland, to this very house, and we know nothing about her. What if they are working with the DeSimones?" I had no idea why she surrounded herself with a group of men. She wasn't part of any syndicate, nor was she some famous person. Maybe she came from money or imagined herself in danger, but still her little entourage was eye-roll worthy.

"She's not."

"How do you know?"

"Because I do."

"Oh, well, there you go," I shook my head at my father, "she's been vetted."

"I get this is unexpected and confusing." Francesco tried to reason. "Trust me, I had no clue this was coming now, but it is, so let's navigate this correctly."

"How do we navigate? We are blind here. Unlike you, we know nothing," I threw back at him.

"But I know enough, so please, you have always trusted me, as I have you. We are family. If the two of you would take my word that they are fine to come here, it would be better for all of us. This must stay within our protection."

"How is Sienna doing?" my father asked me. I knew he trusted Francesco with his life, as did I, so the argument was over, and we needed to let things play out.

"I don't know." I sank onto the couch, hating the timing of this new catastrophe. "Confused and hurt, I guess. Mariano sure isn't making things easy. I'm sending him to the dockyard, so we can keep him in a contained area. I don't want him here when they arrive tomorrow."

"Smart." My father nodded as he thought, then glanced at Francesco. "Elio, could you please give us a few minutes?"

"Yeah," I huffed, feeling all mixed up inside. As I closed the door, I heard my father's chair creak as it did when he leaned, then Francesco's voice.

"All right, so, here's what's going on."

It didn't bother me that I wasn't in the room. I knew my father would steer the family correctly with whatever Francesco shared.

FIVE

Sienna

Andrea handed me two aspirins and a tall glass of lemon water before joining me on the porch chairs. We both sat and looked out over the gorgeous winery. The rain had cleared up, and the sun was quickly taking its place. "Mariano can be—"

"Intense, selfish, pushy," I cut in.

"Don't forget arrogant and self-centered." She chuckled as she rolled her bracelet around her wrist. "He wasn't always this bad, which really leads me to believe he's changing."

"It must be daunting to know he's been burrowing his way into your lives for so many years. Wondering how much he knows and what he could use against you."

"We've been very careful not to share too much, but Mariano is not my only concern."

"Then what is?" I loved that the Capris trusted me enough to let me in. I missed it terribly, and now that I had moved past my own trust issues, it meant the world to me.

"That there's a storm coming." She looked over at me, and I could see there was a lot more going on than I knew. "We've been able to come out in front of them in the past, but this time…" She let out a controlled breath. "I'm not sure if we'll be able to see it coming, especially if we are only now spotting the lion in the mist."

I moved my gaze back to the sunflowers. It really hit home that if we were going to come out on top, I should start to listen more around Mariano. Maybe I could catch something helpful, instead of always focusing on all the annoying things he did that pissed me off.

If someone had said to me months ago that I'd be involved in a syndicate who were chasing down leads on a human trafficking ring and flushing out a mole's plan to destroy the people I loved, I would have laughed out loud, then run like hell. Yet here I was, right in the middle of it all. Maybe one day I'd write about all of this and get the big break I'd always wanted.

"We'll figure this out, I promise." I covered her hand, giving it a squeeze, and meant every word of what I said.

Leaning back against the bright orange cushions, I closed my eyes and hoped the aspirin would kick in soon. The breeze was light and provided just enough relief from the damp heat that I could relax. As much as my mind wanted to dwell on what was to come with Elenora, I forced it to focus on the chirps from the chubby birds that were playing in the puddles.

I didn't hear footsteps, but when Andrea whispered to someone, I instantly felt my state of wishful bliss evaporate.

"She just needs a few minutes."

"Thanks, Mama." I heard him let out a long sigh.

The wood on the railing squeaked as he leaned against it, and I forced my eyes to flutter open, finding his back to me and his hands in his hair. "Mama, if anything happens to her because she's back here…" He trailed off, unable to finish the sentence.

Andrea's eyes met mine, and she threw me a kiss then left us alone. With a quick glance around to see if we were truly alone, I pushed to my feet and ran my hand up his back. At my touch, he turned and caught my lips with his. His hands ran through my hair and massaged the back of my head.

"Hey," it took all my self-control to pull away, "how much time do you have right now?" His lips curled playfully.

"I canceled everything, once I knew we were having company tonight."

"Good, come with me." He didn't question me and followed without hesitation. When I didn't head upstairs to the bedroom, though, he made a funny noise and looked at me, confused. Still, he played along and followed me into the library.

"Sienna, I don't think I could read right now." He chuckled.

"I know." I locked the door and motioned for him to follow me to the back where I knew a comfy couch was. Pulling my favorite book from the shelf as we whisked by, I sat down and opened it to where the yellow ribbon marked my page. "Lose the jacket, Mr. Capri, and come here." I patted the soft material next to me as he shimmied out of his jacket and tossed it on a chair. Once he was next to me, I gently pulled his head to my lap, and he curled onto his side and pulled his feet up.

I knew he was exhausted, but I also knew he would never stop and take the time to rest on his own.

"Wait." I pulled back his sleeve and admired the two beaded bracelets he had wrapped around his wrist. "You still have these?"

"Of course." He yawned. "You gave them to me."

"Well, yes, but I was fourteen at the time." I chuckled.

"It was the nicest gift anyone ever gave me."

"Somehow I doubt that." I eyed the gorgeous library that any book lover would die to have.

He rolled over to look at me then reached up and wrapped a piece of my hair around his finger as he thought. "I don't wear them every day, but when the mood strikes, I like to wear them. Do you remember what you told me that day when you gave them to me?"

"No," I lied, embarrassed that he did.

"You told me that you had nothing to your name but these rosary beads. You said that you kept them in a jar with a gold lid. That Father Thomas at the church let you collect them from the floor in the common room and explained that they were still blessed even if they were from broken chains. We were on that flat rock next to the pond, and I watched as you strung each bead with such care and explained that something can come from nothing. When you were finished, you took my hand and wrapped both around my wrist and smiled that gorgeous smile of yours and said they would protect me because I was a good person." He kissed my fingers as I blinked back the emotion. "Now," he shimmied back onto his side and got comfortable, "are you going to read to me?"

"I am." I gently stroked my fingers through his hair, remembering how he had looked at me after I said those words to him and how he took my hand and gave it a squeeze because he couldn't speak. That moment meant just as much to him as it did to me. I still couldn't believe he kept them.

When I didn't start reading, he nudged me and nestled in closer, sliding his hand up my leg and stroking my thigh with his strong fingers.

Sending my gaze down the page, I found where I had left off. He made it through two chapters before his breathing evened out and his muscles finally relaxed.

We stayed there like that for a long while, my fingers fiddling with the beads on his wrist, hanging on to the memory of that day, until the time caught my attention, and I felt my own anxiety take over. Elio had been asleep for nearly three hours, and I had the finished book well over an hour before. I hated that I needed to move and wake him. The moment I shifted, his hand clamped down hard, and I jumped.

"What's wrong?" His eyes jolted open.

"Nothing," I said in a soothing voice. "I just need to get ready soon."

"Okay." He sat up and rubbed his eyes.

"You can sleep a little longer. There's still time."

"No."

"You're kind of jumpy," I teased to see where his head was.

"Can't imagine why." He closed his eyes and shook his head, then smiled as he realized how grumpy he sounded. "I don't nap, ever, so thank you."

I leaned over and kissed his cheek. "Anytime."

"Wait." He stopped me from leaving. "Will you take a walk with me?"

"A walk?" I studied the time on the wall. I was still okay for a bit.

"I want to show you something."

"You do?" I found myself intrigued. "Lead the way."

He led me out the back door of the Hill House, down a stone pathway and along the edge of the vineyard. "I know that, right now, this place doesn't feel like home, and I know how important it is to have a place to go, especially when you just need to be left alone. Years ago, I felt that way, too. So, I made a special place where I felt at peace." He glanced over at me, gauging my interest.

"All right." I smiled encouragement.

He threaded his fingers through mine and walked me down the hill a little way to where two weeping willow trees stood. He led me through their draping branches into a small grassy area fronted by a bed of lovely sunflowers. A canvas hammock swung between two sturdy trees shaded by the wispy branches of the weeping willows. The protected area was perfectly placed. It had a lovely view beyond its sunflower border down over the vineyard, but it couldn't be seen from the Hill House or from the side that looked over Elio's and Mariano's homes.

"No one can see you here unless they are coming straight up on you from below. It's a place to come whenever you need to be alone or just want to think."

With a huge smile, I let go of his hand and admired the magical spot. The weeping branches of the willow brushed over my shoulders as I felt the smooth fabric of the hammock.

"You did this?" He nodded. "Back when you first came here?"

He nodded, but his face fell as he came closer and joined me in the shady hideout. He leaned his shoulder against the tree and folded his arms as though he found it hard to explain.

"A year after we moved here, I had the roses that lined the area dug up and replaced them with sunflowers. Much like your necklace, I also needed something that reminded me of you. It took a few years to get it the way I wanted it." He looked over at the hammock that hung between the two trees. "I planted the sunflowers myself, every spring. I never pictured myself as a gardener." He laughed softly and looked down at his fingers, and I noticed his edges of his nails looked stained. "I just figured if we were ever to be here together, I wanted you to like it. Maybe it sounds foolish, but now I know I was preparing it for you."

I was speechless. How could a man be this thoughtful when he'd felt all hope was lost?

"Climb in." He pointed to the hammock, and I slowly eased into it and was pleasantly surprised when he joined me, slipping an arm under my shoulders. I tucked my head against his neck.

"I love that you never gave up on us. Thank you." He turned and kissed my forehead, and we snuggled in and spent a few more blissful moments enjoying a spot that was reserved just for us. Just as I got comfortable, he lifted his free arm and checked the time.

"I hate to say it, but we should get going." He offered me a hand, and we headed back toward the Hill House.

Back at the house, I examined the purple sun dress I had decided on in the mirror, then threaded a favorite pair of dangly earrings through the tiny holes in my earlobes. I headed downstairs to the kitchen with my stomach in knots. I wasn't sure what events would come along with the company tonight. I leaned over the counter and lowered my head to suck in a deep steadying breath, trying to calm my nerves.

"Knock, knock." Andrea stood in the doorway, looking very pretty in her slacks and pink blouse. "They've arrived. Will you join us out back?"

I nodded, but as she turned to leave, I called her back. "Andrea?"

"Mm?" When I couldn't seem to find the right

words, she smiled warmly and moved closer.

"You know how much you mean to me, right?" I blurted, just to have it out there.

"Sienna," she gathered my hands in hers, "no matter who comes in and out of your life, you will always be the daughter I'd dreamed of having. Perhaps even one day, my daughter-in-law?" She winked, and I let go some of my tension. Regardless of what might be heading my way, I had the Capris to ride out the storm with me.

She tucked her arm through mine as we walked toward the French doors that led outside. "Surely, it can't be all bad," she whispered.

"And if it is?"

"I've been known to hide a body or two." She chuckled darkly, and I smiled at her humor. Elenora spotted me and rose from the garden chair where she sat. Her men nodded politely at me as I approached but kept their distance.

That's right, keep your wolves on their leashes.

Taking in my surroundings, I spotted a few more of her men by their cars and a couple more down the driveaway. Suddenly, I felt my heartrate speed up. Why so many of them? Where were Piero, Niccola, Vinni, and...

"Andrea?" I started to panic.

"He's here," she squeezed my hand, "you just have to let yourself feel him."

I nodded once and squeezed back.

She stopped and gently removed my white-knuckled grip on her hand. Elenora was once again dressed to perfection in a white blouse and flowy skirt.

"Welcome to our home," Andrea greeted her. "Please take a seat."

"Thank you." Elenora kept her eyes on me as she eased down into her seat, and I mirrored her actions.

"I will just go and get us something cool to drink," Andrea offered and smiled. Then she gracefully walked back toward the Hill House.

"Sienna—"

"Do you know where my father is?" I didn't want the pleasantries. I wanted—no, needed—answers.

"Yes," she nodded, "I do."

I wanted to ask where he was but held off on that, as I guessed the answer would come later.

"You told me you left because you were in danger and that you're back now because of the article I did, but," I blinked back the hurt, "did you ever even check on me?"

She cleared her throat as she mulled over my answer. "I knew where you were."

"How?"

I watched as her gaze swung over to Francesco, who was now standing by a lounge chair. I couldn't fathom that he'd known things about me that I didn't and that he'd never once breathed a word to me in all the time I had been at the Capris' home. I would address that later. Right now, my mother needed to understand that forgiveness wasn't about to come easy. She needed to see how her actions had affected my life.

"After I finally ran away from the terrible family I

had been placed with, I had to live on the street. I had to sleep in alleyways. I went days without eating. But you say you knew where I was." I tilted my head to look at Francesco. "Apparently, you both did."

"You blended in. It was a good thing."

"I was alone. I had no one."

She leaned forward, resting her arms on her thighs, and hung her head. "I just…" Her voice cracked, and I found myself full of emotion. "I just needed you safe."

"I may have been safe," I leaned forward, "from whatever was after you, but I wasn't from everything else."

"I chose the lesser of two evils," she quickly dried her eyes and sat straight again, "and what good did that even do?" She looked over my head.

Suddenly, his hand slipped over my shoulder. It was as though I was thrown a lifeline, and it felt wonderful as it rested there on the curve of my collarbone. Elenora's eyes widened for a split second, but she quickly pulled her mask back down.

"Are you two together?"

"If we were?"

"That would pose a problem."

"What does that mean?" What was her damn hang-up with the Capri family, anyway?

"These people are murderers, Sienna. Stone cold killers."

"I disagree," I stated simply.

"You need to trust me on this, Sienna."

I snorted as I shook my head at her words. "I have

no trust. Not for anyone." Elio flinched, and Elenora caught it. I could see it as her eyes narrowed in on him. To my surprise, he made no comment, and she let it go and directed her attention back to me.

"I want to earn it back." She placed a hand on mine and stared into my eyes. "I know it needs to be earned, and I'm willing to do that."

My knee-jerk reaction was to say no, but she was my mother, the person who had given me life. I needed more from her, and I knew she could fill in the gaps of where I came from and who I was.

"It'll take time." I wasn't going to give in easy.

"I know."

Andrea arrived and passed us each a frosted glass of bubbly water. She settled into a chair next to Elenora.

I waited a moment and took a sip, then turned to Elenora.

"You need to accept that the Capris are in my life too."

Her neck contracted as she swallowed hard. "I'll have to work on that."

"You can't disappear on me again."

"I won't."

"I want answers. I deserve them."

"You do, and I'll do my best to tell you whatever I can."

"All right." I felt unsure, but what other choice did I have? "What now?"

"Come to our party tomorrow night," Elio suddenly said. "See for yourself that we're not who you think we are. My cousin, Vinni, turned twenty-seven today. We're hosting a party for him. It would be a chance for you both to relax and get to know one another in a less formal setting."

I noticed Elenora looked unsure, but when she caught my expression, daring her to say no, she slowly started to nod. "All right. If it's acceptable to the rest of your family, I think that can be arranged."

"Any family of Sienna's is family of ours. We'd love to have you," Andrea said. "The party starts at eight up in the main house." She pointed to the Hill House behind us.

"I guess we'll see you tomorrow." She smiled politely at me while I digested the little progress we had made. While we walked them back to their cars, I couldn't help but notice Oscar was watching me intently. It could be that he was actually watching Elio, who had become my shadow lately. Either way, I felt strange and a little uneasy around him, and wondered just who he was to my mother.

"Thanks," I said over my shoulder once our guests' cars were all headed down the driveway. "You didn't need to do that."

"Yeah," Elio came into my view, "I really did."

"What are you thinking?"

"I don't like how cryptic she's being." He turned to look over at Francesco. "I don't like secrets. They are kept from people for a reason."

"You kept secrets from me." I hadn't meant to lash out, and I saw the hurt on his face.

"And look where it got me." He kissed my hand then tucked it around his arm as we walked back into the house.

Later that evening, after Elio slipped out, I found myself hanging around the kitchen with Donte, who was busy cleaning up from dinner.

"What do you do when you're finished?" I asked as I dried the remaining mixing bowl.

"I normally take a walk, or maybe drive into the city to visit friends. As long as the kitchen is clean, and the meals are prepped for the next day, I'm allowed to leave. However," he removed his chef's jacket, "there's always someone on standby if someone is hungry."

"What are your plans for tonight?"

"A walk."

"May I join you?"

"Sure," he smiled, "as long as you clear it with the Don first." I looked him, confused. "You should ask the boss's father for permission."

I nodded and made quick work to find Piero, who thought it was a lovely idea to go for a walk. I grabbed a light sweater, and we headed out.

"When did you start working for the Capris?" I asked and admired the glow of the sunset over the rolling hills in front of us as we strolled along in relaxed conversation.

"I've known them since I was ten but never officially worked for them until I was seventeen."

"Wow that's pretty impressive."

"Mafia, remember? When you work for the family,

you are treated like family. My father worked for the Don's brother, Bosco, when he was thirty." He paused to make sure I was following, and I nodded for him to go on. "But it was actually Mrs. Andrea who hired my father. She happened to be here on vacation and found him cooking at a small restaurant. She made him an offer, and not long after, we went from a small little place in a poor neighborhood to a three-bedroom villa on the Capri property. Do you know what it's like to see your parents worry?" His face suddenly dropped, and he closed his eyes for a moment, clearly knowing a little of my story. "I'm sorry, Sienna, poor choice of an example."

"Don't be." I shrugged. "It was hard for me, but that wouldn't mean that it wasn't hard for you too, just a different kind of hard." I chuckled. "Sounds very poetic, doesn't it?"

He laughed with me and let it go. Again, it was something else we connected on.

"Let me ask you this." I let my curiosity about what it was like living in a mafia house get the best of me. "Were you ever scared? I mean, they are mafia."

"I think I would have been, if I had known better." He nodded as he spoke as though he agreed with his wording. "I was too young to know much, anyway. Plus, Mrs. Noemi loves kids, so the odd time when I was around, she was really nice. Mr. Vinni and Mr. Niccola were hilarious. They were always pranking their father and getting into mischief wherever they went. As I got older, and I realized what kind of world I was surrounded by, well, let's just say I understood it by then." He lifted a finger. "But it was all because I listened to my papa as he groomed me to not only be the best chef I could be, but how to keep safe in this life. Head down, be polite no matter who you're speaking to. But most of all, he taught me to be loyal."

"Sounds like your papa is a wise man." He smiled at me, and we went back to admiring the evening.

"You're a good person, Sienna. You really fit in well here."

"That's nice of you to say." I twisted my lips as an emotional wave washed over me. I longed to feel I belonged.

"Can I ask you something?" His eyes held mine as I nodded. "You knew the boss when he was younger, right?"

"Yes."

"What was he like then?"

I leaned back and looked at the sky as the box that held all my memories deep inside cracked open just a little. A picture book of memories started to flash in front of me, begging for a chance to reveal themselves. I knew they so desperately deserved to be viewed, but when I went to speak of them, I hesitated. I knew I needed to tread very carefully with what I shared with anyone going forward. I knew things about Elio that no one in the world did.

"He was very kind." I smiled as my body grew warm. "One of the kindest people I ever knew."

"I wish I'd known him better then."

"Yeah, you would have liked him. Did they visit

very often before Elio's family moved here?"

"Sometimes, but since they are the head of the family, their visits here were very hush-hush. That is until the cousins showed up, and then all hell would break loose." I laughed, wishing I could have been there for that.

We walked a little farther, enjoying each other's company.

"What was your favorite thing to do in the summer in Sicily?" he asked as he brushed a little flour from his arm.

"I suppose that would have been an old swimming pond in the woods not far from where I lived."

His eyes popped open as though at a memory of something. He stopped to face me with a funny expression of disbelief on his face. "Oh, wow…" I looked at him, confused.

"Are you expecting me to follow that train of thought?" I half laughed.

He looked away and shook his head, then continued down the hill.

"Hey, don't stop now. You have to finish sentences for the other person to follow, Donte." I picked up the pace and hustled up to his side. Before we could continue the conversation, Vinni pulled up behind us in his car.

"Hey, Sienna," Vinni said through a half open window. "Andrea is looking for you."

"All right, thanks." I turned to Donte and gave him a wave as I hopped in the car, not wanting to keep Andrea waiting. "You want a ride?"

"No, thanks. I need to walk."

"See you later."

Donte never did finish his thought.

I woke early and went down to the kitchen. I walked out to the patio with a bowlful of grapes and watched the hustle as the house prepared for Vinni's birthday dinner. I wished I had known sooner so I could have had more time to buy him something nice. What could I get? I had no idea. A new gun? One with a flashy handle, like the ones from the *Godfather* movie.

"Forgive me yet?" Wyatt sat down next to me on the lounge chair as I tried to stay in my thoughts.

"Nothing to forgive." I popped another grape, keeping my eyes on the workers. No one could have predicted what a storm my mother would bring with her.

"What's going through your head right now?"

"Thinking about what kind of gun I would get Vinni for his birthday."

"Oh, sure, okay." He reached over and stole a grape. "My friend wants to buy a flashy gun. What's unusual about that? Well, let's see. Vinni's kind of a flashy guy. Maybe all white, with a gold handle."

"My thoughts, too."

"Maybe some kind of engraving on it?" He warmed to the topic.

"Mm." I shrugged but moved my attention over to Elio, who was dressed in his normal attire. His black suit and tie looked wonderful on him, and this time he had paired them with a navy-blue dress shirt. He ran his hand through his hair as he spoke to one of the workers, then he caught sight of me. His lips twitched into a sexy, slow smile.

"It's a little unfair that he was made that good looking." Wyatt sighed.

"Indeed."

Something about his tone gnawed at me, and I pulled my attention away from Elio. I knew my best friend struggled with something, and I had a fairly good idea what it was. I was simply being patient because I knew he needed to discover it for himself.

"You mentioned to me back in New York you wanted to talk, Wyatt. As you can see, just now, I'm free as a bird. So, is now a good time?"

"You have enough going on."

"I do, but that never means I don't have time for you."

He turned to face me, but with his sunglasses on, all I could see were deep lines in his forehead, and his jaw looked locked in place.

"I broke up with Rosa," he blurted.

"You did?" I wasn't surprised, but again, this was his story to tell. "How did she take it?"

"Same as always, although this time I'm not going back."

"Good." I shaded the tops of my glasses. "I never thought you two were a good match."

"I have, I mean, I think I have someone else in

mind."

"Oh?" I sucked on the cool juice of the grape while he came to terms with it.

"Only problem is, he's a he. Other problem is, I don't think he's gay."

Resting my bowl on the table, I moved around to face him dead-on. I knew it would only be a matter of time before Wyatt admitted the truth to himself. "I'm proud of you, Wyatt. You've never really been happy with any of your relationships. Now I think you will be. You've got this, my friend."

"Thanks for letting me figure this out on my own time."

"Of course. It's not my path, it's yours."

"You've known for a while, I take it?" He removed his glasses, pretending to wipe them clean with his shirt as he studied my face. "I'm scared. It's new territory for me."

"If you weren't scared, I would be a little worried," I rubbed his arm lovingly. "Here's how I would look at it. You're referring to Vinni, right?" He nodded, not even questioning how I knew. "What is it about him that you find attractive?"

"He's good looking, kind, and funny."

"That's your starting point, but I do believe he's straight." I watched his brows as I spoke, trying to gauge how my comment might affect him. "But at least now you know what you're looking for, and you just go from there."

"True." He let my words sink in, and I was relieved

to see his shoulders sag with relief.

"It's not going to be easy." I covered his hand. "But remember how terrified I was when we met, and how you promised you'd always be there for me? No matter what, I will be at your side."

"You've always been there for me." He stopped suddenly, and I felt his mood change. I instantly knew it wasn't Elio as a pair of cool hands landed on my shoulders.

"Good morning, Sienna." Mariano's attempt to massage me felt creepy, but of course I had to play my part. "I had someone cover my bitch shift at the dockyard tonight so we could spend some time together."

"It's Vinni's birthday tonight."

"So?"

"So, I'm attending."

He sat down on my chair and pressed against my legs so he could sit with me. His hand slid up and down my leg as he settled there, and it took all my self-control not to brush it away.

"There are family parties monthly. Skipping one won't insult them. I doubt they'd even notice if you weren't there."

Gee, thanks.

"It's my last night here," Wyatt said, and my jaw dropped. This was news to me. "Our boss offered me an assignment that will take me south for a few weeks. It's big, and I couldn't say no. So, if it's all right with you," he smiled his hope at Mariano, "I'd love to have one more night with my best friend before I go."

Mariano looked at him for a beat or two then back at me.

"Fine," he ran a frustrated hand through his hair and forced a smile, "but you better keep all the slow dances for me." I cringed at the thought and spotted Elio on the phone staring at us. Mariano gave my hip a painful slap and stood. "Well, I have to go meet someone, so I'll see you tonight."

"Mariano," I called after him, "maybe you should work tonight and take another off? We could go for dinner."

"And miss seeing you in a party dress? There are too many wolves circling you as it is." He made a point of shifting his gaze to Elio, who missed his death stare.

Damn.

Once he left, I flopped my head back against the chair then jerked it over to Wyatt. "I appreciate the save, but tell me you're not really leaving."

"Sorry, friend, but this story can't wait, and I still need to work to keep the lights on. Besides, I've already cleared it with Vinni."

"Of course you did," I pouted. I hated the idea of him leaving.

"Look," his expression changed to an easy one as he pulled a duffle bag onto his lap, "I asked my sister to send me a few things so I could leave straight from here. I thought maybe, since things were going in your favor with Elio, you might like to keep these close." He set the wooden box I had always kept so close to my heart next to me on the chair. "I don't want to overstep."

"Wyatt," I brushed a tear away, feeling like a missing part of me had returned, "thank you."

"I know what they mean to you." He smiled as I hopped into his arms for a hug, loving that he thought to bring these to me. "No matter what, if you need me, call me and I'll come back. Okay?"

"Okay." I squeezed him hard then ran my fingers over the design on the box. "All my precious memories are in here." I peeked inside and sighed with relief at the sight. Feeling better, I pulled myself away, not wanting to get lost in my box just now. I turned my full attention back to Wyatt. "Tell me, what's the story you're going to be chasing?"

"Well," he leaned back, "let me tell you."

Chapter

SIX

"Do you have eyes on her?" I was hunched down using the reflection of the window across the street to watch Stefano's men outside his hotel. Thankfully, he had a ground-level room, and the maid-service closet was only three doors away from his. Any sounds we made going in would, hopefully, be covered by their chatter and wouldn't alert any of his men. We had eyes on Antonio's niece, Val, and were about to make our move.

"Yes, she's sitting on the couch, wrists tied together." Vinni grunted as he shifted his position. "All things considered, she seems all right."

"Any sign of Stefano?"

"No, boss, just two of his men are watching TV across the room from her."

"Do you really think Stefano left her?" Niccola joined my side and lifted a skeptical eyebrow.

"No, he is impulsive and stupid, and in the right situation, maybe, I think he would leave her."

"I have eyes on Stefano," Vinni broke in. "He's with a blonde at the pool bar."

I glanced at Niccola as if to say *case in point*.

"Good, keep eyes on him. Niccola and I are moving in."

"Got it." Vinni hung up, and we raced across the hotel parking lot and straight up to the door. We got inside quietly, with the help of a master key Vinni managed to get yesterday. I popped both men in the forehead. My silencer only allowed a quick *pfft* sound as it sent blood spatter across the scenic painting on the wall.

Niccola leapt forward to wrap Val's mouth with his hand to muffle her screams. I leaned down with my knife and cut the zip ties.

"You're fine. Your uncle Antonio told us what happened."

Her wild eyes stared at me, and she nodded but then squeezed her eyes shut again as she took in the scene of the massacre.

"You want to get home, right, Val?" She nodded and seemed to gather herself. "Then focus on me because we don't have much time." She nodded again.

"Mr. Capri, wait!" She suddenly darted to the bed, dropped to her knees, and pulled out a duffle bag. She fished around inside and took out a small notebook. "Stefano is always writing in this."

Smart girl.

I pulled her to her feet and tucked the notebook into my breast pocket. My phone vibrated, and I saw it was Vinni warning us that Stefano was on the way back toward the room with the woman.

"Which direction, Vin?" I said quickly into the phone.

"South side."

"All right." I motioned for the others to follow me, and just as we turned the corner, I caught sight of Stefano with the blonde on his arm.

"Hey!" One of his men came out of the office in front of me, chomping a mouthful of potato chips. I launched forward, bringing him to the floor, away from view, and wrapped my arm around his neck, causing him to suck in hard. His face went red as he tried to cough the chips from his lungs. Not wanting to waste any more time, I snapped his neck and dropped his fat body at my feet, then I glanced around the corner. We had only seconds to make our escape.

"Holy shit," Val gasped behind me.

"Better him than you," Niccola muttered.

"Go." I signaled for them to race across to the open car door, where Vinni was waiting. The second my feet were off the ground, he pulled away.

"We're good, Val." Niccola gently rubbed her shoulder, trying to soothe her as she cried. "Your father and uncle are waiting for you back at the house."

More tears came, but I could tell she was trying to hold it together in front of me. I made a few calls to my father and Francesco, explaining that things went well and to alert the others we were on our way home. I knew we might get some unwanted company after that, so I had a few of my soldiers on the lookout, ready to deal with whatever aftermath might come.

Antonio and his brother were waiting on the steps when we arrived. They both looked as if they had aged ten years since Val was taken. I would be adding more security to cover the families that were protected by our name. This couldn't happen again.

Val stopped me as I began to get out.

"Mr. Capri?" She tucked her hair behind her ear and used the dirty sleeve of her shirt to dry her cheeks. "Thank you." She cleared her throat. "I know what you must be thinking, but my father and uncle had no choice. They—"

"They did," I cut her off, annoyed at how all of this could have been avoided. "But the air has been cleared, and it's now up to them to keep it that way."

"Understood." She nodded but still didn't make a move to leave.

"What is it, Val?" I noticed she had begun to wring her hands.

"I wasn't supposed to be rescued, and…"

"And what?"

"And I heard things."

I closed the car door, and Niccola caught my silent order to stop the others from coming over.

"You have my attention. Use it wisely."

"Someone named Mikey called him a lot."

"Mikey?" That name didn't sound familiar.

"He never came around, he only called, but whoever he was stressed out Stefano. Sometimes, I think he was scared of him by the way he would curse and begin to sweat a bit before he answered the call." Her hands rubbed together. "Strange, right? Because isn't he, you know, like you? An underboss?" She wouldn't make eye contact with me.

"Anything else?" I avoided her question, not wanting to get into details about the positions in a syndicate. "Did you ever see any other girls?"

"Girls?" She paused and looked confused. "As far as I knew, I was the only girl there."

Interesting.

When she tried to thank me, I opened the door. That was enough for now. "Go see your family, Val, and no more walking home alone from school or to the dockyard."

"Yes, sir."

I let the family reunite and motioned for Vinni to take us home to get ready for his party. My phone vibrated, and I cursed at the caller ID, knowing what it was about. I motioned for Vinni to take a detour and listened to Donatello prattle off about what was going on with the situation.

"Where is he now?" I patted Vinni's shoulder and let him know to hang a quick right. "We'll be there in twenty."

"All good?" Niccola asked from the front seat.

"We just need to pay someone a visit before the party. Call in some soldiers. I want to make sure he knows I'm not messing around." I rubbed my head and stared out the window.

"Sure thing."

When we arrived at the location, I nodded at the soldiers to stay put. They'd know when to step in if needed. Undoing my jacket, I slid my hands along my sides and pushed the back of my jacket out as I took a seat on his front steps. I didn't have time for this, but I also knew that if you didn't keep a finger on the heartbeat of our business, you'd soon lose control. So, visits like these, no matter how frustrating they were, had to happen.

Moments later, a limo arrived, and a young woman stepped out. *Great, more company*. I glared when I spotted the chain around her neck. We all had our kinks, but Cavaliere was a sick bastard.

"Mr. Capri." He nodded at me, and I gave a signal to Niccola to alert my soldiers to pull into the driveway to block his exit. I flipped my coin between my fingers, wondering if I'd let him live or die today.

I could see him vibrating with fear, and I was pleased to see he knew who was in charge and who wasn't. "It's a pleasure to see you again. What can I do for you?"

I flipped the coin in the air and slapped it on the top of my hand.

Tails. He would live to see another day.

Slowly, I rose, buttoning my jacket as I did so. I

slipped the coin into my pocket as I made eye contact with the dirty little shit in front of me. I had to curb my urge to drill my knee into his skull, but the coin had spoken…for now.

"Cavaliere, it's good to see you again." My words were like acid on my tongue. "I didn't realize you were accompanied by such beauty." I grinned at his guest, wondering if I should have them followed or, at the very least, investigate who the hell she was. My paranoia grew, and I wondered if she was one of Stefano's girls from my dockyard.

"I came to show her the upgrades on *our* new home." Cavaliere stressed the word *our*, like he was trying to prove to me she was his. Which was as pathetic as the girl with a chain hanging from her neck. She looked like some kind of a pet. By the way her hands twisted together, I could tell she was in no way thinking they were a couple.

"How's the wine cellar coming along?" I stepped closer, flashing a killer grin. "From what I've heard, it's filled with my wine," I crossed my arms over my chest, "as are both of your restaurants."

"Of course. We only want to serve the best," he replied, trying to sound smooth and calm.

I chuckled and looked at Niccola. "You hear him? He wants to serve the best." I shook my head. "The problem is you seem to have a hard time paying for the best. Both of your restaurants are ninety days past due, and no one from your office is answering my calls."

"I'm sure there must be some misunderstanding."

Cavaliere rubbed his neck uneasily. "My men would never try to take from you."

I nodded. "Do I need to remind you of what happens to those who don't pay?"

Cavaliere dropped his hand and lowered his head. "No."

I tucked one hand in my pocket and rubbed my chin with the other as I leaned down to make my point. I made a show of looking at my watch. "Your time starts now."

Vinni opened the door as I started to walk away, but not before I stopped and gave one last warning. "Be good to her. It would be a shame to ruin such beauty." With that, I slipped inside the car.

"Nic," I pulled out my phone and secretly snapped a photo of the girl and sent it to him, "find out who she is and if she has any connection to Stefano."

"Will do." He started to make some calls, and I leaned back to soothe the ache between my eyes. I hated it here, and my next visit would be his last.

"Everything is set up for Wyatt's return home." Vinni revved the engine as we headed up the hill toward my house. "There will be two men outside his apartment, and another will tail him wherever his assignment takes him."

"Good."

"He seemed happy and confident about the arrangements."

"That's good."

He pulled into the driveway, and I got out. I turned back as his door opened and he stepped out as well.

"Can I ask you something?" He had my attention.

I leaned my arm on the roof and let the other drape over the open door of the town car. "Yeah."

"Does something feel off with Sienna's mother?"

"A lot does."

"Like the timing of it." He tucked his hands in his pockets as he thought. "We just find out about Mariano, and practically the next day her mother shows up and knows Francesco? It just seems a little too coincidental." I opened my mouth to speak, but he wasn't finished. "I still can't believe Piero agreed to let her come to the Hill House." He rubbed his face as though to shake off the feeling. "I don't know, I'm just thinking there's something right in front of us we can't see."

"Paranoia is part of the job. It's what keeps us on our toes and keeps us alive." I stepped aside and closed the door. The truth would reveal itself in time. The real question would be how much blood would need to be shed before we saw it. Until then, we just needed to keep our eyes and ears open.

"I know you're right. It's just playing on my mind." He rubbed his face.

"Go get ready, or Auntie will have my head."

"Right, party time." He rolled his eyes, hating attention just as much as I did.

"You only turn twenty-seven once." I smirked.

"That's true." He chuckled and slid in behind the wheel. "See you soon."

I waved and headed inside.

I was soon deep into Stefano's notebook, trying

to make sense of his random scribbles and marks. His writing looked like that of a serial killer, which was ironic, as he was one. With the book in hand, I moved about the kitchen to fix myself a drink and noticed Sienna hadn't responded to my morning text. It wasn't like her not to.

Elio: Bella, how was your day?

I enjoyed the sharp bite of the rum as I made my way to the window. I stared out at the stream of headlights that approached the house. I took a moment to appreciate the way our property was designed. The way the winding road provided us protection and allowed us to see cars as they approached from miles away. It gave us time to prepare. Or, in this case, to see just how many people my aunt had invited to the party. Vinni was a great guy, and he deserved a night off, especially with all that had been happening. We all did.

My vison blurred, and I focused on the book in my hand, back to scanning the messy cursive handwriting. As I'd seen on the front cover, I once again saw the name "Mikey," only this time there were tally marks next to it. Seventeen marks in total. Maybe they were kills? I wasn't sure, but before I let my mind go any further, my phone buzzed. Mama reminded me I should have already arrived. I snapped the book closed and locked it away in the safe, then hurried off to the party.

As always, when we held an event, I slipped through the back entrance to avoid the guests who were getting their names checked at the front door.

I greeted my mama to assure she knew I had arrived. Niccola was at the bar with two drinks in his hand.

"Hey," he handed me one, "at the risk of having you bury me at the bottom of the hill, check out the goddess in white."

"Who?" I scanned the faces in the crowd and nearly choked on my drink when I caught sight of Sienna and Wyatt surrounded by a sea of men. She had left her hair long and straight, brushed to one side to tumble over her bare shoulder. Her white dress barely covered her breasts and had two very high slits. Gold strings zigzagged under her cleavage and wound around to tie behind her back. The gold in the strings paired beautifully with her gold-bangled cuffs. Though it was revealing, it was incredibly classy. Niccola was right; she did look like a goddess.

"Yeah, that was pretty much my reaction, too." He chuckled into his glass. "So, the suspense is killing me. What was in the notebook?"

"The name Mikey came up a few times, some addresses in their territory, and some dates that are coming up. I want to cross refence them with our shipments and see if that's when their next move might be."

"Wow," he shook his head, "nice job, Val."

"Indeed."

"Elio," Aunt Noemi wrapped her arms around my shoulders and kissed my cheeks, "looking handsome as always."

"Thanks, Auntie," I found my gaze shifting back to Sienna.

"Did Mariano find you?" That pulled my attention away.

"No, why?"

"I just know he was looking for you." A deep burn burst through me with the idea of him being here and not at the dockyard.

"I'll keep an eye out for him." I kept my voice even.

"Niccola," she addressed her son, "I spotted a lovely brunette over by the door, who, I just so happen to know, is single."

"Thanks, Mama, but I can handle finding my own dates."

"Can you?" I teased him. "Because you seem dateless tonight and, despite the last party, you're not coming home with me."

"First, screw you, and second, don't act like you don't love my company."

"What's not to love about your bare ass on my new couch or your shit tossed everywhere throughout my place?" I shook my head at Auntie. "He's a mess."

"I'm sorry I brought it up!" She tossed her hands in the air, exasperated, and Niccola and I smirked at one another as she muttered, walking off. In our family, you had to wear the mothers out or they were relentless with finding us a woman. They all pictured the grandkids on their knee. Luckily for me…my woman was right here across the room.

"I know that look." Niccola chuckled at me, and I rolled my eyes.

Making my way through the crowd, only stopping to greet a few friends along the way, I joined the sea of gawking men and smiled when Sienna spotted me.

"Good evening, Mr. Capri."

"Ms. Giovanna." I nodded and drank in her heavenly scent. "You look lovely this evening."

"Thank you." She gave me a flirty smile then remembered our situation and dropped her gaze to the floor.

"There you are." Mariano suddenly appeared and draped an arm over Sienna's shoulders. She waited a beat then stepped aside, moving a little closer to me. Alcohol wafted off his breath, and I saw her cringe at the stench.

Why the hell is he here and not at the dockyard where I told him to go?

"Everyone," he took a sip of his drink as he addressed our small crowd, "I want you to meet my girl, Sienna."

"Actually," she cut in, "we're not dating. I'm," she paused, "single." The word hit my chest hard, but I knew it was what she needed to do. "Mariano has been a lovely host and friend the last while, and I'm thankful I was introduced to the Capri family."

"You might be the only one." Mariano snickered, trying to make the other men laugh, but it really just came off as backward and disrespectful. "Ah, man, I'm only playing."

I rubbed my short beard, trying to navigate my temper.

"Mariano," my tone was clipped, "I believe I gave you a direct order yesterday as to where you were to be tonight. Yet here you stand."

"I couldn't miss Wyatt's last day, or Vinni's birthday." He laughed like he was strung out on something, and Wyatt shifted uncomfortably. "Besides, she has been spending all her time here lately, even though I've asked her repeatably to come to my house."

I licked the inside of my dry mouth, barely hanging on to any self-control I had left. He kept making it seem that they were together.

"Wyatt," Sienna said softly, "isn't that Joseph, the one you were looking for earlier?"

"It is, thanks." He took her exit and raced across the room, disappearing into the crowd.

"If you all would please excuse me." Her dark blue eyes looked up to mine for a moment then she turned and left the room.

"Niccola," I said over the buzz of the party as he approached me on cue, "where did you say you spotted my father last?"

"By the pool."

I left, but not before giving him a warning to watch Mariano. Once in the hallway, I spotted Francesco, who pointed out the French doors to where Sienna was walking into the garden. I wanted to ask when Elenora would arrive, but he answered the phone, quickly walking away.

I headed around the side of the hedge and dipped under into a small hollowed-out spot that Niccola and Vinni had made to hide in when they were boys. Twinkle lights were woven through the branches and provided a soft glow, but you were completely hidden from view. As soon as she was close enough, I reached out and pulled her through the soft branches.

"Oh, my goodness!" She yelped but sagged into my

arms and let me nuzzle her neck. "My heart nearly leapt out of my chest, Elio."

"You're not playing fair, Sienna," I growled, running a hand down her side. "I can't tell the world you're mine, yet you wear something like this," I fisted the fabric near her hip, "and I'm expected to behave?"

"Never behave with me, Elio." She tilted her head and kissed my jaw line.

"Sienna," I warned and moved the fabric out of the way to stroke across her silky skin, "your company will be arriving—"

"You never did finish what you started in the closet at the last party." She ground her backside into the painful erection that had suddenly developed, and my eyes rolled to the back of my head.

I stroked the back of my hand down her shoulder and pressed my lips to the nape of her neck, sucking ever so softly. Lapping, I drank in the fresh scent of her shampoo and resisted the urge to sink my teeth into her delicate skin.

"Mm," I moaned from the bottom of my chest, "ten years I dreamed of this."

"We have a lot of time to make up for."

"We do," I whispered, sending my hot breath over her sensitive shoulder, and watched with fascination as goosebumps burst down her arm.

With both hands moving quickly to her hips, I whirled her around, holding her chin as I sucked in a sharp breath, trying to control my animal instincts. The desire to feed on this woman positively consumed me.

My gaze plummeted to her chest that heaved and

strained against the fabric of her dress.

"Seeing all those men around you—"

"But yet, here I am, with you." She freed the button on my pants and stoked my erection while I groaned with a curse. "Offering my body to you."

She barely had time to think before I had her panties moved aside. Careful of her dress, I pushed inside her. I hooked her leg over my hip and covered her mouth to muffle her gasps. I stared into her gorgeous eyes as they clouded over with need.

"This is mine, Sienna." I dragged my gaze down her gorgeous body. "I don't like them looking at what's mine." I watched as her pupils dilated. She always loved it when I became possessive of her. It made her feel wanted and loved.

"Elio," she huffed as my hand brushed her lips.

"Shh," I warned, knowing that if we outed ourselves now, we would have lost our only leverage with Mariano. "You're here with me, like a gift from God, and I hate that no one knows it," I whispered, leaning back to better balance us and to make sure our shoes wouldn't scuff the gravel.

I lost all thoughts while I pushed myself in and out of the woman I loved, each stroke bringing us closer and closer to the edge. Though nothing mattered while I was inside that woman, I did keep one ear open for visitors. Our eyes locked again, and I saw her desperate need for release. I lowered my guard and gave her everything. She was the only one who could ever love and destroy me at the same time.

Chapter SEVEN

Sienna

"Is that a new blush?" Wyatt teased with a pointed look at my pink cheeks. "I don't blame you, though." He sipped his drink and checked out Elio as he walked past me toward his father. "I realize I wouldn't say no to that either."

"Nice to know we have the same taste."

"That we do."

"Any sign of—"

"Your mother? Yes," he pointed toward the bar, "she and her entourage arrived ten minutes ago."

"Am I all right?" I stepped back for him to give me the once-over in case I was missing something.

"Sex looks good on you." He winked at my startled

expression. "You look stunning as always. Go on."

"Oh, no." I took his hand. "You're coming."

Elenora turned when Oscar let her know I was coming up from behind. I wasn't sure how to greet her, so I kept a small distance between us.

"You look lovely, Sienna." She beamed at my dress. "How very fashionable."

"Apparently, I get that from you. I love this fabric," I reached over and fingered the stretchy silk that flowed from her peacock blue dress. "How chic."

Were we really having a normal moment? I wanted to freeze time and savor it.

"How's the party been so far?" She shifted her gaze around the room in discomfort.

"Good. It's fun seeing Vinni the center of attention. Normally, he just pops up out of nowhere."

She studied me for a moment. "You seem to get along well with the Capris."

"I do."

"What are your feelings on Piero?"

I knew she was digging. I just wasn't sure why.

"He's pretty amazing. He's welcomed me into his home with open arms. They all have, actually."

"When did you first meet them?"

Before I could answer, my shoulders tensed at a sound behind me.

"There you are." Mariano draped his heavy arm around me and leaned into me. My heels fought to distribute his weight. "Every time I turn around, you're gone." He finally acknowledged those around me and offered his free hand. "Mariano."

"Violetta." Elenora offered a polite nod as her men drew in closer. "Tell me, Mariano, are the two of you dating?"

"No—" I sputtered.

"Not officially, but I'm wearing her down." He gave me a blurry-eyed grin.

"And how did you two meet?" She dug for information.

"She was on the cover of a magazine, and I fell in love."

I noticed she gave Oscar a side glance, and something passed between them.

"Actually," I glared at him, "Mariano hired me to write his story. Sadly, that came to an end, but another article landed at my feet and has kept me here." I wasn't about to go into the details, but my version sounded better than Mariano's.

"And now she's staying here as a guest of the Capris and not down at my house."

Elenora's expression fell, and she blinked at me like this was all news to her.

"Mariano," Wyatt peeled him off of me, "why don't we go get you a rye and Coke?"

"Can we make it a double?"

"Double Coke, sure, coming right up." He rolled his eyes at me, and I mouthed a *thank you* as he drew Mariano toward the bar.

"Sienna, please tell me you're not living under the same roof as these monsters."

Where in the world had she thought I was staying?

"This might be hard for you to hear, but they're my friends, my family." She started to speak, but I shook my head, stepping closer. "You weren't here. I had to do life on my own, and that brought me to the Capri family. Whether you can swallow it or not, they saved me when you didn't come back."

"You don't understand—"

"You're right, I don't, and I'm right here standing in front of you waiting for anything you can offer me. Why are they monsters to you? Maybe if you give me something, I could understand your feelings better."

"They…"

"Elenora, maybe not here," Oscar warned.

"Are you my family, Oscar?" I was angry that he was stepping in the way of something.

"No, I'm not."

"Then you don't need to be here right now, do you?"

His jaw flexed when I didn't show any sign of backing down. He stepped back a few steps at a glance from Elenora.

"The Capri family put a hit on your uncle years ago. They killed him."

I took a moment to digest the information and tried to stay neutral on my gut reaction.

"What was his name, and when was this?"

"You don't believe me?"

"I don't know you well enough to believe or not believe you, but I will find out if what you say is true before I ever think of judging them."

She softly said the name and the date, and I typed it into my phone so I wouldn't forget.

"Sienna," Vinni popped up looking like he was having a great time, "you promised me a dance, and it's about that time." He held out a hand and did a little jig as the song switched over.

"I'll find you later," I dismissed my mother.

"Please do." She quickly dabbed at her eyes then waved me off.

Vinni had moves that I didn't think were humanly possible. It was a combination of the robot, country, and some kind of worm roll. How he didn't hurt his back was beyond me. All I did was laugh while he spun me around and made a horrible attempt of teaching me the steps. I considered myself a coordinated person, but Vinni was not.

"Wow, Sienna," Niccola handed me a large water after the song ended and Vinni claimed another friend as his next victim, "you should win a medal for sticking out the entire song. Most bail, and he doesn't even notice."

"It's his birthday. It's the least I could do."

"You're good people."

"We'll see about that."

"Meaning?" he asked through a long sip of his water.

"I don't know. I thought having my mother back would be so different. But it's all dark and mysterious." I shrugged. "She really hates your family."

"A lot do."

"I get that, but why would my mother?"

"What did she say about it?"

"She only alluded to something about a hit that happened years ago."

"Do you know when?"

"Yes."

"Did it happen before 1999?"

"It did."

"In that case, you'll have to ask Piero. I only could help with the more recent ones."

"Can I do that?"

"What, ask? Of course. If he can't share it with you, he won't, but asking never hurt anyone."

"Thanks. I appreciate that a lot, Niccola."

"Any time, but," he lowered his voice when the waiter came toward us, "Sienna, we don't ever take a life easily. We would only call a hit because that person deserved it. It is not for the sport of it. So, maybe your next question to Elenora should be, if we did do the hit, why?"

"Yeah." I chewed on the inside of my lip.

"Just something to think about." He patted my hand before leaving me.

My head spun, and I felt like I needed some air, so I headed toward the French doors when suddenly I slowed my walk. I watched as Elenora brushed a hand down Francesco's arm, and his expression softened for a hair of a second. Goosebumps broke out on my body as I continued to study them. I started to walk through the sea of people, the entire time keeping my gaze on them. He seemed to comfort her, and what was even more strange was she was doing it with Oscar nearby.

Could he be…I couldn't finish the thought. How could I? That would mean my own flesh and blood had been near throughout my younger years. I couldn't go there.

I stopped mid-step when Elio's Aunt Noemi came into the room. She froze like a deer in headlights as she glared at Elenora.

Wait. What?

When Elenora spotted her staring, she quickly dropped her hand from Francesco and looked like she'd seen a ghost.

All the noises around me faded, the guests disappeared from my view, and all I could hear was my heartbeat and air rushing through my lungs as I watched the interaction between them.

I felt *his* eyes on me, and it took all my strength to meet Elio's worried expression.

"What's wrong?" he mouthed. I pulled his gaze with mine over to his aunt and my mother, who were now glaring at one another fifteen feet apart.

He was across the room before I could even blink. He leaned over the bar with his back to them.

"What do you know?"

"I'm not really sure." I was still frozen in place.

"Where's Vinni?"

"I-I don't know." I stumbled over his question.

"Look around," he ordered as he calmly sipped his drink.

I closed my eyes and tried to focus on what he wanted me to do, then opened them and searched the crowd until I spotted him rocking out with a friend.

"On the dance floor."

"Good, now keep your eyes on him and only him."

"Why?"

"Because I said so." I let out a frustrated breath but did as I was told because Elio only got bossy when something was going on.

"Wait, what do *you* know?"

"I understand enough that you shouldn't have seen what you just did, so keep your eyes on Vinni until whatever you saw is finished."

"Why?" I leaned back and studied Elio's stony expression, frustrated that he had stopped sharing.

"You want to be a part of this life, right?" I nodded as he spoke through gritted teeth. "Then you need to know how to deal with situations like these when they happen. I see what you're seeing, but like you, I know nothing," he explained. "Elenora arriving is like a spider spinning a web. It's catching lots of attention, and flies are getting tangled up in it. So, for now, we sit back and watch and gather as much information as possible, because moving too fast will only scare away the truth."

"Was that so hard?" I couldn't help the hurt in my tone.

He lowered his drink and finally looked at me now that Elenora walked away.

"You also need to know how to take orders." His gaze skimmed my cleavage as his tongue darted out to catch a drop from his bottom lip. Everything inside me coiled tight as the memory of him inside me made my skin heat. "I've spent a lifetime keeping this part of my life away from you. It's not ingrained in me to share it easily."

"But look at how much I listen when you do." I held my dirty expression for another beat then pushed off the bar. I stopped short when my mother suddenly appeared in front of me.

Jesus.

"I was hoping we could spend a little more time together."

"I'm willing."

She looked at Elio then back to me. "As long as I'm not interrupting anything."

"Not at all." Elio smiled warmly then left us alone.

"Do you mind if we step outside?"

"Sounds good." I followed her outside and along a small path that led us away from the music and constant chatter. Crickets chirped happily, and tiny fireflies flickered through the sunflower fields. As dark as the mafia life might be, there were many aspects of living here that were absolutely stunning.

"I love these." She brushed her finger along the petal of a six-foot flower that stared up at the night sky. "These and white roses are my favorite."

"Me too, but I like red roses."

"My mother always had a dozen red roses on the dining room table." She lowered her head. "She died a few years after we left."

"Do you have any photos of her?" I was so desperate for something from my past.

"Just one." She cleared her throat. "I wish I had more, but I didn't have much time."

"Why did we leave in such a hurry?"

"Sienna—"

"Please," I closed my eyes and felt the burn of tears coming on, "you may have the painful memories of knowing everything, but I have the painful hole from where those memories should be. I know that something big happened. I know this because a mother doesn't just abandon her daughter then show up randomly half a lifetime later. I'm not asking for it all right now. I'm only asking for something to ease the lonely ache that grows inside of me."

"I wish you would stop saying I abandoned you, Sienna," she finally said as we continued deeper into the field. "I thought you were safe. I was led to believe you were safe. You had a roof over your head, food, clothes. I wanted you with me, but I couldn't, so I made sure you at least had all you needed at the time."

I stopped in my tracks, shocked by what she said.

"All I needed?" I wanted to shout, but I also didn't want to have another fight. "What I needed was my mother. I needed to know who I was and where I came from. I feel like a blank canvas with the edges all smudged and pinched at the seams. When I was a child, there were times I could barely hold it together. Then you finally show up with the key to my past and judge me for who I have surrounded myself with."

"I'm sorry, Sienna."

"I don't want your apologies, Elenora, I want you to

be my mother." That hit home for her because her mouth shut and her chin quivered. "Give me something," I whispered. "Prove to me you want this."

"I want to. I really do, but there is so much, and I need time to figure out how to protect you." Her eyes narrowed in on mine.

I felt like I might just open Pandora's Box and I wouldn't be able to stop it.

She hesitated. "You're looking for the truth about your past from me, Sienna, but perhaps you should open your eyes and look to the people you now call your family." She slowly took her hands and placed them on my shoulders and turned me toward the Hill House. "Quiet secrets lay in places where you might think you're safe. Perhaps with those you love." An icy chill raced up my spine.

"Sienna." Niccola suddenly stepped out from between a row of sunflowers, as if appearing from another dimension. He eyed my mother with a cold expression. "Wyatt's looking for you."

I stared at him for a moment, trying to gather myself. "Okay, I'll be right there." I turned to my mother. "I need to go."

As I began to make my way to the house, I felt a strong urge to look up. When I did, I stopped short as a man, dressed in a gray suit, stood close to the wall. He was watching me. I couldn't bring myself to smile or say anything to him as I brushed by him. I just blinked, startled by the intensity of his stare. The lights from the party caught the pin on his lapel, and I squinted to see a gold crown. I tried to shake off the unwanted chill both from him and from my mother's words.

"You look pale," Wyatt commented as I joined him. "Are you all right?"

"Never better." I shook my head at him, not wanting to get into it right now.

As the night went on and the world's biggest birthday cake was devoured, I found myself out by the pool on one of the big puffy lounge chairs with a few friends of Vinni's. Wyatt was laughing so hard at one of the guys he was turning red while I savored the moment that my best friend got to meet, live, and party with some of the most important people in my life.

"*Pssp*, Nic!" Vinni raced out of the guest house with his shirt open. "There's a girl in my bed."

"Yes, there is." He laughed.

"I didn't do that." He suddenly grinned ridiculously at Niccola. "Did you do that?"

"Happy Birthday, little brother."

"Best brother ever." He mauled Niccola's head. "Well, I should get back."

"Good plan."

We all laughed when Vinni nearly missed the door and clipped his shoulder on the frame.

"Well, Vinni's got company tonight. What about you, Sienna?" One of the guys, who had been really nice, leaned forward.

"Nope." Niccola shook his head. "Not happening, man. Nope, nope, stop talking."

"Why?" He shrugged. "She's hot, and she said she

was single earlier."

"This is so awkward." Wyatt covered his mouth.

"What's awkward?" The guy looked around, not at all feeling the vibe.

"As flattered as I am—" I paused as Elio sat down next to me and wrapped an arm around the back of the seat.

The guy stared at him then leaned back and raised his hands for a moment then let them settle nervously on his thigh.

I smiled at him in sympathy. "Gentlemen, I've been through a lot this past week, and sleep is the number one thing on my mind at the moment."

"Understood." The guy gave a glance at Elio then cleared his throat and stood. He sputtered an excuse and hurried off toward the house.

It wasn't long before we all were saying goodnight and heading up for some much-needed rest. Who knew what tomorrow would bring? But my experience as a reporter had come to the surface over the past few hours, prompted by all I'd observed tonight. As off as I felt, I was ready to hone my skills and do some digging.

I stripped out of my dress and slipped on a gray silk robe, easing onto a chair that was placed to look out over the hills. I kicked my feet up on the chair next to me and watched some guests pile into their cars. I saw their lights as they wove along the winding roads and disappeared into the dark night. The moon peeked out from behind the clouds, and as I relaxed, I wondered what in the world I had witnessed tonight between my mother and Aunt Noemi. I tapped my nail on my lip as I let my mind run through all the possibilities that it could have been about.

"Hey." Elio was standing in the doorway, and his gaze positively burned as it dragged down my body to where my robe had fallen away from my hip. "I just wanted to check in before my meeting with papa."

"I'm good." The heel of my shoe dug into the fabric of the chair, a dead giveaway I was lying. He stepped inside the room, closing the door behind him. His hands were in his pockets as he approached me, but as he got closer, he reached out and dragged a finger from my ankle up to my knee and down between my legs, brushing over my arousal. He moved behind my chair, brushed my hair back, and started to gently rub my shoulders.

I moaned at how good it felt.

"No matter how bad this gets," he whispered, "we always have us." I nodded, unable to speak. I needed to hear that. "I'm sorry I can't stay." He kissed my neck.

"I'll be here if you can."

"Leave the heels on." He chuckled before he left me, slipping out of the room just as silently as he had appeared.

Morning came, and the sun shone brightly through the window. Wyatt had left to chase another story, and there was a part of me that wished I could have joined him on the assignment. I loved being a journalist as much as he did, but my own leads were about to take me in a very different direction. Right now, my attention needed to be here.

My thoughts wandered back to last night. I had hoped Elio would come to me, but his father's meeting must have gone late because he never returned. My need for him was strong, but sleep eventually overcame desire, and I needed that too. It was a new day, and I wanted to get digging on my mother and what she had told me, not to mention Mariano and what he was up to.

After a long shower, I slipped on a sun dress and headed downstairs where I found a very hungover Anna wearing sunglasses and one hell of a scowl.

"I know that look." I gave her a sympathetic smile as I waved at Donte, who was prepping something green in a blender. "Can I get you anything?"

"If I wanted your sympathy, I would have asked for it," she muttered hatefully. "Donte, for God's sake, are you growing that fruit for the smoothie or what?"

Donte rolled his eyes and smirked as he turned up the blender to full speed. Anna groaned and covered her ears at the shrill sound of frozen fruit being roughly puréed.

I handed her a bottle of aspirin from the cabinet, but she swatted my hand away, sending the bottle flying across the room.

"I said I don't need your help, orphan girl!" My mouth dropped open at her words. "Don't give me that innocent look. I've been on to you since you arrived here."

"Ms. Anna." Donte shook his head with disbelief.

"You're the help, Donte. Know your place." She

slipped off the stool and stuck a finger in my face. "I have been part of this family since they arrived here a decade ago. Elio is mine. Mariano is my good time." Stale bourbon poured out of her pores. "I will not let some alley cat from the streets come in here and screw it all up. I know all about you and your rise to success, but the truth is, your parents didn't want you, and guess what, everyone here is just being nice because you had your face on a magazine cover. Do you really think Andrea and Piero are okay with who you are? Open your eyes, Sienna. This family has an image to uphold, and having some orphan hanging around doesn't look good for their reputation." She pointed over my shoulder. "So, there's the door."

I shook my head as her words cut through to my lifetime of insecurity. How could she say something so incredibly hurtful without even knowing me? I wanted to snap back something witty, but sadly, the word "orphan" rocked me off my game.

"I believe you were going to go pack?" She flicked her wrist at me and snatched the jug from Donte before sitting back down at the island.

"Right," I muttered with a nod. "Got it."

I turned on my heel and came face to face with Francesco.

"Are you okay?"

"Yeah," I swallowed back my emotions, "I just need some air."

"Ms. Sienna," Donte called after me, but I was too embarrassed to face him.

Elio

"I know when they're going to move their next shipment. It's in three hours." I handed my father Stefno's notebook. Our meeting had started late as we had waited for Francesco, who eventually cancelled on us. It wasn't lost on either of us that it was the first time in twenty years he had missed one of these meetings.

I had been in my office in town all day making calls and preparing for our oil shipment to arrive. I needed things to go smoothly this evening. I had spent considerable hours trying to connect with Stefano's mind before I was able to work out how his notes were kept. "It's the day, then month," I explained.

"This could be old."

"It's not. My guess would be he has one for each year. Flip the front cover and look at the spine."

"Yup, there's the year." My father squinted at the tiny writing.

"And he marks the pages that have been dealt with by splitting the page at the center bottom." I pointed to a Post-it that marked a page from a few days ago. "That was the shipment where we found the girl."

"And how many detective shows did you watch to figure this out?" Vinni chuckled.

"It's more than looking at the book," I explained. "You have to look at the pattern of events, and then cross reference them with his writing. He has a big ego in real life, and it shows on paper as well. Look how he writes the letter I." I reached for the book and showed them. "See how all the I's are bigger than the others. It took a little while, but after I started to think like him, I could figure out the rest. It helps to know his character."

"And what about this Mikey person? Any thoughts there?" Niccola spoke up.

"That, I don't know. All I can find is the name written a few times and some tally marks. What is strange, though, is every time Stefano writes someone's name, he runs the pen over it a few times to make it be bold. Not once in the four times that he wrote Mikey's name was it bolded."

"Maybe he isn't that important?"

"No," I shook my head in thought, "I think it's just the opposite. But whoever it is, I don't think Stefano likes him."

"Niccola and Vinni, you two start digging on who the hell this Mikey guy is," my father ordered. "Elio and I will get the men ready to intercept this shipment. Circle back here in sixty for further instructions."

"Sure thing." Vinni started on his phone, while Niccola went for his laptop.

An hour later, there was a cavalry of men at the dockyard, all in different locations, well hidden from view.

I had dressed for the encounter, with several handguns hidden under my clothing. My mind centered on the bloody business that was about to happen. As I reached for the handle of the town car, my father stopped me, then asked our temporary driver to step out of the car.

"Son, I want you to stay back with me. I can't risk you getting shot. The family business needs both of us, especially now, and you don't need to be on the forefront risking your life. Our soldiers will leave their mark. They're well trained."

I knew he was right, and the day would come that I might stay back, but not this fight. This fight was mine.

"I'm different than you, Papa. I need to be in it, to see it. I'm not reckless, and I believe I've proven that to you time and again. This is quickly getting personal, and the fact that Stefano's been spotted at the dockyard means I should be there too."

My father looked out the window, digesting my words. He could order me to stay; he had that authority. He had always held me as an equal to him, but for some reason right now he was in the mind space of a worried father, not the head of our syndicate.

"It's not just about us anymore," he added.

"I know, and her face is what will be driving me home tonight." I put a hand on his arm to assure him that my mind was in all the right places tonight.

"All right." He nodded, and I saw the moment was over and his tone was all business once again. He glanced at his watch. "One hour."

I rushed out of the car, pulled my weapon, and headed down the hill to where Vinni and Niccola were waiting for my approval to move in on the containers. Row by row, we cleared the area. We had a visual on a few of the Coppola men down by the water in a dingy. What we didn't know was if the container of girls was here now, or if they were being dropped off somewhere else and then being loaded onto our ships a few at a time.

"Nic." I nodded at a door that looked to have had the lock cut off. Niccola slowly opened it, and Vinni used his flashlight to peek inside. It was empty. I made a note of the container number to have the lock fixed later. We moved in unison. The water lapped at the shoreline, drowning out any noise of our approach. Trouble was it also covered any sound that might have helped us locate the girls.

As Vinni disappeared around a corner, I heard footsteps behind me. I pulled out my knife as a man suddenly charged me. Once he made contact, I jammed the blade into his neck and removed it as he fell to the ground in a slump. I felt another pair of arms wrap around me from behind and was pulled backward. Using my elbow, I knocked him in the ribs, bent down, and popped his shoulder out of the socket, freeing myself. As he yelped in pain, I sensed someone else behind me and instinctively ducked at a swoosh of air over my head as a fist swung above me. I threw my weight onto my hands and kicked his knee as he dropped. I tossed my knife, done with this shit, and popped him right between the eyes then followed up with his buddy. My silencer helped to not give my position away. I leaned down to the man I had knifed in the neck. He choked as he gurgled and fought to speak, his hands clenched tightly to the deep gash. I pressed my foot into his windpipe to open the wound wide, and the blood flowed freely.

"I have no sympathy for demons that prey on young children," I whispered. "You're getting off easy."

"It's not what you think," he gurled with his last breath.

I rushed to catch up with the others, wondering what his comment meant. After a few turns, I stumbled right into an ambush on Vinni. I shot two in the back then punched the one who held my cousin around the neck. Vinni gasped for air as the man released his hold and fell. We both jumped him and punched until he went slack.

"Where's Niccola?" I panted.

"That way." Vinni shook himself and snatched up his gun from where it had fallen. We headed in the direction of the water.

I heard a groan and held my hand up to stop Vinni, who was hard on my heels. Something alerted me to danger, and I knew Niccola was ahead of us.

"Make the call," I ordered and turned to stop Vinni from moving forward. If Niccola was seconds from death, the last thing his little brother needed was to witness it. I knew the call would spook them, and it might risk our chance at locating the girls, but I would not chance losing one of my own to the Coppola family. I could not carry that on my shoulders.

"The call is in." Vinni appeared behind me again before he raced off in a different direction. Suddenly, it was as if someone pulled the plug on a levee, sending a tsunami of destruction onto the town below. My men swarmed the army of Coppola men at the dock's edge, gunfire lit up the night, and screams filled the air as I carefully scanned the area.

I knew he was there. I could feel him.

Something cold prickled my back, and in one swift motion I whirled around, but not soon enough. The back side of a shovel smoked my head and sent me backward. Pain shot through my skull, but I managed to catch my footing and get into my fight stance. This was what I had trained for, why I had spent all those hours in the ring with my trainer, and I hoped it would pay off.

I blinked to clear my vison, and he caught me off guard and rammed me into a container, sending all the air from my lungs.

"Ahh, the mighty Elio Capri." Stefano laughed like a crazy person as he held me down. "I should have known you were too proud to stay up on the mountaintop like your father."

"And miss this?" I relaxed for a split second then sent a punch into his gut and head butted him hard sending him back. "Where are the girls?" I lunged, and he grabbed my arms, using my momentum to send us both into the wall. Again, I was on my feet ready for more. Blood dripped into my eye, but I blinked it back. My vision was now blurred in the left eye.

"Girls?" He chuckled, shaking his head as he limped backward. As I followed, my fingers twitched for my gun. "Oh, please, Elio, you need to see the bigger picture here."

I spat the blood that pooled in the corner of my mouth.

"See what?" I yelled, feeling the anger fuel my adrenaline. "Entertainment?"

"Though I've been known to be theatrical, my dear rival, I knew sweet little Val would share my phone call performance with you."

No, she didn't, actually.

"I figured we should meet face to face, since this is, after all, our fight."

So, no mention of the notebook.

"She also mentioned Mikey." I was pleased to see the corners of his eyes widened at that, and the creases in his forehead deepened.

"Well, sir," he slipped his mask back down and held his arms open wide, "I believe this is where we part ways." He glanced over his shoulder then turned back to me. "Tell Sienna I'll take her out riding sometime." He dove sideways behind a container.

I pulled my gun and fired off a shot as I charged after him, but he had disappeared.

The sound of a boat engine caught my attention, and I raced toward the water's edge only to see its light disappear from view.

Fuck!

I swung around and looked for Niccola and Vinni and was relieved to find both of them safe. Our soldiers had rounded up any of the Coppola men who still could stand and had them lined up next to a pile of their dead cohorts. Frustration and fury at the situation filled me as I walked toward the car, and I shot two of the men in the head as I passed by. "Clean this shit up." I spat the words at one of my men.

The car ride home proved to be a difficult one. My father got his rundown mostly from Niccola, as I stared out the window with my anger building over what had happened. Stefano's words about taking Sienna for a ride bounced around my head. What the hell did that mean? Had Mariano told him about Sienna and her love of horses and how she enjoyed riding? Did Mariano know who Sienna was to me? Had I been underestimating Mariano this entire time?

"Elio?" My father drew me from my internal war. "Coming?" He looked down at me as I sat like stone in the car. I hadn't noticed we were in our own driveway.

"Yeah," I sighed.

"Is there something I should know?"

I closed my eyes and touched the cut on my head, glad to feel the sting. I used the pain to center myself before I exited the car and answered him.

"Stefano mentioned that he would be seeing Sienna very soon."

"What?" Francesco said as he approached from behind my father. His face looked as jacked up as I felt.

After we entered the house, my father quickly filled him in on what had happened. He then brought him up to speed on the afternoon's meeting.

"What about Stefano's comment about Sienna?" Francesco brought us back to the main issue.

"Either I'm way off and Stefano is looking to take Sienna from Mariano, or," I lowered my voice, "Mariano knows who Sienna is to me."

"Both could be plausible." My father rubbed his face.

"I'll see what I can find out." Francesco hurried away, and I rolled my shoulders to relieve some tension.

"If Mariano does know who Sienna is to me," I whispered, "I can't promise my actions, Papa."

"Until then," he motioned me to follow him, "let's join Mama and let her see you're okay."

Donte caught my attention, and one look at his face made my stomach drop.

"Boss, may I speak to you?"

Chapter
NINE

I fiddled with the tassel that dangled from the spine of my old journal. It was a lovely deep yellow and made me think of the sunflower fields next to me. I still couldn't believe Wyatt had asked his sister to send me my box of memories. I had kept every note Elio had ever written me and the three journals that had carried me through most of my childhood. Some might think I should have tossed them away, not wanting to relive such pain and confusion, but for me it was not about the pain. It was about the good memories tucked between the bad times. The questions to my mother about life, friendship, and boys, or how much I loved Cara. I was so thankful to have saved all those memories of our friendship. Then there were my thoughts about when I first met Elio and how I felt so safe and free around him. It was my personal time capsule, and I relived each moment as I leafed through the pages, breathing in the heavenly notes as I let my mind wander.

I loved it here at the Hill House, minus a few exceptions. The hurt from today's nasty conversation with Anna still burned at the insecure spots in my heart. I had no doubt that Elio loved me, and I knew Andrea and Piero did too, but I would never want to overstay my welcome or be a problem in general. It bothered me a bit that I had allowed old wounds to crack open at what I knew was only said out of jealousy.

My phone buzzed against my leg, and I saw it was a text message.

Mariano: Taking a quick shower, but drinks at my place in thirty?

I dropped my head back against the chair and wondered what I should do. Maybe Andrea would have a suggestion.

A loud bang had me on my feet and inside the living room where I caught sight of a battered Elio as he raced by the doorway in a fit of rage. I followed as he marched right up to Anna, wrapped his hands around her neck, lifted her off her feet and slammed her into the wall.

Andrea waved her hands to whisk the kitchen staff away from him. I glanced over at Donte who was also watching things unfold.

Oh, no.

"Who are you," Elio growled at her, "to talk to my

guest that way?" Anna tried to speak but couldn't. "Just because your father did what he did for us doesn't give you the right to throw stones. For this, you owe me." He lowered her to the floor but waited a beat before he let go of her throat. "And, Anna, I will be collecting on that real soon."

"Are you okay?" Niccola asked over my shoulder. I nodded, unsure if I should move and draw attention to myself. "Anna's father was the one who warned us about the hit on Piero. Needless to say, we tolerate Anna's behavior as a thank you. However, I think that gesture may have an expiration date."

"I can see that." I could barely hear my own words as I watched Anna rub her throat. Her eyes streamed with tears. No one moved to help her. In fact, Andrea turned on her heel and left the room. Anna just stood there, frozen, not at all registering my presence. "Where is Elio?" I muttered to Niccola. When he didn't answer, I looked over my shoulder and realized he was gone.

I moved to open the freezer to get her some ice, but Donte pulled my arm toward him.

"Don't," he warned. "Trust me." I nodded. He was right, because if she lashed out at me again, Elio just might kill her.

"Why did you tell Elio?" I had hoped he would keep it quiet.

"For two reasons, really." He rubbed his arm as though uneasy. "If the boss found out I was there and didn't tell him, I would be out of a job, and second, she'll only get worse. Anna has had her eyes on the boss since the moment he arrived here, which means you are her number one target."

"Elio and I aren't even together."

"I'm the head chef, Sienna," he raised an eyebrow at me, "which means I see and hear all." I brushed a hand through my hair, unsure what I should do next. "But don't worry," he smiled, "I learned quickly that I know nothing."

"Good," I huffed, letting go a little bit of tension.

"She's wrong, you know, about you not being welcome here. I know for a fact that Andrea and Piero hope you stay. And, well, the boss…" he pointed to the still gasping Anna, "the proof is in her bruised vocal cords." I smirked, and he laughed.

"Thanks, Donte."

"Anytime." He started to leave then turned back. "I know Wyatt left today. So as your *person* is gone for a bit, if you ever need company, you know where to find me."

"I think I'll take you up on that."

"I hope you do." He shot me a genuine smile and headed for the walk-in pantry.

"Oh, wait."

"Yeah?"

"When we were on our walk the other day, it seemed like you remembered something when I told you about my favorite thing to do in Sicily." His smile widened. "What was that about?"

He moved closer and lowered his voice, but his eyes danced with excitement. "When the boss first moved here, there were countless women who wanted his attention, but it was as if he didn't even see them. As you can imagine, over time, many theories were put out there about why the boss wouldn't date anyone." He warmed to his story. "One night, I was working late and wanted to run the menu by Mrs. Capri when I overheard Niccola telling a story about the boss's great love. I mean, they were right outside the kitchen." He shrugged with an unapologetic grin and tapped his temple as a reminder that he did see and hear all.

"I know, I know." I laughed and grinned back at him. I urged him to continue with a roll of my hands.

"Well, Niccola's point to his story was to try to explain to another family member that it wouldn't do any good to bring her daughter's friend to the house to try to introduce her. He said the boss had met his love at a swimming pond many years ago and had to leave her behind. He said it was as if he was cursed to never love another." He stopped and placed a dramatic hand over his heart. "How romantic is that?" He gave me a look but, when I said nothing, he continued. "At the time, we all wondered if it was true or if he was just bitter over what happened to his family." He paused. "Then you arrived, and suddenly he was so different. It was almost as if the part of him that could love was reawakened." He shrugged. "As if all those fairytales you were told as a child might actually come true if you searched hard enough." He laughed at himself. "Forgive me, I really am a romantic. When you told me about how you loved going to the swimming pond, I connected the dots, and

I was so happy for him. I genuinely care what happens to the boss. Mafia or not, he's a good person, and so are you."

I felt a tear slip down over my cheek, revealing how deeply his words hit me.

"I wasn't expecting that."

"Well, for what it's worth," he leaned in, "I'm on Team Sienna." He winked then turned to the shelves and made a show of trying to select the right spices.

A small laugh escaped my lips as I stepped out and saw Anna on unsteady legs, her face a study of fury and tears. As I slipped around the corner to go look for Andrea, I let a little bubble of happiness rise through the hurt of my Anna wounds.

"Okay, where could she be?" I said to myself as I continued my hunt for Andrea. It was as if everyone in the family had disappeared, and the staff scurried about like mice.

It made me think about Elio's loss of control. Talk about a mood change. I wondered how often he lost his cool. I couldn't imagine it was the norm, so the staff probably weren't sure how to handle it.

"There you are!" Mariano shouted from the end of the hall, sending my heart into my throat. His voice echoed over the marble flooring, making me cringe at the sudden intrusion. "You never texted me back."

"I must have missed it." I slapped on a smile and tried to act normal. "How was your day?"

"Better now." He leaned in for a kiss, but I moved my head, sending his lips to my cheek. I felt his shoulders sag at my lack of affection. I didn't care. I had reminded him many times that we were just friends. "Are you ready?" I loved how I didn't even give him a yes or no, but he just made the assumption it was a yes.

"Where?" I shot him a glare.

"Drinks at my place."

"Oh, that sounds fun." I stepped back and called into the kitchen, "Vinni, drinks at Mariano's?" And just like that, my perfect plan of flushing out a barely recovered Anna worked like a charm. There was no way I would allow myself alone with this asshat.

"I'm game," she said as she cleared her throat. Mariano's face twisted but soon smoothed out as something else seemed to come to him.

"Yeah, Anna?" He squinted at her red eyes. "You okay?"

"I'm fucking great." She snickered.

"Great." I made a halfhearted attempt to be cheery. "Let me grab my things, and I'll meet you back here."

Oh, boy, an evening with a woman who hated me and a man who would love nothing more than to get me alone. I was flirting with disaster.

Once inside my room, I ran a brush through my hair then paced the floor. I didn't have much time, but I hoped if I could get them drinking, something just might come out. Besides, Elio's house wasn't far from his. I could just race up there if I needed to.

Sienna: I'm at Mariano's. I'll explain later.

With a plan in mind, I grabbed my sweater and purse and headed down the stairs.

"Finally," Anna snapped, and I rolled my eyes as I followed them to the car.

Not even an hour later, Mariano and Anna were three quarters of the way into their beloved bottle of grappa. I had already tipped two glasses of wine into the planter next to me. If I was going to do this, I needed to act like I was holding up to their level of drinking. How anyone could drink as much as they did made my liver ache.

"So, Sienna," Anna had sprawled herself out on the couch, her skirt hiked up her thigh, it was sure to gain Mariano's attention, "I don't know much about you."

"That's true, you don't." I made a show of downing the small quantity of red wine left in my glass and poured myself another.

"Why is that?" She rubbed her face.

"Because you chose not to like me."

"That's true." She laughed, looking at Mariano, who chuckled while staring at his phone. "I don't like most women."

"I get that impression."

"Mostly, I don't like women I can't read." She leaned forward and blinked a few times, no doubt trying to clear her blurry vision. "And I find you very difficult to read."

"It's a safety thing," I admitted, thinking if I said some truths maybe they would too.

"So, tell me, if you're as quiet and reserved as you seem, why would you do something as risky as that article? Especially that half-naked photo on the front."

"I am reserved to a point." I felt the need to defend

myself. "The article was about hope and strength. When you grow up the way I had to, that is all you have. As for the photo, that was me being brave enough to let people really see me, who I am and how proud I was of who I had become. I can see how it might make some women feel insecure, especially if they don't see themselves as beautiful on the inside." I held her annoyed gaze.

"Well, if you don't mind the idea of that picture being in multiple men's bedside tables, I guess." She laughed with Mariano.

"Yeah." He wiggled his eyebrows at me. I shook off their childish reaction.

"Tell me something about yourself." Anna awkwardly poured herself another drink spilling more than a good shot onto the wooden table. "Tell me about why you won't sleep with Mariano."

So, he shared that, and we're going there. Okay...

"I've rushed into relationships before getting to know the person well enough, and it didn't end well. My last boyfriend reminded me I don't need a man to be happy."

"Are you gay?"

I squinted at her crassness; if I was or wasn't, it certainly was none of her business.

"No, I'm not."

"That would be a shame," Mariano muttered.

"My turn." I filled up her half-full glass. "You're clearly interested in Elio. What's going on there?"

Her face twisted into a painful expression, and she took a moment to lick her fingers free of the spilled grappa.

"We've been on a few dates." My stomach sank. "We are supposed to…" She paused like she was stopping herself from finishing her sentence. "I'm too close to the family, I think, for him to see me as much more than a friend, though. At least at this point."

"I see. Well—"

"But that doesn't stop me from removing fake women like you from his life. He'll wake up one day and see I'm the best fit for him."

"That's a great plan you got there, Anna." I couldn't help but chuckle at my sarcastic tone, which in turn made Mariano laugh too.

"You're one to talk," she tossed at him.

"Yeah," I chimed in, "you'd need to break up with your phone first to even see the women around you."

"I see you," he shot back as he slid the phone onto the table then moved closer to me.

"And I need to pee," Anna groaned, leaving the two of us alone.

Dammit.

"All right," I turned to look at him dead in the eye, trying not to show any weakness, "what is it about me that you like?"

"Your smile." He beamed like a child, but there was something else there I just couldn't pinpoint. It was in his expression. "I like that you're nice, but I do think you need to loosen up a little." I swatted at his hand when it went for my shoulder strap. "And I think you'd be a good secret keeper." That caught my attention. "Your turn. What do you like about me?"

Oh, boy...

"I think you're nice, but you could work on your manners."

"Meaning?" He studied my face as I leaned forward and snagged his phone.

"This is always in your face."

"I have a lot of people who need me." He slurred the last word. "I have many hats to wear, and some have to be worn at night." He grunted the last bit.

I tucked that away.

"Okay, but what's going on in here?" I stood and held up his phone. He stood too, nearly falling into to me. "Is it really as important as spending time with someone you claim to care about?"

He leaned back and had to grab the chair for balance. He was completely out of it. "My life is like a game." He started to stumble over his words as he followed me over to the bar. He leaned to one side and grabbed some chips from a bowl and shoved some in his mouth as he spoke. "Like one of those teeter totters that children play on, each side has something I want. I'm just trying to figure out what side is better."

"I've been there."

"Not like this, Ace." He laughed but started to choke on the chips and held the bar top as though to stop the spins. I worried he would pass out on me.

"You want to talk about it?" I tried to act sincere. "Is there anything I can do to help?"

He smirked and shook his head then took his phone

from me. "I'd say I'm sorry, but I'm not."

"I'm not following. What are you sorry for?"

Anna came back then, in only a towel, announcing she wanted to go for a swim. He looked up from his phone and started to cheer.

"Yes," Mariano tossed his phone on the bar, "let's skinny dip!"

"Give me a sec." I rolled my eyes and pretended to make myself another drink. "Ice?"

"Freezer." He waved toward the kitchen as he followed Anna to the pool. Mariano didn't even remove his shirt, he just fell into the water, with a naked Anna right behind him. Quickly, I scooped up his phone before it turned off and headed into the kitchen. With the fridge door as a barrier, I used my phone and started to record what I was looking at. Many contacts were made up of numbers or one letter. It was pretty cryptic, but I was hoping Elio could make sense of it all. After a minute, I decided to go into his pictures and scrolled through.

"Need any help?" Mariano was suddenly behind me, and I froze. "Getting undressed?" He sounded like he was a sleezy teenager.

"No." I turned his phone over and quickly slid it under a bag of cherries while using my other hand to hide my own.

"Have you seen my phone?" He patted down his wet pockets then eyed me as he took a step toward me. I pulled the last weapon I had on me, thanks to Niccola and his little tip. Removing the packaging, I popped the round little red lollipop in my mouth and sucked on it loudly.

"No, I haven't."

He came closer, and water dripped off his hair and sent goosebumps down my arms. "Can I ask you something?"

"Sure." It took everything in me not to step away.

"Can I trust you?" His expression changed, and I was unsure of what he was about to say or do.

"I don't see why not." He pushed my hair back over my shoulder, and the other pushed the fridge door shut. I sucked louder, and for a moment my mind went to Elio leaning back in the hotel chair in New York.

"What would it take for you to open up to me? Just to give me a chance?"

Here was *my* chance.

"I'm not sure." I pretended to think, slurping around the little white stick. "Maybe you could try to do the same with me. Sometimes sharing something personal can break down barriers." He leaned closer, and I held my breath, not wanting to ruin the moment, his gaze dropped to the lollipop, and I saw his disgust and annoyance by the way his lip curled and his brow wrinkled.

"I hate those things. Let's get rid of it." He pulled it from my mouth and tossed it in the sink where it broke into sticky pieces. Then his hands moved up to my breasts, and I grabbed them, pushing them away.

"Personal boundaries are to be earned, Mariano. I'm not an Anna, and you should be thankful for that."

"Anna is only here because of what her father did."

"What did he do?"

"Her father figured out there was a going to be a hit on Piero. That's what saved his life."

"Who was behind the hit?" I shifted, and his eyes dropped to my breasts.

"There was speculation."

"Oh, yeah?" I wanted him to keep going. "Do you know who it was?"

He smirked, but when he went to speak again, Anna came in looking fit to kill.

"I didn't realize the party had moved to the kitchen." She glared at me. "Can I cut in?" She dropped her towel, and her skinny body shone in the dim light from the other room. Her tiny nipples were taunt, and her ribs poked out from her chest as she sucked in a sharp breath. I had to admit she wasn't sexy to me. I would think a woman needed meat and curves to grab my attention.

Mariano was like a cat in heat as he twisted away from me and moved over to her. As they went at it, I grabbed my purse then opened the fridge door to retrieve Mariano's phone. I slipped out the side door of the kitchen and dropped the phone near the pool. There was such a part of me that missed the investigation part of my job. I really should touch base with Georgio to see if there's anything small I could work on.

After finding Elio's house empty, I raced up to the Hill House. It was midnight, and the place was quiet. A light in the study told me someone was awake. Removing my heels so as not to risk waking anyone, I made my way down the hall and found Piero bent over a stack of papers. He had his thick, black reading glasses halfway down his nose. I leaned into the doorway, thinking how nice it was to come home to a family and not an empty house.

"You're out late, my dear," he said quietly as he licked his finger to turn a page.

"I am." I nodded. "Have you seen Elio?"

"He's handling some…" he paused, "business and won't be home until around noon tomorrow."

I found myself disappointed that I hadn't known that, but I remembered he hadn't responded to my text about going to Mariano's.

"Come, sit." Piero indicated a chair.

"I don't want to bother you."

"You're not." He smiled warmly. "Normally, Andrea spends the evening with me, but she's tired after spending the day with Bria."

"I can understand that." I chuckled and moved into the room. Spending more than an hour with Mariano's mother would drain anyone. I watched as his eyes scanned the pages and as he made little red marks by numbers. "May I ask you something?"

"Of course." He slid the paper he had marked to the bottom of the pile as he moved another one on top. It was relaxing to watch how methodically he did things.

"Now that I know your family is the head of a…" I wasn't sure how to word it.

"Syndicate."

"Yes, a syndicate, does that change things between you and me?"

"In what way do you think it would change things?"

"Well, I mean, am I still allowed to call you Piero? Are there things I should and should not say to people? Should I really be here, or am I here because I know things?"

"Yes." He nodded while keeping his head down.

"Okay." I felt strange suddenly and made a move to get up.

"My dear Sienna." He removed his glasses and pulled himself away from his work. "You've always been the exception to the rule with our family. I've always allowed you to call me by my first name. But yes, there are things you need to know, and we'll get there. I haven't pushed it because of your mother arriving. I know you wouldn't share anything with anyone, because you never have. It's not who you are. And as for your last question, you're here because you are part of this family. Life may have kept us apart for a decade, but it also put us back together, stronger."

"Thank you." I played with my hands and thought about his lovely explanation. "Not to be bold, but I wonder if I might ask a question?" He nodded. "My mother mentioned something about a hit that took place back in the nineties. Would I be allowed to ask you about it?"

He leaned back in his chair and dropped his pen on top of the paperwork.

"I'm all right with that."

"My mother said the reason she hates your family so much is because of a hit that was put on her brother back then."

"Do you have a name?"

"Yes." I pulled out my phone with the name and year he was killed and handed it to him. He said nothing but fixed his glasses on his nose and scribbled it down.

"I will look into it in the morning."

"I appreciate that." I stood then sat back down, and he looked over at me. I knew it was wise to share Mariano's information too. I would never want him to think I would ever hold a secret from him. "I'm not sure, but I think Mariano might know who was behind the attempted hit on you."

"What?" His face went from shock to no emotion while I filled him in on the conversation. "And there's this," I opened my phone and showed him the video I took. He absorbed the information being played out in front of him.

"It was very dangerous doing what you did tonight. The information you have is invaluable to us, but please, Sienna, you must be careful. You have no idea what evil looks like until it has you in its hold."

"He had no idea. He was drunk, or I would never have done it. However, please know that I did let Elio know via text where I was going. I was not trying to be reckless, only helpful."

"I'm glad you did that. I know you were trying to help. Just please don't do anything like that again. I don't need my son losing his mind."

"You have my word I won't do anything careless. So, I'll tell you now that Mariano is taking me out tomorrow. He says he has something he wants to share."

"Any idea what that is?"

"No, but I've shared the location of my phone with Elio and Vinni, so they can track me whenever."

"Smart girl." He nodded with approval. "You might catch on to this life faster than I thought."

I couldn't help but glow at his comment. I wished him goodnight and headed to bed.

Chapter
TEN

Elenora

Time passed us by in funny ways. Some moved on quickly from the wounds they got along the way and learned from them, while others dwelled on them. I wasn't too proud to say I dwelled, but I did for good reason. As anger festered below the surface, and I let my mind slip back in time.

I stepped out of the way of the stampede of students steaming from their last class of the day. Often, I'd wait outside his class and listen to the professor go on about the human body and why it did what it did at a crime scene. It was fascinating, and I only wished I had attended college, but I had no choice. My parents had insisted I work in the family business. No one enjoyed working for an insurance company, but it did pay the bills and then some. It was a very successful business. We had two main offices, one here in southern Sicily and another over on the central mainland. My brother and I raced to be the one to run Sicily, as soon as we were old enough to help manage the business. We both wanted to get away from our parents, but to our despair, our parents switched off and spent six months at one site and six months at the other. So much for some freedom.

"Hey, there." Francesco tucked his book away then wrapped an arm around my shoulders and kissed my cheek with a sigh. "God, I missed you."

"I walked you to your first class." I grinned, loving that he missed me.

"That was five hours ago. That's a lifetime to me." He tugged me toward our favorite spot under the tree next to the coffee cart where I found my brother Angelo waiting.

"Hey," he jumped to his feet, excited, "how's my favorite sister?"

"I'm your only sister." I gave him a hug. "What are you doing here? Does Papa know you're not in the office?"

"Yes and no. I kind of told him I had a doctor's appointment and a few errands to run before he and Mama arrive tomorrow." We both made a face. Our parents were so old fashioned and kept us on a short leash. "I wanted you to hear it from me first, but I've met someone."

"Oh?" I pulled him down on the blanket. We sat in

a circle as I pulled out the sandwiches I had made and shared them. "Tell us all about her. How did you meet?"

"She actually chased me." He chuckled and selected a carrot from the container. "She kept coming into the office on days I worked, selling things she made. She got to know that I loved her butter tarts. She was persistent, and apparently that's a major turn-on for me."

"Good to know your turn-ons," Francesco said through a mouthful of sandwich, and I smirked at his comment. The three of us were very close, so the idea that my baby brother had found someone who was just as interested in him as he was in her was pretty great. Besides, having another girl around would be a refreshing change.

"When do we get to meet her?"

"Soon, I hope, but can I ask you for a favor?"

"Of course." I would do anything for Angelo.

"Can both of you be there when she meets our parents tomorrow night?" He made a face as both of ours dropped into grim expressions.

"Look, man," Francesco brushed his hands free of crumbs, "you know I have your back no matter what, but let's be honest here. I'm not exactly welcome at your house."

"Which is total crap," I added angrily.

"It is, but it doesn't change anything." Francesco's hand landed on mine. "Despite what people think about the Capri family, they've done good for Sicily."

"Screw my parents." Angelo's face went red. "You're a great man who loves my sister, and that should count."

"It should." Francesco took my hand and pulled me closer. "But it doesn't change anything. Your parents made their minds up about the Capris long before they ever met me." He leaned back and rested his head on the tree trunk. "I'm sure the fact that they met me for the first time with Piero didn't help."

"I'm still really sorry about the way they acted." I lowered my gaze to my hands as I remembered how furious my parents were when we bumped into Piero Capri and Francesco at the shop next door. I was forced to introduce Francesco to them at a less than perfect time. They were very aware of who Francesco was with, and being in the insurance business, they were very aware of the crime that surrounded us. They forbid me to ever see Francesco again. Of course, I couldn't stay away from him. I was madly in love, and we were now desperately trying to figure out what our next move was going to be.

"Fine, then. I get it." My brother let it go. He knew there was no way Francesco could be there. "But you'll come, right?" His eyes pleaded at me.

"You, in the hot seat with a girl, meeting our parents for the first time." I laughed. "You couldn't pay me to miss that."

If only I had known the storm I would walk into when I arrived that night.

The sudden feeling of not being alone drew me from my memory.

"How long do you plan on watching me?" I asked without turning around. I felt the vibration as he pushed off the frame of the French doors and stepped out onto the hotel balcony with me.

"You always had a sixth sense when I was around." He took a seat next to me and rested his ankle across his thigh. "What were you thinking about just then?"

"Angelo." I flinched as I said his name, still feeling the sorrow that nipped at my core. "I miss him so much."

"Me too." He shifted and dropped his foot.

"Do you?" I murmured a challenge and stared directly into his eyes.

"Don't." He bit back a warning for me not to go there. It was the one topic we ran in circles with each other and had never come to see eye to eye on. It was the one topic that had nearly finished us many years ago. Only our strong love for one another held us together then, but, sadly, even it had run out along our painful path. He took a deep breath and changed the subject.

"I wanted to check in and see how you were after… last night. I saw that exchange with Noemi Capri." The hairs on my arms stood when he said that Noemi was a Capri. The words started to come, but I locked my jaw, unsure I could trust him not to shut this entire thing down when he found out the truth.

"Don't you do background checks on everyone?"

"Yes, and she had nothing to show."

"Neither did someone else we know," I countered then shifted my gaze off him. "We had a few run ins before. It's nothing that important." I waved it off.

"All right, Elenora, I'll leave it for now." He cleared his throat and waited a beat. "What do you have planned for today?"

"Well, I'm stuck in this hotel until I figure out what my next move is."

"It's not so bad." He shrugged, and I ignored his comment. I was used to something much better, and I wanted it back.

"Have you spoken to Sienna since the party?"

"No."

"Why?"

"Because she's always surrounded by *them*." I tasted the hate on my tongue and let the comment linger in the air.

Francesco leaned forward and rubbed his face. "You're back, Elenora, only you can choose what that means for her."

"I planned on reaching out to her today."

"Good." He stood and checked his phone.

"Do me a favor and call off the watchdogs."

"Elenora." He leaned down low, bending at the waist, and placed his hands on the armrests of my chair. "My patience with your attitude will only fly for so long." His eyes widened, and it took me back to the days when he would put me in my place because I went too far. "You'll be kind to those who looked after her when you weren't around. You have a second chance here to make things right." He shook his head as I tried to cut in. "You will not hurt my young girl, or you will have to answer to me."

"Are you quite finished?"

He waited a beat then slowly rose and left me alone with a racing heart.

Chapter
ELEVEN

Seriously? I sent another text to Mariano. For about the sixth time.

Sienna: Like I said, I can't come today.

My heels clicked on the floor as I raced into the kitchen and found Donte working with some fresh herbs. We had become fast friends, and I really enjoyed watching him whip up delicious things to eat.

"Morning." I took a moment to inhale the heavenly scent of whatever he was working on today. "Have you seen Elio? It's been nearly two days since I've heard from him." I was starting to get worried, as he and Piero had disappeared without a word. Even Niccola seemed to be absent. I thought I had heard his voice yesterday but couldn't confirm it. I knew Andrea was off visiting her sick cousin. It was crazy quiet in the house.

"No, sorry, but Mr. Vinni raced by here not that long ago. He might know where he is."

"Oh, yeah?" I turned and headed to see if he was out by the pool, but there was no sign of him.

Mariano: I'm heading up your way.

"No, no, no!"

I rushed back inside. "Donte, I'm not sure what to do here."

"What's wrong?" He wiped the herbs off the counter with a cloth as I panicked, not sure what I was allowed to share with him.

"Can you pretend that I have to stay home today? Mariano wants to take me out, and, well…"

"Not a problem." He raised a hand, and I was pleased he didn't make me have to explain further.

"There's my girl!" Mariano boomed through the front door as a few of the female kitchen staff bolted for the pantry.

Lucky.

"Mariano." I slapped on a fake smile and shook my head at him. "As I told you earlier, I'm not able to get away today."

"I don't take the word 'no' very well." He winked and hopped up on the counter right in Donte's way. "And I've been patient with you moving in here and me not seeing you as much, but all things must come to an end. So here I am, not taking no from you."

Here we go again, that balance where I shouldn't be

going off alone with him, yet I need to act normal with him at the same time.

"Mr. DeSimone," Donte stepped in, "The Don had asked Ms. Sienna to stay home today and help him with a few things."

It took me a moment to remember that Don was a name for Piero.

"I'm sure he did." He waved off Donte's comment like it was a joke and went for my hand. "Come on, we have to make one stop along the way, but then we'll have some fun."

I scrambled for something. "Let me grab my purse."

Once in the study, I scribbled on a notepad what was going on, folded it in half, and headed for the kitchen, handing Donte the note. "Can you give this to Elio, Vinni, or Niccola?"

"Of course. Are you sure you're okay?"

"Yeah," I shook my head, "I just want them to know this wasn't my decision."

"Oh, trust me, I'll tell them what happened."

"Thanks."

Mariano jumped in the car, and I barely had my safety belt fastened when he slammed the car into drive and took off down the winding road.

"Listen, Sienna. I try not to take you leaving me to live up in the Hill House too personally, but I'm starting to think you might be tired of me." *Wow, so we're jumping right into it, are we?* "I felt a little better when you joined me and Anna last night, but then you disappeared."

Stay the same, don't act like anything has changed,

echoed in my head.

"You know, Mariano, you keep asking what it takes to be with me, but you don't listen," I shot back, tired of the same conversation. "I'm reserved. I like respect and a little chivalry, but I get none of that from you. You say you want to date me, but in the next moment you have your tongue down Anna's throat. I don't drink to get drunk, but you do. You have such tunnel vision of what you want that you can't see what others might need from you. So, don't sit here and give me shit about me pulling away. You've had chances to change things, but you didn't take them."

I took a deep breath in and was shocked at my candor. I pulled out my purse, flipped down the visor, and reapplied my lipstick for something to do.

"Well, that's a lot to take in." He chuckled, and I fumed with anger. "Who knew that was inside of you?"

"You do push my buttons."

"I wonder what else I can do to make you pop off like that." He poked my arm, and I slammed the visor up with exasperation. He was hopeless. "Well, if you're finished, I need you to tame the wild horse and come inside." He parked outside Elio's aunt's house. "I have to speak with Elio's uncle. I won't be long. He's a real ass, but what boss isn't?" He made a face, and I knew he was referring to Elio.

The green vines that hugged the walls moved like a wave in the breeze. The house was a spectacular stone structure with two chimneys on either side. Mariano was already inside by the time I made it up the stairs, leaving me to hover outside the door.

"Are you coming?" he called, and suddenly Aunt Noemi appeared with an annoyed face.

"Hello again, dear." She waved me in. "I'd apologize for his behavior, but then I'd be apologizing too often."

"It's all right." I laughed, thinking how true that was.

"The boys' father will only need him for a few moments, so why don't we sit in the sunroom and enjoy a little girl time?"

I followed her through the long hallway, down two little stairs that led into a pretty river stone room filled with potted flowers. She offered me a drink from a small table designed to comfortably sit three, but I declined. I felt awkward enough at being there unannounced.

"Did you enjoy the party last night?" I fought for something to talk about, but as soon as the words came out of my mouth, flashbacks of the look that had passed between my mother and her hit me hard.

"It was eventful." She broke off a piece of cookie and popped it in her mouth. "I never stay long at those events, but it was fun to see Vinni let loose a little and have fun."

I chuckled. "He's quite the dancer."

"That's all his father, Bosco." She fiddled with the cloth napkin she had pulled onto her lap. "Would you mind maybe spending some time with the poor girl who was found at the dockyard? I'm teaching her Italian, but I think she's very lonely."

"Of course, I'd be happy to." I was pleased she asked. I could only imagine how scary this entire experience had been for her.

"I'll set something up maybe next week." She seemed pleased with my answer.

I couldn't help myself as I felt the probing questions form on the tip of my tongue. "Have you always lived here? It's gorgeous."

"Bosco, Vinni and Niccola's father," she repeated, reminding me who Bosco was, "was born and raised here. After we met, I moved in, and the rest is history."

"How did you two meet?" I wondered at her choice of words when she referred to him, as she never said "my husband" very often, if at all.

"It's no fairytale." Her smile seemed strained. "Our paths kept crossing, and finally one day he made the move to talk to me, and nine months later Niccola was born."

"Love at first sight." I smiled.

"Something like that, yes." She looked away and dabbed the corner of her eye. "Will you please excuse me, dear?" she apologized. "I will be back in a few moments."

"Of course." I stood when she did. I felt completely uncomfortable and now was even more confused. Wrapping my arms around myself, I wandered the room, admiring the different plants and trinkets that were placed here and there. Little ornaments were nestled into the soil or between the pots. The urge to just ask how she knew my mother tugged at me hard. As a journalist, I was never one to beat around the bush, but this was a whole new situation and a very personal one. The painfully careful way my mother imparted such tiny tidbits of information made me tread carefully.

"Well, hello, there." I spotted something familiar as it glinted in the light. It was buried right to its tiny head. "Don't you look familiar, little teddy." I went to brush some soil from it but retracted my hand quickly at a sound. A clinking like someone tapping together two stones became louder as it got closer. It was the same sound I had heard when I was here with Elio.

What is that?

I poked my head out the door and saw nothing, but when I turned back around, I gasped.

"Oh!" A flinch ricocheted through my core. A set of the coldest gray eyes met mine. They were set in a face wrinkled with age. The skin around the eyes creased as if to read my soul. At least that was how it felt. "Hello." I tried to find my manners. "I'm Sienna, a friend—"

"I know who you are." The anger in her raspy tone made me step backward, and I hit the doorframe with a thud. "And where you've been." She stuck her finger in my face, and I heard the sound again. It was her rosary beads clinking together. "You can't be here."

"I'm-I'm not sure what's going on here." I tried to shake the nervous tone from my voice. The woman was terrifying. She looked old, but you could tell from her eyes she was sharp as a tack.

"Leave." She drew out the word and pointed to the door.

I reached back and flung myself around then raced out of the room and down the hallway, the word 'leave' still screaming inside my head. I turned as I ran to see if she was watching when I smacked into someone. "Oh!"

Elio grabbed my wrists to steady me and glared.

"What the hell are you doing here?"

"I—" I stumbled, completely rattled. "Mariano brought me, and—"

"So I heard," he snapped, and I was confused by his mood.

"I didn't want to come. I had no—"

"You always have a choice."

I ripped my arms away, annoyed. "Lovely to see you again."

"You have no idea what my last forty-eight hours have been like."

"How could I? You left without saying goodbye and didn't text or call."

His angry expression softened when he suddenly looked over my head.

"Nonna," he brushed by me and leaned in to give her a kiss on both cheeks, "I want you to meet Sienna."

Oh, sweet Lord, no.

"Hello, child." She offered me a friendly smile, and all signs of psycho Nonna were gone. "Lovely to meet you."

What the hell was happening? "Nice to meet you, too." *I think.*

"Where are you from, dear?" She waved us to sit down. "I detect a slight accent."

"She's from—"

"All over." I cut Elio off, not wanting her to know.

"Elio?" A man who looked a little younger and wider than Piero stood in the doorway. "Excuse me, but I just need a quick second."

No, no, no.

"Do me a favor and stay put," he murmured.

The moment he turned the corner, Nonna glared and leaned forward.

"If you knew what was good for you, you'd pack your bags and leave my family alone. If you don't," she pulled herself up to her full height and hissed, "I will get rid of you myself."

"I think you may have me confused with someone else."

"No, Sienna Giovanna from Sicily, I certainly do not." My mouth dropped open while a ton of bricks dropped down on top of me. "She's quite the beauty, isn't she?" My head shot back at her sudden change in tone.

"That she is." Elio still sounded annoyed, so I quickly stood and headed for the door.

"Hey." Elio came up behind me and snagged my arm. "Where are you going now?"

I glanced at Nonna's tilted head and could see she was interested in my answer, so I closed my mouth to rethink my words. "I think it's best if I leave."

"What?" He pinched his nose in frustration. "No, we have to talk."

"If the young lady wishes to leave, Elio, let her leave."

He shook his head at Nonna's words, and I stepped toward the door, only to have him stop me again.

Mariano's voice echoed down the hallway, and I wanted to disappear. Elio took my hand and marched us outside. I glanced back at a very pissy Nonna glaring at me.

"I don't have the mind space for whatever is going on, but you are not to be alone with him."

"I'm sorry. At what point did I say I wanted to be?" I pushed him away and walked a few feet in order to take a breath. There was so much happening right now, and from all different directions, and I was having trouble sorting through it all. My nerves were on their final edge.

"Hey." Mariano came down the stairs and slowly eyed both of us. "What's going on?"

"Sienna has a friend in town wanting to meet her," Elio said. "I called Vinni to pick her up."

"But we have plans." He directed his confusion to me.

"I tried to tell you there was a possibility, but…" I trailed off.

"Can't he reschedule?"

"*She's* only in town for one day." I wanted to correct the gender, so he didn't flip out.

"Oh, I see." Then he looked at Elio. "How did you know about it?" One look at Elio's face and he held up his hands and backed off

"Fine. Then we'll meet up tonight." He took out his phone as Vinni pulled in the driveway.

"Okay." I gritted my teeth, avoiding Elio's stare. "I'll see you both later."

Vinni had barely come to a complete stop when I jumped inside and covered my face with my hands and loudly growled into them.

"Wow, you don't sound happy." I heard Vinni twist in his seat. "Are you okay?"

"Would you mind taking me to the market? Or maybe a gun range? Is that okay?"

He thought for a moment. "Gun range. Ahh, no, but the market, yeah, I think I can do that. Do you need to go back to the house first?"

"No, I'm good."

As we pulled away, I caught sight of Nonna in the doorway and closed my eyes in confusion at just how I could have so upset a woman I had never even met.

"Vinni? Can I ask you a question?"

"You can ask." He grinned playfully.

"Your nonna, she seems pretty sharp. She doesn't suffer from any kind of dementia, does she?" I hoped the fact I had my fingers crossed would give me a pass on my one-way ticket to hell.

He laughed as he made a wide turn. "Nonna is one of the sharpest tools in the entire family. People might underestimate her because she doesn't leave the property often, but trust me, she knows everything that goes on and then some."

Great.

"That's pretty impressive."

"She really is. Let me guess, you met her?"

"I did."

"She might come off a little protective, but she'll warm up. She just needs to get to know you first."

Mm, that's it.

"I'm sure." I sank into the seat and tried to push the terror of dear old nut-job Nonna out of my mind.

The market was just what I needed, friendly people, yummy food, gelato, and no lover or crazy wanna-be lover to deal with. I found myself drawn to the fountain and sat at the table Piero and I had used once before. Pulling off a little piece of sweet bread, I let my gaze drift over to some children tossing coins into the water. They looked so carefree while their parents watched over them. It drew me to thoughts of my mother. I should call her, but her hint that the Capris might have some answers to my past held me back. I just didn't see it. Perhaps she just wanted me to hate them as much as she did?

"*Scusa*," Vinni sat down suddenly. "Sorry, I know you were deep in thought, but I just got called to the dockyard. So, Jimmy, over there, will drive you home." He pointed behind me to a man in a tight t-shirt and sports coat who now leaned against the car. He looked like he should be on the cover of some men-over-forty sports magazine.

"I'll grab my sweater."

"No need, you'll continue in my car. I'll take his."

"You sure?"

"All good." He smiled warmly. "Take your time. He's been told to wait until you're ready."

As he walked away, I called after him, "Hey, Vin?"

"Yeah?"

"Your Nonna, I think—" I stopped myself, unsure if I wanted to pull harder at that thread just yet.

"She what?"

"Never mind, it's not important."

He looked at me funny, then his phone started to ring, so he waved and raced off.

I spent another forty minutes enjoying my alone time as I tried to collect my jumbled thoughts. I almost needed a notebook to jot down all the twists and turns that were coming at me. My phone rang, and I pulled it out with a groan. I wondered who wanted to yell at me next.

"Oh." I saw Georgio's name on the caller ID. "Hi, Georgio, how are you?"

"I'd be better if you'd return to work," he huffed. When I didn't react, he took a breath and started over. "I wanted to talk to you about something that's come up. Do you have a moment?"

"I do." I was curious to know what he wanted, particularly if a story might come along for me. I settled in to listen.

When I focused on my surroundings once again, I realized the place was clearing out and the vendors were closing up. I hung up in a daze, still reeling from what Georgio had just told me. I wasn't sure why I didn't just say no right away. Maybe there was a part of me that was intrigued enough to be flattered. Either way, I just wanted to relish the feeling.

Grabbing my bags, I looked around for the driver. Jimmy was a few yards away, across the street, getting a coffee. I headed toward him but stopped when I caught sight of the man in the gray suit from Vinni's party. He was watching me again from across the street. What was strange was that when I locked eyes with him, he made no attempt to move or to look away, he just stood there. He wasn't at all threatening. I decided I would have a talk with Elio. I wouldn't put it past him to have hired the guy to keep an eye on me, but a heads up on Mr. Stoneyface would have been nice.

Peeling my attention away from him, I focused on the driver who I could now see through the window of the coffee shop was juggling his coffee as he reached for the door. I introduced myself as I pulled the door open for him.

"Thank you." He nodded at me. "So, you're Sienna?" He smiled.

"I guess I am."

"I've heard nice things about you."

"Thanks." I wasn't in a chatty mood, and he must have picked up on it because he didn't ask any more questions.

Several yards away from the car, he pulled out the keys and clicked the unlock button. The next sound that hit my ears took my breath away. A bright flash of light and heat blinded me, and I blew backward, hitting something with a heavy thud.

As though in a dream, I realized I was slumped against a mailbox. Through a haze, I saw a figure lean over me. Then all went black.

Chapter
TWELVE

Elio

"I don't get it." Vinni rubbed his face and tossed the paperwork on the table. "We've been through every tape, every document from here to New York. We've been through the New York videotapes, and the paperwork, and there's just nothing."

"There's always something," Niccola reminded him. "We're just missing it."

I stood in front of the window and looked over the dockyard and watched the workers unload today's shipment. I had my guys combing through every nook and cranny of the ship. If there was something there, they'd find it.

"All right." Niccola sighed loudly behind me. "If I

was going to smuggle a girl or girls from Siberia through Italy, why go through the States? Are they just stopping there or going farther? How much does a girl go for?"

"It really depends on a lot of factors," I muttered, "virgins, body type, eye color. There are about four million victims around the world every year. America is one of the top three places to pick up girls. I know they're easily snatched from foster care, so maybe that's where they found her. They rarely look very hard for them." I shrugged, disgusted with the thought of it all.

A stretch of silence fell over us as we took a moment to think about what could be happening in our dockyard. I had no problem taking someone's life, but women and children needed to be left out of it.

"The boss of a major syndicate chooses to traffic girls through our dockyard. Why?" Vinni pondered out loud.

Niccola joined in. "If he gets the operation moving through here, he could easy call the Feds and have us all taken down."

"It just doesn't seem like Stefano. He's vindictive, but to set all this up just to have the Feds take us down… Sounds, I don't know, off somehow. He'd want more of a show," Vinni countered.

"Maybe it's nothing at all. Maybe it's just a distraction?" I thought out loud. "Nothing leads to anything." I pointed to the paperwork. "We're here chasing our tails and killing off our own men for what? What do we really have except the word of one girl?"

Niccola stood and gave me a thoughtful look as his

train of thought linked with mine. "Maybe we should question that girl again. See if she remembers anything else."

I sent a text off to my translator giving him a date and time to meet the next day so we could question her further.

"Boss?" One of my soldiers stood in the doorway. I gave him a nod to report his findings. "We scoured every inch of the ship, twice, and we came up empty."

I tossed the glass across the room, sending it into a billion pieces. What the hell was happening?

"Stop everything. Gather everyone below," I barked at him.

"I think you may have been right, cousin." Niccola joined my side. "Either it's a distraction, or we caught the whole thing early and screwed up his plans. Either way, there are no girls, money, or evidence here."

I fumed with anger, knowing what I needed to do. I headed outside to the steps and looked over the sixty-some employees who gathered with interest.

"We have a problem," I called down to them. "So, hear me now, as I will not repeat myself." My voice boomed over the quiet yard. "Anyone who has seen anything unusual or hears anything at all of Stefano Coppola or any of his men needs to come forward. There'll be no repercussions if you speak up immediately. As of today, the dockyard will be shut down, except for a few remaining ships that are on their way to us. You will not lose pay. Consider it a small vacation." A dull whisper could be heard. "If you know anything, come forward. I will keep a small number of you on to search the returning ships." I turned and addressed my cousins. "Anyone who might have something to say, bring them to the warehouse. All ships returning to the dock will be searched and held until I say otherwise."

Niccola nodded. "Understood."

"Understood, bo…" Vinni trailed off as his phone rang in his hand. "Yeah?" His eyes jumped to mine, and suddenly my phone rang as well.

"What?" I snapped, not reading the caller ID.

"Elio," my mother's voice broke, "you need to come home."

"Not a good ti—"

"It's Sienna…"

I went cold as my hearing became super acute. "What's happened?"

"There was a hit." I hung up and raced out the door, down the stairs, past the sea of stunned bodies, to my car. As I peeled out of the gates, I swung onto the road and nearly clipped another car. He gave me the finger as I slammed the gears and shot off, leaving him to shrink in my rearview mirror.

Niccola's name popped up on my dash screen, and I tapped the button.

"What do you know?"

"Someone planted a bomb under Vinni's car. When Jimmy unlocked it, luckily from a few yards away, it triggered it."

Anger raged through my veins, and I had to clamp my jaw tight to bring it under control.

"How bad is she?"

"I don't know." At his pause, my anger turned to fear in my gut. "We can't find her."

"What do you mean, you can't find her!"

"She's disappeared. Don't worry, Elio, we're on it. Just get there safe."

I knew he could hear the screeching of my tires as I drove like a madman. I would break every single bone in Stefano's body but his neck. He would suffer pain like no other, and my face would be the last thing he would ever see.

I took the main road, riding the shoulder most of the way. Cars honked, but nothing registered. My mind swirled with horrible scenarios. Did someone take her? Could she have been so hurt and afraid she started running?

I could barely think straight when I skidded to a stop at the Hill House. The door flew open, and Mama came out with my papa right behind her.

"Hang on, son." He threw up his hands to stop me as Mama dabbed her eyes. "Let me tell you what we know." He stood in front of me to block my path. "Jimmy had just stepped out of the coffee shop, and she met him, then the car exploded. Witnesses say the smoke was so intense that you couldn't see anything, and once it cleared, she was gone. Jimmy is getting checked out now. You need to take a moment and get yourself together for Sienna's sake." He held my arm. "Son. Before you rush off, let's get the footage. I have soldiers scouring the streets as we speak. The footage should be arriving any minute. Let's be smart about this before you rip this city apart."

He was right, but it didn't tame the rage inside. I headed for the door, hearing my mother's worried sobs behind me.

"Out." I ordered the kitchen staff to disperse as I grabbed a water from the refrigerator and downed all of it. I wanted something stronger but knew I couldn't risk clouding my judgment. I tossed the plastic bottle and took a moment to steady myself. Then I pictured her in her blue dress, and I could see her eyes as I'd last looked into them at my uncle's house. They had been a darker shade than usual, and then I remembered she'd seemed rattled. I wished I had pushed my frustration at the meeting away long enough to have asked what was bothering her. I wasn't used to checking in or calling when I worked. I was learning what it meant to have her back in my life again.

"Elio," Francesco appeared on the other side of the island, "your father needs five minutes before you go anywhere. He said to show you this." He held out an iPad. "It's the footage from the corner store, next to the coffee shop."

I pressed play and watched the video feed of Sienna sitting at a table in the market. Vinni joined her and pointed at Jimmy. I sped up the footage, and heat radiated through my core as I saw Sienna, a while later, have to go and look for Jimmy, and then seconds later the car exploded and they both flew backward. I backed up and replayed the video again and again as I studied the area around the car.

A man could be seen. He bent down as he neared the car, then he quickly walked away.

Wait.

I backed up the footage and saw Jimmy check the time on his watch. He glanced at the coffee shop and left the car. Immediately after he left was when the mystery man planted the device.

I tossed the iPad on the counter and spun to face the wall, infuriated by Jimmy's obvious lapse in judgement. His training should never have allowed him to leave the vehicle unattended.

"Take a moment here, Elio," Francesco said calmly, but I could tell by the white around his mouth that his anger was equal to mine. Sienna might be one of us, but she was the only one who didn't deserve this. "If it *is* Stefano, flipping out on a murderous rampage is exactly what he would want."

"Who else would it be?" I hissed.

"Here's my problem with what happened." Francesco took a seat on the stool and waited for me to join him. When I didn't, he held up the small notebook taken from Stefano. "Stefano's notebook has all these little S marks." He opened the book to a marked page. "Look, the S's are for Sienna. He's been following her since she arrived here. See, here and here, they are all times when Sienna was there." He pointed to another scribbled location and the letter S.

"He might be planning something, but the timing of a hit on her right now just doesn't make sense. Unless I'm missing something in the bigger picture." He lowered his voice as he glanced at the door. "However, you did get in someone else's way today, remember? Mariano isn't one to overlook. Jealousy and love can make a person do crazy things, but drugs, jealously, and love, well, that is a cocktail for disaster."

I lowered myself to the stool and let that sink in. Was this my fault? We all had agreed that we'd play the next few months as normal with Mariano, but my head had been so messed up with Stefano that maybe I hadn't played the cards correctly.

"I know you and I have been off lately," he continued, "but despite what your feelings are about her mother being here, it's time for some truths to come out. The good and the bad." He twisted his hands together. "You have my word, if I'd known she was coming, I would have said something. It was a shock to me, too, and I'm still unsure how it will all play out. But it is what it is, and we need to be strong enough to weather this storm."

"Tell me something." A dark hate lined my soul. "How do you know what happened today wasn't *because* of her mother?"

"Because I have eyes on her too." He held my gaze, and I believed him. "She hates the family, but it's because she believes we killed her brother, Angelo."

"Did we?"

"No, but she was fed full of lies while she was mourning him, and it did a lot of damage. Some of it was repairable, but some of it, not."

I leaned forward, resting my elbows on the counter, and held my thumping head.

"You know Sienna better than anyone," he whispered. "Where would she go if she needed help?"

Suddenly, the restaurant where we had our first date popped in my head. She didn't know many people here, but she had really liked the owners. "Tell Papa I can't wait." I grabbed my keys and raced out.

THIRTEEN

Sienna

"Ouch." Pain flickered across my eyes as I tried to pull myself from a groggy sleep. My entire body felt like lead, and when I tried to move, the pain that shot from under my right lung made me gasp and break out in a sweat.

With all my might, I pushed the heels of my hands into the hard mattress, and I pulled myself up against a wooden headboard.

Thump, thump, thump, the hammer in my head was relentless. When my vision finally cleared, I looked around in confusion. I took in the room. It was tiny. A small bookcase sat by the door, and next to that was a rocking chair with a wicker basket full of yarn. Paintings sprinkled the walls, and an old square rug lay in front of the television. A delicious smell of some kind filled the room and heightened my senses. My eyes went to the door that looked like it led to a kitchen.

"Rest, dear, rest." An older lady hobbled in holding a tray with a teapot and cup. "You have been asleep for a long time."

"Where am I?" A bubble of panic rippled through me. "Who are you?"

"A friend."

"I don't have any friends here." I tried to move again and winced at the deep burn.

"I didn't say I was a friend of yours." She poured the tea and set it on the table next to me. "Drink."

Suddenly, the day came rushing back to me, and I swallowed back the fear that someone had tried to kill me.

"If I wanted to hurt you," she sensed my fear, "I would have by now."

How comforting.

I did another quick assessment of the room and saw two possible ways of escape. My heart beat loudly in my chest, and I wished the pain in my head would leave so I could think.

"Where is my purse?"

"Here." She pulled it off the table and handed it to me.

I dug through it. "What happened to my phone?"

"I have no idea."

Tears quickly formed, and I knew this was it. All my years on the streets, and this was how I was going to be taken out? By some wizened old lady.

"I'm a friend of the Capris." She eased into the rocking chair, reached in the basket, and started to knit. "I was told to keep you hidden until they came to get you."

"How long was I out?" I didn't believe her. Elio would have been here within an hour of hearing the news.

"Five hours."

Sweat broke out across my neck, and I tried to keep calm, but my shaky hands gave me away, and she glanced at them.

"Have some tea, Sienna. They'll be here soon."

What the hell was happening here?

My mouth was like cotton, so I took a few sips, desperately needing to wet my throat. I knew I needed to keep sharp. The warm liquid felt nice as honey coated my taste buds, giving me a natural boost of sugar. When I was finished, I leaned back and wondered how I was going to get out of here. I knew I could take her out. She was old, and even in pain I could outrun her, I thought as my eyelids got heavy. The sound of the chair as it rocked at a steady rhythm made me drift off.

"How much?" I heard her say as I started to come to. The hands on the clock were hard to focus on, but after a few blinks I caught it for a split second.

Four hours. I'd been asleep for four hours!

"You better make this right. If I'm going to go against the Capri family, it better be worth it," the old lady's voice snarled from another room. "She's out like a light, so I suggest you come now."

That was all I needed to hear as I ignored the pain and sat up. I slipped on a pair of shoes, briefly wondering where my own were, grabbed my purse, and raced out the door. I stopped at the top of some stairs as a wave of dizziness came over me. I shook it off and used my hands to guide myself down then out the main door to the street. The smell of baking was almost overpowering.

I knew she must have drugged the tea. I could still feel it in my system. Not knowing where I was, I decided on a direction and hobbled away as quickly as I could. My battered body protested at every step. I quickly realized it was the wrong decision. The smell of smoke and beer hit my nose, and I opted to cross the road to keep in the shadows of the side streets. The thought of the old biddy following me or in case she had someone else follow me had my nerves on edge.

The sun was setting. It would be dark soon, and the last thing I wanted was to be out here alone at night with a bunch of drunk people as they headed home from their barstools.

"Hello there, darlin. Where are you off to tonight?" a man called out and whistled for his buddies. I stumbled over my heavy feet and used one hand on the wall of the building for support as I hurried away. Everything hurt, but I sure as heck wasn't going to make it easy for them to catch up.

Keep moving. One foot in front of the other.

Two more turns, and I found a small opening and

tucked myself into it and held my breath as I knew the group of them were headed in my direction. I realized the light above me might give my location away, so I pulled off a shoe and shattered it just in time. I dug in my purse and fingered the rip in the fabric at the side seam and eased my phone out. It often slid inside the fabric, and for once I was pleased I never got that purse fixed.

"Shit." I wanted to scream. The phone was dead.

I could hear their footsteps and their drunk mutterings to each other about how fun their night had been. One kept calling out for me, and I shut my eyes and prayed for them to leave. I didn't want violence, but it wouldn't be the first time I'd fought for my life.

Not long later, I risked a peek and saw they were now headed back toward the main street.

Thank God.

I took off up the hill farther and farther away from anything that looked remotely familiar. I kept reminding myself that I'd survived for years on the streets, and although I was strong mentally and could be scrappy when I needed to be, I was much happier with who I'd become. I loved having a home, with a lock, fresh clothes, and food to eat.

I thought of how close I'd been to losing my life today in that bomb blast. I remembered it all clearly now. Elio was right. I was in this deep, and I knew it was because of who I was to him. I knew the life he led was scary, but the feeling of that blast as it shot toward me was a fear I could definitely live without.

Just as I reached the top of a hill and the pain in my

ribs could no longer be ignored, I allowed myself to stop and rest. I was holding on to a wall for support when a set of headlights lit me up. I knew I could run no farther as the car stopped a few feet from me, so I slowly turned, wondering what I'd have to fend off now.

"Sienna, is that you?" Ugo, the new cousin my mother had introduced me to, squinted at me then pulled his phone out and made a call. "Yes, ma'am." He hung up and made another call. I was so relieved to have found someone I knew I let myself go. I pressed my back to the wall and slid down until my bottom felt solid ground. His voice seemed a million miles away. Another car came roaring down the street in the opposite direction, and when I heard *his* voice, I broke out into a sob.

"Sienna!" Elio raced toward me and dropped to his knees. He began to pat me all over. "Are you hurt?" He turned and spoke to Vinni and Niccola. "Give us a minute." I was a mess and could barely understand him.

"I'm okay, but I think my ribs are bruised." He grabbed my hands and held them tightly. "Please, Elio, get me out of here," I sobbed, and he wasted no time lifting me into his arms, then he sat in the back seat of the town car still holding me. I tucked my head under his chin before he ordered Vinni to drive.

"Where to, boss, the hospital?"

"Yes, she'll need to be seen."

As the car sped away, I allowed myself to totally relax and pressed my face into his neck.

I was examined by a very kind doctor who, I was sure, was worried for his own life by how intense Elio was being. The doctor began to give me the results of the x-ray and exam when Elio stepped impatiently from behind the curtain. He hesitated and licked his lips but continued, only this time he spoke directly to Elio.

"She has two bruised ribs, a good bump on her head, some bruising to her left shoulder, and a first degree burn on her arm. She will need rest and should be watched for signs of a concussion."

Elio nodded as the doctor handed him a prescription for pain meds and began to explain how they should be taken. I drifted off a bit, grateful to have Elio handle all the information. They had already given me something for pain, and I was beginning to feel the benefit of it.

"Thank you, doctor," was the last I heard as I drifted off.

The next thing I remembered was being back in the car. Elio's arm was around me.

"You scared me." He leaned in and hugged me gently.

Andrea and Francesco met us at the door, and he reached out to hug me.

"Careful, Francesco," Andrea warned, "she has bruised ribs."

Elio shot me a concerned look, and I closed my eyes, not wanting any further attention.

"Really, I'm fine," I tried to reassure them, but I could see it wasn't working.

"Come on," Elio wrapped an arm around my back and moved me toward the stairs. "We can talk later, but you need to lie down." I nodded and glanced at Andrea.

She smiled and put a hand on Francesco's arm to draw him back.

With Elio clucking away like a mother hen at my bruises in the shower, I finally felt half-human again. I lay down in bed, and he covered me with a soft blanket then lay beside me. He didn't ask any questions, but I knew they would come. I knew they would need the details of what happened. At the moment, I just needed time to breathe, now that I was back within the protection of the family. He slipped his fingers through mine and squeezed my hand as if making sure I was really here. With the warmth of his body molded to mine, I let go and gave in to sleep.

When I woke, Elio was gone. I clipped up my hair, as I'd fallen asleep with it still wet, then slipped into a new dress and flat shoes. The painkillers had done their job, so I felt better as I made my way downstairs. Even though it was around ten at night, the house was wide awake and in full swing.

Andrea started to rush to my side, but Piero placed a hand on her shoulder to give me a moment. I gave him a thankful nod as I came into the kitchen where Elio was sitting at the island. As he looked up, I could see he was fit to kill. Not sure exactly what the conversation was before I arrived, I decided to speak up.

"I promise, I will share everything with you, but first, is Jimmy, the driver, all right?"

"He's been dealt with." Elio's tone made me shiver.

"And what does that mean?"

"He's alive but won't be able to walk for a while." I

shook my head at Piero, confused about what Elio meant.

Piero spoke up. "He broke a number one rule. He left the car alone, out of sight. That's forbidden."

"So, he was," I tried to find the right word, "disciplined?"

"He's lucky that's all that happened," Elio barked. His dark expression told me he was in a bad place. "You could have been killed."

"There are rules, Sienna." Piero gave Elio a look. "Our drivers are responsible for the safety of the family. Breaking a rule, especially such a basic one, is completely unacceptable. The only reason he is still breathing at all is because of Vinni."

"You must be starved. Here, try these, Sienna." Andrea stepped forward with a warm plate of pastries.

"Thanks." A few bites in, and I felt mildly better. More than anything, I wanted my nerves to settle, but I figured that would take a few days.

"Nobody stood out to me," I started mid-thought. "I didn't feel like I was being watched. I didn't notice anything out of the ordinary at all. I just made my way over to Jimmy as he was coming out of the coffee shop. He pressed the unlock button on his key, and boom." I swallowed hard, hating that I felt tears coat my eyes. "You hear about those people who go through something traumatic and they lose the memory of what happened…" I trailed off, thinking how different my situation was. "Why couldn't I have that? I remember every single detail of that blast. The way the blast looked, and a second later the ear-piercing sound, the moment my feet lifted off the ground, even the impact of the steel mailbox. I must have blacked out for a few seconds, and when I woke, I…" I looked at Elio as I remembered something, but as I started to speak, there was a noise at the door.

"Where is she?" I heard my mother's voice in a high shriek. Her shoes clicked as she hurried across the floor.

"Please, Elenora, wait!" Francesco was on her heels, and I met them both in the hallway.

"What happened? Are you all right? Do you have any idea who did this?" Elenora came at me like a firing squad.

"I'm okay," I assured her as I felt Elio come up behind me. "It was close, but I'm all right."

"See," Francesco threw his hands up to calm everyone, "she's okay, you're okay. We're all okay."

"We," she spun and pointed a finger in his face, "are nowhere near okay." She turned back to me and gave me a pointed look. "I think it's time we spoke."

I looked at Elio, whose jaw was flexing, and his neck strained with the effort to keep calm. "I'll be right back. I promise."

"She must not leave the property." He spoke over me, and my mother's face twisted in anger.

"*She* can leave at any point." Elenora stepped forward, but Francesco pulled her back as Piero joined my side. "She is not your family. She does not need to obey your rules."

"Elenora," Francesco warned, "you're in their house, and she is very much a member of the Capri family. Whether you choose to recognize that or not."

"That was your doing," she shot back, and his face turned to stone.

"Don't," he growled, and I felt like leaving the entire lot of them to find a quiet corner.

"Everyone, please." Andrea came to my rescue. "Elenora, of course you can speak alone with your daughter, if it's all right with her." I nodded. "Feel free to go out by the pool, and I'll make sure we all give you the privacy you need."

"Thank you." My mother muttered as she immediately headed for the big French doors that led out to the pool.

"It will be fine." I ran a hand up Elio's vibrating chest, and his hand covered it and gave it squeeze.

"Not too far away," he grumbled as I gave him a reassuring smile.

Elenora paced by the marble stairs that led down into the shallow end of the pool. She looked pale and stressed.

"You wanted to talk?" I wasn't sure how to start the conversation.

"There's something you need to know."

"All right." A quick response about there being a lot of things I wanted to know leapt to my tongue, but I didn't want to risk that she might change her mind. I twisted my hands together nervously, yet relieved she was finally going to share something with me.

"I'm worried that the people I've been running from might be the same people who blew up your car."

"What?" I was completely thrown that she might

have a connection to all this. "I need to tell Elio."

"Sienna!" She grabbed my arm, and I cried out at the sudden stab from my ribs. "I'm so sorry!" Her eyes went big, but she didn't let go. "I think," she rushed her words when Elio suddenly stepped out of the house, "these are the same people who killed your father."

"My father is dead?" I whirled and found Francesco had also appeared next to Elio. The worry on his face mirrored my mother's.

FOURTEEN

"Enough!" I ordered once I saw Sienna's white face. "She's been through enough, and whatever the hell is happening here needs to stop!"

"Who are you to get in the middle of me and my daughter?" She lifted her chin at me.

"I'm the man who has loved your daughter my entire life." I moved inches from her face, and her mouth dropped open as she looked from me to Sienna.

"Elio." Sienna's face was shocked that I would boldly share such a fact in front of the others.

"I've tried to be patient with this entire situation, but I'm done," I said to both of them, then I addressed her mother one on one. "The secrets you keep are damaging, and you picked the worst time to show up here. You have horrible timing."

"You *can't* love my daughter."

"You don't have a say in the matter."

Sienna had whirled around with a hand over her mouth and tears streaming down her face. "Please, stop," she pleaded with her mother.

"What did you say to her?" I yelled at Elenora. I was wound so tightly I could snap her neck right here in front of everyone.

"I didn't want her to find out this way," she pleaded. "Sienna. If you just come with me, we can talk more about this."

"No," Sienna took a step back, "I need a moment."

"You've overstayed your welcome, Elenora." I nodded at Francesco, giving him a warning that if he didn't deal with her I would.

"Sienna?" Mama called after her as she ran inside. I wanted to follow, but I also wanted our guests to leave.

"How could you?" Elenora marched up to Francesco and stuck a finger in his face. "You knew letting her near the Capris was the one thing I could never handle. The one thing you promised me you wouldn't do."

"What choice did I have?" he snapped. "You might've been able to walk away from her, but I couldn't."

Hang on, what?

"That's unfair." She drew back as though his words had hit deep. "You were the only one I trusted. The only one who truly knew what was happening."

"And I was the only one who kept her safe."

"Safe?" She looked around at all of us with a dark chuckle. "Yeah, I can see that." She motioned for her two men to follow as she left by the side gate.

"Son?" Papa grabbed my attention, "Sienna just left."

I quickly headed for the door and found Vinni coming inside. His expression showed concern.

"She's walking, toward your place. She didn't take my offer to drive her. She looks…"

"I know." I hurried out the door.

I slowly drove behind her but kept well back to give her the time she needed. When I pulled into the driveway, she leaned against the house.

"I just need," she sniffed as I came up to her, "a quiet place to think."

I didn't say anything, just opened the door and let her go inside. The motion lights that lined the floor clicked on as she went and provided her a soft warm glow as she drew further into the house.

"Take a seat, and I'll make us something to drink." I removed my jacket and unbuttoned my dress shirt, feeling instantly more at ease in my own place. I flipped over two wine glasses and uncorked a bottle of Sunflower Fields. As I tossed the cork in a wire basket on the bar, I glanced over at her. Sometimes I had to shake myself in disbelief to realize she was now here at all, let alone in my home, close enough that I could touch her.

It was amazing how the world could change. I took a moment to study my home. Thirty-foot ceilings, windows that looked over part of a vineyard and some of the countryside. The large chocolate-brown beams lined a cathedral ceiling that supported a cast iron chandelier in the center of the room. The room was warm and inviting, but what I loved most was the custom fifteen-foot bar I had built out of stone. I kept it fully stocked with every kind of scotch and brandy I could find. An added bonus was a well-planned panic room behind the bar where I kept all types of weapons and gear for any and all situations that might arise. One could never be too careful, even if we were protected by an army.

"Are you hungry?" She shook her head as I came toward her, and she took the glass of wine I offered.

"I'm not sure what I am." She sighed. "And you…" She stopped and seemed to gather her thoughts. "You were so mad at me at your uncle's house. Elio, you know me. I would never knowingly do something that was against the rules. Mariano doesn't take no for an option, and don't even get me started on your…" She stopped herself and swallowed back her words.

"Get you started on what?" I found myself curious as to why she stopped talking.

"Nothing, just forget it." When I tried to take her hand, and she stepped away. "I get it. This is your life, and now mine is tangled up in it and whatever. That's fine, because I love you, but I can't have you getting mad or frustrated with me all the time."

"I'm mad and frustrated because I've had to watch the woman I love be pursued by a man I want to kill with my bare hands. It's not easy for me, Sienna."

"Oh, I know," she shot back with a sarcastic laugh

as she took a sip of her wine. I could tell she was in need of a good fight. She had been pushed to her breaking point.

I set my glass down and opened a small wooden box on the side table. I pulled out a joint, lit the tip, and sat on the couch. My legs were open, my arm ran along the back of the couch as I kicked back and watched her annoyance grow that I wasn't taking the bait. I loved that even after all these years I could read her.

"What are you doing?"

"Sitting."

"I've never seen you do pot."

"You've never seen me snap someone's neck either, so there's a first for everything." I grinned and enjoyed the sudden red flush to her face. If she would just lose it and run her mouth, she'd feel so much better, but instead she huffed and turned away. Her hand went to her ribs, and I caught her pained expression in the window.

I suddenly remembered our earlier conversation. "What happened to you after the blast?"

"Which part?" She snickered, but I could tell she was close to tears again. "I'm so tired," she murmured after a few moments. "I've fought to keep things inside for so long that sometimes I'm just not sure how much more I have in me."

That hit a spot in me. I was so used to taking each day for what it was, letting out my frustrations on the men who deserved it, that sometimes I forgot she didn't have that kind of outlet.

"I don't know." Her shoulders sagged, and she

winced. "Maybe I shouldn't have wished so hard."

I decided to hold off on the questions. "Hey." I was on my feet standing behind her, and I gently wrapped an arm around her chest and held the joint to her mouth. "It'll help with the head and the pain." She leaned forward and sucked the tip, drawing in a huge breath. "Careful, you don't want to cough."

She took another and, to my surprise, she seemed to handle it well. After a moment, she sank into my hold and let out some more tears.

"You aren't in this alone, my *bella*." I kissed her shoulder. "Your wishes worked because I was wishing, too."

"Nothing comes without a cost," she muttered and turned in my arms.

"When we were created, we were one person," I whispered. I inhaled another deep breath of the smooth smoke and placed my lips to hers to let her take in my exhale. "They may have torn us away from one another, but you got my heart, and I got the memory of our love and the will to fight." She exhaled as she leaned into me. "We were never supposed to be separated. Souls cannot be kept apart. It's why you're back. You take as much time as you need to process what happened tonight." I brushed my fingers through her hair, exposing her slender neck. "But the darkness that's creeping around the edges of your heart, if you let it in, it can change who you are, in here." I slid my hand down her back.

She was calm now, so I led her to the couch and draped a blanket over her lap for comfort.

"Did you speak to Francesco?"

"Yes. Elenora wasn't forthcoming, but I know he'll look further into it. Just give him some time."

"It's just strange."

"I know Noemi used to travel a lot, so it's possible their paths have crossed before."

"Well, Elenora doesn't make the best first impressions, so if there's tension there for some reason, I don't blame Noemi."

We sat in silence, letting the drug turn off all anxiety and pain to our brains. Today was one of the worst days I'd had yet, and while I seemed okay on the outside, I was anything but on the inside.

"I was almost sold today," she sighed as she stared out the window, "like I was an item, rather than a human."

"What?" I tried not to raise my voice.

"The old lady I was with." She rubbed her forehead. "Someone took me there. She drugged me while I was trapped in her place. I heard her on the phone talking to someone who made her an offer. She said it better be worth it to go against your family."

"What the hell?" I sent a quick text off to my papa so we could start hunting down who this woman might be.

"I wanted to share all this before, but we got interrupted." A flicker of pain raced across her face. "It smelled like fresh-baked pastries." She sighed. She handed me her glass then shimmied down the couch and farther under the blanket. I removed her shoes and pulled her feet up on my lap in hopes she'd continue to share.

"I ran. The guys scared me, though, they got bored when they couldn't find me. Which reminds me we need to replace that back light I broke." She rambled.

"What guys?" I urged her on, not wanting her to go to sleep.

"Some bar was right around the corner. They followed me, but I hid." She groaned, and I knew more was weighing on her. "Who do you think did the bomb?"

"I'm not sure, but I will find out."

"I think it was Stefano."

"Why?" I twisted so my leg was along her side and the other was on the floor. I tugged up her legs so they rested on my groin.

"Because he seems like he would be cocky enough to stand over me right after the bomb went off."

"Wait," I wanted her to keep her train of thought as she told her story to me, "are you saying Stefano stood over you after the bombing?"

"Hmm," she nodded, "at least I thought it might be him, but maybe it wasn't. Oh, wait." She remembered something. "He tucked something into my pocket before he left me to, I don't know, be kidnapped by some old lady?"

"Do you still have what he left you?"

"Purse." She pointed to the table. I leaned over and pulled out a piece of paper.

"Death only has so much patience, and life only has so much time," I read out loud.

"What do you think it means?" Her eyelids grew heavy.

"I'm not sure." Anger and confusion mixed with the drug in my system, and I closed my eyes to stop the urge to share it all immediately with Papa.

"Elio?" Her eyes were closed now.

"Mm?"

"Can you mourn someone you've never met?" She was almost asleep.

"Maybe. Why?"

"Because I am."

"Who are you mourning?" I tried to follow the jump in her story but saw she had now fallen fast asleep. I let her be.

Once she was out, I checked my watch and sent a quick text off to Aldo, my trainer. Twenty minutes later, I was downstairs in my personal ring with my hands up, ready to shed the tension that had its nasty claws around my chest.

"You look like shit," he said, deadpan.

"I feel it." I ducked when he swung.

"Seems that way."

"Meaning?"

"Your head is elsewhere."

"Hence why we're in the ring." He studied my face as I swung, and I smoked him in the jaw, not that he felt it.

"You're different." He blocked my kick. "Something's different this time."

"Nothing's different."

"Oh, fuck," he chuckled, "it's a girl, isn't it?"

"Yup." Vinni popped out of nowhere and sat down

on the bench against the wall.

"What the hell are you doing here?"

"I brought Sienna something to eat." He forked some pasta and jammed the entire thing into his mouth. "But I couldn't find her, so now it's mine."

"Vinni, tell me about this woman." Aldo laughed as I went in for a three-punch sequence.

"She's," he sucked back a long noodle, "great, gives him shit, and makes him work for the rest."

"Are we fighting or having fucking girl time?" I grunted.

"Both." Vinni slurped louder.

I shook my head, trying to clear it, and Aldo took the opportunity to plough one into my shoulder. The pain felt good, and I purposely missed blocking his second hit, feeling my bones vibrate from the impact. He glared at me, knowing what I was doing, so I got my head on straight and came at him, punch, punch, kick, punch, punch. I went in hard and used my speed and strength to work out my aggression, and all the while I heard my cousin slurp on his damn noodles.

"There," Aldo coached me, "harder, yes, just like that. Twist your body and clench your stomach to add more power." I knew most everything there was about fighting, but there was something about having someone yell in your face that helped block out the mental white noise that wanted to creep in and control me. "Good. Again."

Slurp, slurp…

I dropped my hands and pivoted toward the ropes

with clenched teeth. "So help me Vinni, you either eat your damn dinner somewhere else or I'm going to tape you slurping up those noodles and put you on every gay site in Italy."

He slowly slurped the noodle hanging from his lips and swallowed. He leaned down and carefully placed the bowl next to him.

"See what she does to him!" He grinned then raced out the back door, laughing the entire way.

When I turned back to Aldo, I met his fist as it hit my chin. When my eyes could focus again, I saw he had a shit-eating smirk on his face. I guessed I had that one coming. I lifted my hands, and we started back up again.

Chapter

FIFTEEN

Sienna

I woke to sunshine. It warmed my entire body as it shone through the window. The sweet smell of coffee met my nose, and for a brief moment, I felt wonderful. I controlled my head from going to a dark place as I unwrapped the blanket and carefully sat up. The house was quiet and calm. Just what I needed, a moment for myself. I knew a ton of questions were waiting for me at the Hill House, and I would give them everything I could, but for now, I would just enjoy the morning.

The air unit above me kicked in, and a cool breeze brushed over my skin. My guess would be that the temperature outside was quickly heating up, and I wondered if I would be able to get into the pool with my aching ribs.

A piece of paper caught my attention, and as I reached for it, butterflies fluttered in my stomach just like they did when I was young and saw the sight of the familiar printing.

Imagine waking up to a dream only to discover it's real life. I didn't have the heart to wake you, but I have a meeting at the Hill House. Come and join us when you're ready. I've instructed all to leave you be. Coffee is set to brew in an hour, and there are fresh towels in our *bedroom. Take* your *key from the bowl by the door. I want to wake up next to you every morning. – E*

I loved that he underlined the words *our* and *your*, the fact he had written a note and signed it just the way he used to.

I folded the blanket and fluffed up the pillows then decided I should get the lay of his house. It was strange to think that for as long as I had been staying here, I hadn't really spent much time here. But first, I headed to the kitchen and poured myself a big fat mug of coffee and snagged a pastry from the plate he had left out.

My phone vibrated, and I saw it was a missed call from Wyatt. I tapped on his number, hoping to catch him.

"Hey, you!" He sounded out of breath. "I have like five minutes before I head into a meeting."

"Where are you? What meeting?" I was dying to get back into the field.

"Washington. I went down a rabbit hole, which dragged me to the US, but, girl, I am not complaining because—"

"Well, fuck me sideways," someone called out, and Wyatt laughed.

"Who was that?"

"That was an army man, dressed in camo, who I think was quite literally plucked from every fantasy I've ever had."

"I'm jealous."

"Your fantasy wears James Bond outfits and is basically a badass outlaw. Don't talk to me about jealously."

"Fine," I laughed.

"One second, Si." He paused then let out a long sigh. "Sorry. Poor Spencer is trying to get hold of her Aunt Lisa. I guess she's gone MIA for a while."

"Anything I can do to help?"

"No, I guess she's been doing this a lot lately. She seems a little nutty, if you ask me."

"I'm sorry to hear that. Tell Spencer if she ever needs to talk…"

"I will." He seemed distracted for a moment. "Oh, they're waving me in, I'll let you know how everything goes. Bye!"

I hung up and laughed at how happy and free Wyatt seemed. I pulled my focus back to the task at hand, exploring Elio's house.

I let the vibe of his house take hold of my senses as I looked around. Everything was modern but had a simple, rustic feel. I knew all the lights were voice and motioned activated and other updated tech stuff was behind the walls, but it didn't interfere with the old-style look. The view from the kitchen of the winding roads within the property line was like a child's game of Snakes and Ladders. I left the window and sipped my coffee as I continued to explore. A small bathroom was tucked away at the end of the hall just off the living room area and stairs.

As strange as I felt climbing the stairs, I knew the only way I would ever feel comfortable here was to take the time to explore and get to know the place. I ran my hand along the deep chocolate-colored wooden railing that curved like a wave ahead of me as I took each step toward the top. Another bathroom was on the left, and two guest rooms were on the right, and the last room on the left was the master. Pressing down on the thin handle, I stepped inside Elio's most intimate room.

"Wow."

The back wall was all done in dark-gray brick, like subway tiles, from floor to ceiling. Up against it was a frameless king-sized bed with white bedding and a silver blanket that matched the lightshades on each bedside table. A rectangular leather headboard looked to have been bolted above the bed. Huge windows were on one side, and a big master bathroom was on the other.

I smiled when I saw that he had our picture next to the bed. So, his side was on the right. I liked that I now knew that little thing about him.

Exploring the bathroom next, I found two stone bowls for sinks with the neatest little levers for faucets. A mirror hung from the ceiling, and a stone tub that matched the sinks doubled as a base for his shower.

I looked at my battered body in his full-length mirror and decided I needed to pull myself together and get on with the day.

Once I got to the Hill House, I changed out of my dress and into another. Vinni grumbled about how I should have called him to come get me, and I just shook my head at him, thinking how ridiculous that sounded. It was, after all, only about a three-minute walk up a hill.

"Good morning." Elio strolled into the kitchen at the same time as I did with a sexy smile. He looked mighty fine in his normal business attire. He leaned in as he brushed past me. "You smell like my shampoo," he said softly with a heated look.

"I hope that's okay."

"You in my shower? I've dreamt of that."

"Well, in that case," I smirked, "I also borrowed one of your dress shirts while I dried my hair." He let out a puff of air as he closed his eyes. "Speaking of which, and don't change this up," I referred to his outfit with my finger, "but I must ask. Do you even *own* a t-shirt?"

He laughed. "You just didn't look hard enough."

"I didn't want to snoop."

"It's not snooping when it's your house, *bella*."

I gave a small smile, unsure how this whole life thing was going to pan out.

He slid the files he was holding onto the counter then trapped me in with both arms. "Here's how you should look at this." He leaned down and brushed his nose by my ear. "I would have had you move in with me if we hadn't had to leave Sicily. It might not feel like yours now, but it will. Anything you want to change, just talk to Francesco, and tell him your plan, and he'll make it happen. Just know this. I've never had a woman live with me, and I've never had a woman overnight there. I always kept my house to myself. I guess I was waiting for you to return to me." He smiled, and I got lost in his eyes. "It's yours, Sienna. I want you to be there with me."

"I want to wake up to you every morning, too." I used the words from his note, so he knew I'd seen it. I leaned in and pecked his lips. His grin was incredibly sexy as it spread slowly across his lips. He entwined his fingers in my hair and pulled me in for a long kiss. I pressed against his chest, concerned who might walk in, but he didn't seem to care. His tongue commanded control, and I willingly gave in, loving his dominant side. He was the only man I could truly be myself with, who I ever wanted to be myself with. I always belonged to Elio. No matter how deep my scars were, he owned me, and given his hungry kiss, he knew it.

"Tonight." He pulled away with a huff, and I could tell he was barely hanging on to his self-control. "I want you home."

I nodded, still trying to find my footing. God, the man could kiss.

"But right now," his face fell, "I need you to join me in the next room."

"Of course." I knew it was time to share what I remembered. "Are you going to get angry?"

"Someone hurt you, Sienna." He shrugged, twisting

a piece of hair around his middle finger. "I have the right to rip them limb from limb."

"Fine," I knew it was pointless to argue, "but maybe I can help with your temper?" I raised an eyebrow at him.

"Try me."

I took his hand as my other lifted my dress slightly and skimmed his hand over my smooth skin to reveal I was going commando.

"Jesus," he groaned and gently pressed a finger between my folds, discovering just what he'd done to me, "I would do anything to be inside y—"

"Why are there meetings that I don't know about?" Mariano called down the hallway, and Elio's hand slipped away with a curse.

"Tonight." He nodded and stood back as Mariano came into the kitchen looking fit to kill.

"Why is it you're always with Elio?" he snapped at me as he reached for the coffee pot, banging everything loudly. "I'm starting to get a complex here."

"Are you feeling okay, Mariano?" I eyed Elio to show I could see Mariano was off this morning.

"Do I look okay?" he barked over his shoulder.

"No, you look like shit," dropped from my tongue, and Elio hid his smirk. I was growing tired of his mood swings. *Grow up*.

"Tell me how you really feel," he muttered. "What time is the meeting?"

"You're not needed for this one." Elio gathered up the files next to me.

"Why the hell not?"

"Pardon?" Elio stood straighter to show his authority and flashed a glare at him. "You're hung over, you're wearing clothes from yesterday, and you need a goddam shower. All before I would even consider bringing you into any meeting we are having."

"I've been worried about her," he blamed me, "because…because." He struggled to remember what happened to me. "She got hurt and shit."

"Nice." I shook my head. "Remember what we spoke about in your kitchen? About how I don't do this." I pointed a finger up and down his painful appearance. "Don't toss your train wreck of a life at me, Mariano. Ever." I left the room and met Piero in the hallway.

"Good morning."

"It was," I couldn't help but snap.

"What happened?"

"Oh, thirty some-odd years ago, the DeSimones decided to reproduce."

He laughed loudly then wrapped a loving arm around me with a sigh. "Elio will deal with him when the time is right, but until then, can we get the full story from you?"

"Of course." I followed him into his office and shared everything I remembered with him and Elio.

Later, spent from talking, I found my way to the special place Elio had made. I sat sideways in the hammock and used the toe of my shoe to gently swing myself. The painkillers I'd taken were soaking in my stomach and had begun to push away the hurt from my ribs. I took a moment to envy the way the sunflowers swayed in the light breeze without a care in the world. I could only stand tight and wonder at my unfinished story. I'd always known that finding out about my past would probably not be everything I wanted it to be, but I hadn't been prepared for the fact that my father was dead. The fact that he had been murdered only confused me more.

"May I sit?" I hadn't even heard Francesco come up behind me.

"Of course." I slid over carefully and put my hands on my lap as I tried to curb my emotions.

He eased into the hammock next to me and took over the job of swinging it with his foot. He sat silently as though waiting for me to speak. When I didn't, he breathed heavily a couple of times, allowing the air to puff out his cheeks as he exhaled. He was obviously mulling something over.

"I don't want you to hate me," he whispered. "Things just didn't go as planned."

"I so wanted—" my voice cut out as my chin quivered. "I really hoped you were my father." The words hurt so much that I broke out in a sob.

"Oh, Sienna," he pulled me into his side and wrapped a gentle arm around me, "I wanted to be your father so much. It's why I couldn't give you up."

"Give me up?" I tried to follow.

"I think it's time I told you my part in this whole thing." I tried hard to breathe evenly to stop the pain in my chest as he spoke. "I was in love with your mother. I still am, apparently." He chuckled darkly. "But our happily ever after never came. Things got very complicated, and we were torn apart. She later married and had you. But your mother's, ah, life situation became unbearable. As things worsened, she knew she needed to get you somewhere safe. She turned to me, the one person in this world she trusted, for help. We made an agreement that I would hide you away from danger and," he hesitated, "from the Capri family."

"Because she believed the Capri family killed her brother."

"Right."

"But they didn't?"

"No, they didn't." He turned to look at me. "Piero looked into it. He was going to share that information with you last night. The bombing just threw everyone for a loop." I nodded, feeling better knowing they weren't behind the hit that killed my uncle.

"Do you know who did it?"

"We have our suspicions, but I'll save that for another day. I want to finish my story." He took a deep breath. "I was only supposed to hide you away from danger, but in the first few weeks of you being with me, we became close. It was my hand you needed to fall asleep, I was the one who read the stories right, and you'd latch on to my leg when you were frightened. I never had a daughter, and you were part of my Elenora. I had no idea when, or if, I would ever see her again. Maybe it was selfish, but I just couldn't be that far away from you. So, I did the one thing I promised I wouldn't do. I hid you close by. Next door to where I lived with the Capris."

He drew in a breath and huffed it out. "I promised myself I would drop you off and only check in on you occasionally." His hold on me tightened. "I truly thought they were a good family. I had someone watching you, but he fed me false information. I wonder if he even really checked on you at all. Then months and months went by, and he never showed up to give me his report. He went missing, and I had to know what was happening.

"Remember the day you met Elio at the pond?" I nodded through sudden tears. "Well, I was following the path through the woods and saw you crying. It broke my heart to see you like that. I couldn't believe I had found you there, after so long, and it took every ounce of willpower not to approach you. I knew I had to find a way to see if you were all right. I circled back home and sent Elio to you. I knew he would find you."

"Did Piero or Andrea know about me?"

"No. It's the biggest secret I'd ever kept from them."

"Why?"

"For reasons I can't share right now."

"Did you ever tell Elio about me?"

"Never. And when it was obvious that Elio was falling for you, it was too late. I couldn't take that from you or from Elio."

"Why?"

"Because the love you two have is the exact same as Elenora's and mine. You can't cheat that kind of love. It's like a boomerang effect. No matter how far you separate, one way or the other you will find each other again. I know what that's done to me and Elenora. I couldn't do that to the two of you."

Tears dripped from my cheeks as I let his story marinate in my head. Many questions rose to the surface, but one thing stood out.

"It's strange," I whispered. "Subconsciously, I think I knew you were someone special to me, because when we met, I felt an instant connection with you."

"I'm sorry I wasn't honest from the start. I just couldn't be."

"I am, too," I nodded, "but I appreciate you taking care of me, even though I had no idea you were."

He sniffed and cleared his throat then gave my hand a squeeze.

"Thank you for sending Elio to me." I squeezed his hand back.

"He needed you, just as much as you needed him."

We both fell silent and enjoyed the sway of the hammock as we sat immersed in our thoughts. Then his phone rang. He spoke briefly then slid the phone into his pocked.

"Shall we?" He smiled and held out a hand to me. Wordlessly, I took it, and he walked me back up to the house. We both had to get on with our day.

I was tempted to call my boss and see if there were any stories I could look into, just to feel like I was doing something worthwhile with my time. Then decided I should check in with Wyatt first to see how his research was going. As I went to look for my phone, I ran into Andrea struggling with a big box with a laptop balanced on top of it.

"Here, let me help you." I took the computer and a file she had pressed under her arm.

"Thank you," she sighed, then she looked at me as though in thought. "Sienna, I think it's time you learned some things about the family business."

"Oh." I had wondered when someone would take the time to talk to me about the mafia way of life. "I would love to."

She motioned for me to follow. She led me to one of the sunrooms on the far side of the house. It was a lovely room that looked over the pool and gardens.

My phone vibrated, and I glanced at it, hoping it was Wyatt telling me he would be free for a call soon. I missed him terribly and wanted to know how the story was coming along.

Elenora: I have to leave town for a few days. When I get back, I hope we can meet up again?

My nose twitched at the text. I hated how she was only a short drive away, but I didn't get to see her very often.

Sienna: I'd like that, too. Have a good trip.

"You can help me go through these files." Andrea didn't pry. She opened the box and started to lay out files. "They are all in order by date." She smiled up at me. "We need to find any mention of extra containers that may have arrived in Italy, or of any extra ones that may have arrived back from Libya. There should be three signatures by these three men in New York," she pointed to one of the invoices, "and three from our dockyard, and another three from Libya, where the oil is actually coming from. If anything looks off at all, put it aside."

"Are we looking for the girls?"

"Yes." She nodded. "We are the third sets of eyes on this paperwork. Though she's from Serbia, we run our oil from Libya. I'm just not sure what's happening here." She rubbed her head, looking stressed.

"Then let's make sure we don't miss anything." I smiled and warmed to the task. It was nice to feel useful. She mentioned a few more things about how the family business was run, when we fell into a good rhythm, and I let my mind wander a little with some questions.

"Can I ask something basic?"

"You can ask me anything." She tapped her finger on the wet sponge and swiped through the pages.

"Do you spot syndicates by their family rings?"

"Yes. Only a select few in the families have them. You have to be a direct bloodline from the Don and be the first-born child to get one. There are normally dates engraved inside the band to show it's authentic, along with a little stamp from the first founding godfather." Something caught her eye on the paper, but I guessed it was nothing, as she moved on. "Then from there, the Don of each family has a signature piece to identify who they are."

"Is that the tie pin Piero wears, the one that's almost hidden under the collar of his shirt?"

"Yes, good eye." She smiled, impressed. "He used to wear it further down, but after the attempted hit in Sicily, he tends to not be so flashy with it. I don't blame him. That was a close call."

I wanted to pry more, but I could tell she was still bothered by what happened, so I let it go.

I spent the rest of the day helping Andrea go through the papers. We combed tirelessly through the last three years of all the imports and exports of their oil business. When we broke for lunch, she explained to me about how they laundered money through their wineries. After seeing how it was run, I was amazed and impressed at just how simple it was.

"Simplicity is best." She sipped her grapefruit drink. "The authorities expect to have to dig deep for evidence, so leaving the truth just shaded by a little covering is often overlooked."

"Is it wrong that I find this fascinating?"

"Not at all." She shook her head. "This is how the world works, Sienna. We are a well-run syndicate, and we help keep our country going. We are reserved and know how to rule from the top without letting power or greed get the better of us." She checked the time on her watch. "We should get back to it. Noemi is coming over for drinks later."

We came up with nothing. There was zero evidence of any kind of human trafficking coming in or out of the Capri ports.

A few times, I caught Jacob Raine's name on some paperwork, so I pulled that aside. I decided I was going to think of a way to deal with him myself. I snapped a photo of his address.

As I sat across from Aunt Noemi and Andrea, I found myself remembering that night in the hotel room when Jacob carved his initial into my arm like a rancher branding his cattle. I remembered the smell of whiskey on his breath as he grabbed my breast. I shook it off as I heard someone enter the room.

My body temperature soared, and my skin flushed as the movement of his arm rubbing his cheek gave me a sight that nearly took my breath away. Elio's stance was that of a man who had the weight of what he had to do lay heavy on his shoulders. His white dress shirt was stained in blood. It traveled up his torso and splattered across his cheek.

I wanted to stand, run to check him over, see if all of him was okay, but instead I waited and watched. My heart slowed to a steady rhythm. I read his mood and studied his movements. I was seeing Elio in a whole different light. It was dark, like his yin to his yang.

I gave him a simple nod that I understood he was home and okay. He did the same and nodded toward the window, toward his house. Then he disappeared. I crossed my legs and turned to Andrea, who was watching me as Noemi prattled on about something. A small smile escaped her lips before she went back to the conversation. I saw Noemi give Andrea a look without a break in her sentence.

It wasn't lost on me that a big moment had just passed through the three of us. I guessed I was learning the mafia world.

Andrea gave me the first out she could, and I rushed down the hill to Elio's house. Using my key, I headed inside and followed the lighting that led me to the stairs and up to the bedroom. I gently pushed the door open to find Elio leaning against the wall looking out the window. His blood-soaked dress shirt dangled from his fingers.

I took a steady breath and straightened my spine, wanting to show confidence.

"You've been gone awhile."

"Hmhmm." He kept one shoulder flat against the wall as he watched me play with my key between my fingers. Then his gaze moved up. His bangs had fallen forward and covered the tops of his eyes, deepening the shadows around them.

"Tough night?"

"Yeah." He nodded once.

"Is any of that your blood?"

"No."

"Good." I calmly set my purse and keys on the dresser. "I'd really like it if you'd come to bed with me."

He pushed off the wall and stared down at me through hooded eyes. The blood splatter on his face had dried, and part of it cracked when he squinted. He was trying to read my mind, to see if it bothered me.

"I'm not sorry for what I have to do," he whispered.

"Okay." I knew he wasn't.

"What are you thinking?"

"Truthfully?" I whispered, and he nodded, stepping closer, and I felt the pull he had on me coil tighter inside. "I want to be the person who makes this haunted look," I brushed the back of my fingers down his temple and across the dried blood, "disappear."

He grabbed my hand and held it to his cheek, closing

his eyes. A painful expression flickered across his face.

"I want to make the world better, for you." His eyes shot open, and I was once again held captive by his intensity. For a brief moment, I saw inside him. The good versus evil, the reasoning to do things he did that outweighed the good, and the love he had for me.

"How badly do you hurt?" He referred to my sore ribs.

"I barely feel them."

"Mm." He kissed my lips gently then headed into the bathroom. I wasn't sure what I should do then, so I grabbed my bag and got ready for bed in the guest bathroom.

He was still in the shower when I returned, so I stripped down to nothing, took my nighttime pain pill, and settled under the cool sheets.

I allowed myself a brief moment to relish the fact I was in Elio's bed, naked, and he was only a door away.

The pain pill took no time kicking in, and I felt my eyes grow heavy.

I had just given in to sleep when I felt the covers shift over my bare back, and his lips skimmed my shoulder blade. Slowly, I rolled to face him and stroked my hand down his short beard, seeing his face soften in the low light.

"Do you remember the first time we had sex?" I moaned as he started to kiss his way down my neck and across my chest. "I was terrified of the idea of a man touching me that way, but with you, it was as easy as breathing."

He hovered over me, hooking my wrists and drawing them up and over my head. "I'll never forget the moment I pushed inside of you. Your eyes widened and latched on to mine like an anchor. Then, when you let yourself go and trusted me, they softened just as the rest of you did." He gently pushed my legs apart and nudged his erection at my opening. "I never got that out of my head." Leaning down, he nipped at my erect nipple as he dragged his fingers through my arousal. My breath caught in my lungs as utopian warmth spread across my skin, awakening all the sensitive nerve endings. "As fucked up as our situation is right now," he whispered, "at the end of the day, having you under me like this makes me sane."

"We need to be care—" My words trailed off when he pushed all the way inside me with a hungry moan.

Both of his hands slid down my wrists, arms, to my chest where he palmed my breasts, pushing them together and ravenously licking between them. He began to move inside me to the rhythm of his tongue. I hooked my legs around his waist, wanting him deeper, and held on for the explosion that was brewing in the center of my stomach.

"Yes," fell from my lips, and he suddenly leaned back on his legs, pulling me with him, so I was balanced on his lap. My wild hair fell all around us like a curtain. Both of us were breathing hard when he lifted me and gently brought me back down, stroking all the good spots at a painfully slow pace. Repositioning myself, I used my knees to lift myself and tried to take charge of the thrusts. He buried himself in my breasts again as he squeezed my hips.

"Yes, *bella*," he groaned as my body built and built.

I was so wound by our sounds I could barely think straight. Caught up in the wildness of it all, I reached back and cupped his balls, giving them a little roll through my fingers.

"Jesus, Sienna!" He huffed through a flexed jaw, and when he shot his hips up to meet mine, he hit the perfect angle, and I leapt off the edge, falling to pieces in his arms. He continued to pump into me as he came with a groan.

I vaguely remembered what happened next. All I knew was that I was wrapped up in Elio's arms, and I fell blissfully into a deep sleep.

Chapter
SIXTEEN

Elio

Niccola whisked into the kitchen to pour himself a cup of coffee. He slurped it as he said good morning. He came closer and leaned over the counter to dramatically study me with slitty eyes.

"What?"He held up a finger then left the room, returning a second later to repeat his actions from just a moment ago. He looked me over with a knowing expression.

"You had sex."

"And how did you come to this discovery?" I pulled at the pastry that was sitting in front of me.

"You seem relaxed," he mumbled from behind the lip of the mug.

"As opposed to…"

"Uptight, tense, murderous face, vein in your forehead ticking like a—"

"Thanks." I snickered and went back to reading an email from my phone. I could feel his prying eyes burning a hole in my forehead.

"Morning." Vinni came in and joined us.

"Hey, Vin, do you notice anything this morning?" Niccola leaned over the island again with a shit-eating smirk.

"That Elio had sex? Oh, yeah." He laughed lightly. "I spotted that from across the room."

"You know he could kill you both with the flick of his wrist." Aurora appeared out of nowhere, looking completely at ease in our home.

"He loves it."

I glared at Niccola then turned my attention to our guest.

"What brings you by, Aurora? I haven't seen you since two parties ago."

"That's actually why I'm here." She tossed a copy of *Fab* magazine down on the counter, and Sienna's deep blue eyes stared up at me. Images of last night and my head buried in her plump breasts as I thrust deep inside her made me shift. I glanced at Niccola, who just grinned and winked at me. "I heard the girl was still here, and I want her autograph."

"Who told you that?"

"Who do you think?" She rolled her eyes. "Mariano has been bragging about his new girlfriend since the party. I mean, I get it. I wouldn't kick her out of bed, but please, we have the same parts."

"Good morning." Sienna came into the kitchen with a bounce in her step but stopped short when she caught of Aurora standing next to me. "Oh, hi there, I'm—"

"Sienna Giovanna. I'm very aware of who you are, sweetheart."

"Okay." She looked at me, confused, and then at the others.

"You may not remember me, but I was Elio's date at the party a month or so ago." Aurora shot me a flirty smile. "We never did finish our night." She batted her lashes at Elio.

"I'm sorry." Sienna cleared her throat, drawing Aurora's attention back to her. "I met so many people that night—"

"It doesn't matter. What does matter is this." She held up the magazine and thrust a marker in Sienna's hand. "It would be really nice if you would autograph it to me."

"Oh, ah, sure." Sienna quickly signed the magazine as Aurora pulled out a phone. She then snapped a selfie of the two of them.

"I've never known you to be so wrapped up with a magazine article." Niccola said, clearly wondering what in the world her obsession was with Sienna.

"There's nothing wrong with appreciating the female body and all that comes with it." Aurora gave Sienna a grin. "Besides, if she does this next story, she's going to drive any man anywhere mad."

"What?" I shook my head. I knew I was missing an important part of the story.

"What are you talking about?" Vinni came to stand next to me.

"Wait," Sienna held up her hand, "how did you know about that?"

"After Mariano told me, I called your boss to confirm. If only I'd known these guys had you up here at the Hill House." She glared at us. "I can't believe you never told me, Elio. I had to learn about it from Mariano?"

"You called my boss?" Sienna's cheeks grew pink with anger and confusion.

"Everyone stop talking." I grew annoyed. "What story?"

"Just that the hottest lingerie company in the United States has requested Sienna to do a full- page spread. We're talking cover, billboards, the lot. The list goes on and on. She's about to be the biggest male fantasy going, and I just got her autograph and a photo." Aurora practically swooned.

Sienna glared at her with a look to kill. My temperature was about to hit max, and I tugged my tie loose.

Aurora looked around the room at all our faces. "Wait. Was that a secret? Because your boss said you didn't say no when he asked you the other day." She looked at Sienna sweetly. "So, I just assumed you were following through with it."

"Oh, look, everyone is here." Mariano rubbed his messy hair as he walked into the kitchen. He instantly perked up when he saw Aurora. Then he leaned over and kissed Sienna. That quickly made her snap out of her daze, and her face flushed even more. "What are we all up to this morning?"

"Got my autograph." Aurora held up the magazine. "This will make me wildly popular later on."

"Yes, darling," he addressed Sienna, "let's talk about your outfits for this next shoot." He grinned at me, and I imagined his neck under my hands.

"When did I lose control of my own life?" Sienna muttered then turned on her heel and hurried out, leaving us to digest everything.

Where does she think she's going?

I waited for Mariano to hone in on Aurora, then I slipped out of the room. I raced off in the direction I'd seen her go, with Niccola on my heels, begging me to slow down and think about what I was doing.

I found her sitting in the library, flipping through the pages of a book.

"What the hell was that?" I barked. She jumped, and the book went flying. "What the hell are they talking about?"

"It's nothing—"

"I very much beg to differ, Sienna." I wanted to kill someone I was so angry. "I forbid you to do any kind of photoshoot."

Her demeanor instantly changed. Her eyebrow rose, and her head tilted to the side as she looked at me. An annoying smirk broke out across her lips.

"Oh, boy." Niccola dropped down next to her and

stared up at me like he was enjoying the show. I dismissed him and went back to Sienna.

"First, you will not forbid me to do anything. Second," she lifted a hand and held it up when I tried to cut her off, "you do not come in here demanding to get an answer out of me. Cool it down, or we're finished with this conversation."

"Oh, my God, she's a female version of you." Niccola chuckled, just asking for a fat lip.

I tried to digest her words, but my temper was getting the best of me.

"You see that right there," Niccola turned to her and ran a finger across his forehead, "that's Elio's beast vein. It pops out when he's about to utterly lose his shit."

"Oh, yeah? Beast Vein?" She played along.

"Yeah. We named it." He laughed like I was a comedy act for their personal enjoyment. "You're pushing the boss to new limits."

"Well, if the *boss* spoke to people rather than yell and demand things, maybe the beast wouldn't show itself so often."

Niccola shrugged. "He is the underboss and should expect to have respect at all times. However, with you, it's different. Hence why I'm here."

"Really?" I snapped. "Whenever you're both done."

"Are we done?" She looked at Niccola, who nodded at her, then at me. "Okay, now we're done."

"Amusing." I dripped with sarcasm.

"I thought so," Sienna shot back as she stood, replacing the book on the shelf. "Yes. I was offered that job. Georgio wanted me to do it, and honestly, I was flattered and wanted to savor the feeling for a while. I'm not saying I will do it." She turned to look at me as she lifted her chin and straightened her spine. "But I'm not saying I won't. Bottom line is, Elio, it's my decision."

"The hell it is. You're going to be my wife. You're mine, and I will not share your body with anyone."

"Again," she sighed, like I wasn't getting it, "not your decision to make, but I will certainly take into account your feelings on the topic." *Excuse me…* "Now, if you boys don't mind, I have to be somewhere."

She walked past me and out the door. Niccola spread out on the couch with a deep, noisy intake of breath.

"Did she just walk away from me?" My mouth hung open while Niccola chuckled.

"She might be my most favorite person yet." He pulled out his phone, no doubt to fill in his little brother.

I spun on my heel and headed for the house. I really needed to work out some anger.

A few hours in the ring, and I was still pent-up, but when Nonna called, I left, knowing we had a lunch date. Plus, I still had to hold some interviews.

I glanced at my watch as I climbed the stone stairs to the house and saw I was ten minutes late.

"I'm sorry, Nonna." I raced out onto the terrace and kissed her cheeks. "Time seems to be slipping away on me a lot lately."

"You sound like me." She smiled as I helped her back down into her chair. "No need for apologies. I just appreciate you taking time for me."

"Always." I leaned back as a plate of food was placed in front of me. I lowered my head and said a quick prayer with her, which I didn't often do myself anymore. The Lord and I had different ideas about forgiveness, but I did try to be respectful for those around me who did rely on him.

Just as I took a bite of the creamy salmon, I noticed Nonna was working over her rosary beads at an extra-fast pace. "Something on your mind?"

"Yes, actually." She took a moment to wet her mouth with lemon water. I glanced at Abramo, her *consigliere*. He'd been in our family for as far back as I could remember. I wondered if he would give me any indication of what was going on. Of course, he didn't. He just held my gaze as he stood there in his classic gray suit with its gleaming crown lapel pin. The pin that was a symbol of working for the elders. "The pretty young lady you had over here the other day."

"Sienna."

"Yes, that was her name. How did you two meet?"

"She is from Sicily. We met years ago, but when we moved, we lost touch and—"

"Now she's here." She finished my sentence.

"Nonna, you've never been one to dance around a topic. If you have something you wish to say, I'm listening."

"Forgive me, but you must understand my questioning. A stunning new female has caught your eye, and you bring her here. In all these years, you've never brought a woman here. I must say, I'm curious."

I gently set my knife and fork down and tried to see it from her point of view.

"This is true, I haven't, but she's different."

"How?"

I thought for a moment before I answered her. "We have a very deep history, Nonna. She isn't after our money or our land. I know she's with me for me."

Nonna dabbed at the corners of her mouth then tossed her napkin next to her half-eaten plate.

"So, you know everything about this girl?"

"Yes." I studied her face and wished she'd relax. Sienna was the last person to be a threat to our world. "I love her," I stated so that she knew where I stood on the topic.

Her face dropped, but she quickly recovered. "I see."

"I know she isn't the woman you wanted me to be with, but I don't have any love for Anna. We are too different, and I'm not going to be pushed into an arranged marriage. I'm sorry. I know that was how it was for you, and I only hope that you, at some point, loved Papa. But, Nonna, I love Sienna, and I will marry her."

Her fingertips worked over her rosary beads as she gazed over my shoulder. I knew she was only looking out for me, but nothing would change my feelings.

"What is her last name?"

"No." I let out a long, controlled breath. "You will not dig, Nonna. You're invading my personal life, and that's not okay."

"I have the right to know."

I tossed my napkin on the table and stood. "I love

you, but I am not my uncle. You can control him, but you can't me."

"Elio, sit." She calmly pointed to the chair, and I waited a beat before I lowered into it. "I lost control once before, and it brought a level of darkness to the family that still needs to be watched very carefully."

"When?" This was the first I'd heard of this.

"It's not important."

"I think it is."

"You must always think of the family first, Elio, even before your heart. Think of your parents, your cousins. As difficult as it might be, it is your responsibility. Listen, all I ask is that if you wish to marry this girl, before you ask her, simply dig a little. There's nothing wrong with that, and it's protection for the family." I started to speak, but she stopped my words as she reached over and covered my hand with hers. "You know you mean the world to me and I'm only trying to protect you."

I pushed away my frustration and tried to remember that Nonna had been in this life longer than any of us. She was simply making sure I did my duty to the family.

"All right. I will."

"Good." She smiled, and sweet Nonna was back. "Now, finish up that delicious salmon. Your men should be arriving any moment."

Once our lunch was finished, I took her by the arm and walked her down to the driveway. I was happy she wanted to join me in my interviews. Nonna and I had always been close, and I trusted her with any decision I had to make. She had always had my back when others hadn't. That was why our conversation bothered me. Maybe I should understand what happened to Sienna in the last ten years. Maybe there was something there that could come back and hurt the family. What kind of an example would I be as a leader if I didn't apply the same rules to my own life?

One of the house maids approached us. She handed Nonna a cotton umbrella, providing her with some much-needed shade. I stood on a step next to the driveway and looked down at the drivers in front of us. If I was going to keep Sienna safe, she needed a driver I could trust.

One by one, I tested the skills of the drivers, and I quizzed them on the many situations that could occur. I even tested their reaction when they understood who they'd be driving. One man's pupils dilated with interest when he saw her photo, and he was immediately eliminated.

Three hours later, I still hadn't found anyone I would hire. I glanced over at Nonna, who was now sitting in a chair Abramo had brought for her. She shrugged as if all were hopeless in her eyes, too.

When the last man was told to go home, Nonna spoke quietly to Abramo, and he quickly disappeared.

"No man will ever be safe enough for the woman you love." She patted my arm. "So, my gift to you is…" She paused as Abramo pulled up in her old classic Paul Brown Jaguar MK2.

"She might be old and a little dusty," she pointed to the car, "but I can assure you those windows have been reinforced, and the doors could take a semi-automatic head-to-head. Abramo's skills are being wasted here at the house, and I think he could be just what you're looking for. Trustworthy, older," she smirked, "and will take a bullet for her, as he would for any of us. There's a reason he's been around for as long as he has."

I'd never thought of Abramo for Sienna. He was, after all, Nonna's right-hand man. He certainly hadn't been on my radar.

"What about you, Nonna?"

"You know I don't leave the property much, and if I were to, I'm sure Sienna and I could come to some kind of arrangement."

"I like the idea of you getting to know her better."

"Me too."

"To a point." I gave her a sharp look.

"Can't blame your Nonna for caring about her favorite grandson."

"Well, when you put it like that." I laughed as I glanced at my vibrating phone and agreed to take on Abramo as Sienna's new driver.

Vinni: We need to leave.

SEVENTEEN

Elenora

We had dropped off the grid for three days and stayed low while Oscar assessed the situation at hand. Before I saw Sienna again, I needed to know we were wrong about the assumptions we had made. It could have been nothing, but my nephew Ugo thought he had spotted someone from our past, and after what happened with the bombing, I couldn't risk anything else happening, especially with Sienna. Though we had come up emptyhanded, something told me the wolves weren't far away.

Oscar opened my door while Ugo retrieved my luggage from the trunk.

"Welcome back, Ms. Violetta." The doorman tipped

his hat at me. "I'll have some hot tea sent up to your room."

"Thank you." I didn't break my stride as I headed to the elevator and pushed the button for second floor.

"I'm good from here." I took my bag from Ugo and nodded for Oscar to stand post at my door. Once inside the dark room, I took a deep breath and let the stress fall away, just needing a moment to myself. That was until I felt a strange prickle up my spine, alerting me I wasn't alone.

"You could call for your men," the calm voice said. I scanned the room and found a pair of expensive shoes in the moonlight. "But by now they have been drawn away from your door and out into the stairwell." The wooden rocking chair squeaked as she started to rock. I didn't have to turn the light on to know who it was. We had met once before, and the fear in me ran deep.

"Given your silence, you have connected the dots." That voice.

"Yes," I whispered.

"Good, then I will make this very easy for you." The clicking of the rosary beads made my stomach churn. "Just like years ago when you tried to burrow yourself into Francesco's life, I give you the same warning. But this time," she paused and stood, just as agile as I remembered, "this will be your last. Take your daughter and leave here. Because if you don't, I will expose the truth, and something tells me no amount of forgiveness will be given after that is shared."

The door opened, and Abramo, her right-hand man,

stood tall in the doorway. She brushed by me, leaving me alone in the dark, with nothing but a chair still slowly rocking in the moonlight.

I grabbed a pillow and covered my face while I let out a long, frustrated scream. My life had always been controlled by puppet strings. Everyone always telling me what to do and who to be with. The fight for power over my own life hadn't been easy, and skeletons from my past showing up in my room made me shrink down two sizes.

I grabbed my bag and pulled out the file I used to remind myself of what I was doing and why. Pulling the article out, I read the headline.

Remains of two bodies found in field. Authorities conclude they are the bodies of a mother and daughter who went missing…

A knock at the door. I shoved the paperwork under the pillow.

"Come in." My voice betrayed me.

"Everything okay in here?" Oscar looked around.

"Yes," I lied, needing a moment to gather myself before I shared what had happened. I could tell he didn't believe me, but he knew better than to push.

"I'll be right outside."

"Thank you." I waited for him to leave then curled into a ball on the bed and remembered the last time I'd seen Greta Capri.

"I'm sorry, I can't stay for dinner, Elenora. I have to go deal with a situation." Francesco spoke quickly as he kissed my cheek in the lobby of the restaurant.

"Seriously?"

"I'm sorry, but you know when the Don calls, I answer."

"And when the girlfriend calls?"

"I promise I'll make it up to you later on tonight." He winked.

"Fine," I huffed in disappointment but understood. He took his job seriously, and I was trying to respect that. "I'll see you later." I waved and headed inside where I spotted my brother, Angelo. He had a beautiful woman next to him. They both rose to greet me.

"Noemi, this is my sister, Elenora, and her boyfriend..."

"Just cancelled, but he sends his apologies." I hooked my purse on the seat next to me.

"That's no problem." Noemi smiled as she took her seat. I noticed she reached for Angelo's hand and gave it an excited squeeze. "I've heard so much about you, Elenora. I feel like we're going to be good friends."

"I think so." My brother beamed, and I couldn't help matching their excitement.

"Tell her." Noemi wiggled in her chair, and I looked at my brother, puzzled.

"I know Papa and Mama haven't met Noemi yet, but things have been happening so quickly, and, well," he grinned at her, "we're moving in together."

"Oh." I couldn't hide my shock, so I quickly reached for my water, taking a moment to recover. "That's really quick."

"Love knows no starting point, and we are in love."

Noemi sighed and looked adoringly at Angelo.

I blinked as I digested what Noemi had said. Love did have a starting point. It was after you spent a little time together. It was when you realized your heart beat faster and expanded whenever you caught sight of each other.

"I know, it's only been three weeks—"

"But when you know, you know." Noemi cut Angelo off as she prattled their order to the waitress. I forced a smile at my brother as I pushed down the thought that Noemi was a tad overbearing.

Dinner consisted of Noemi talking mostly about herself and her dreams of the future. I realized as she spoke her dream required a lot of money. I wondered how my brother would keep up as he ran his side of the family business. The few times I asked about her family, she sidestepped and acted like they didn't matter. Finally, when she paused for a breath, I took the opportunity to take a restroom break. As I headed to the back of the restaurant, I saw an old lady watching me. She sat contentedly while her white rosary beads slid through her fingers. A man stood tall behind her. I dismissed the strange woman's curious interest in me and carried on with my night.

"It was lovely getting to know you, Elenora." Noemi tugged on her sweater and excused herself. My brother and I sat quietly for a moment.

"I know," he laughed, "she's a lot at first, but once she calms down, she's really wonderful and funny."

"Who am I to judge? If you're happy, I'm happy."

"But?" He eyed me.

"All I'm going to say is just make sure she's with you for the right reasons."

"Meaning?"

"Meaning she seems a little controlling. It's only been three weeks, and she's already working out your future and, forgive me, but a lot of what she said puts you behind a desk working, while she plays out her dreams."

"I love her, Elenora."

Love? Yikes.

"Then, of course, I stand behind any decision you make."

We switched topics when Noemi returned to the table, and we gathered our things to leave. Just as I said my goodbyes and was heading to the parking lot, I spotted the old lady again. She stood next to a lovely old classic car. Her white beads hung from her fingers, and her cold, dark gaze made sure I knew she was looking at me.

I wanted to call out and ask what her problem was, but she slipped into the car and was swallowed up within its shaded windows.

I flipped onto my back and stared at the ceiling, trying to decide if I should share the news about tonight's visitor with Francesco. I never mentioned my encounter with Greta Capri all those years ago either. Mainly because when I finally decided to, it was too late, and the damage had been done.

Chapter EIGHTEEN

Sienna

My hand shook as I reached for the doorhandle. The last time I was here, I had come face to face with psycho Nonna, but I had made a promise to Noemi before I ever met Nonna, and I took pride in keeping my promises. Even if it terrified me to my very core.

"Good afternoon." Noemi waved me inside. "I can't thank you enough for doing this. I just feel so terrible for the young girl having no one to talk to."

"I understand the feeling and don't mind at all."

"Good." She pointed to the back yard. "She spends a lot of time in the garden. She enjoys the butterflies." She looked over her shoulder as though someone was watching. "I'll leave you two alone, then."

Okay…I felt incredibly awkward, but I was starting to realize this might be the norm for this house. I headed down, deep into the garden, and spotted the girl. She stood very still as I approached.

"Hello," I said gently, so as not to scare her, "I'm Sienna."

"Hi," she said quickly as she nervously tucked a piece of hair behind her ear.

"Do you mind if I join you?" I had no idea if she understood any of what I was saying, but to my surprise, she nodded. "I used to live on the streets. I had no home, no friends."

I figured I should just jump in. She might connect with me if she understood that I wasn't a Capri. I was just someone she might be able to relate to.

"I was really lonely and felt like I didn't belong." When she didn't react, I dug deep, trying to find something in my life that might spark a conversation. "I remember one time eating out of a trash can, I was so hungry. I'd say that was my lowest point, but it wasn't. I was so hungry once I stole money from a mother on a bus. She had three kids to feed, and I stole from her." I rubbed my head at the guilty feeling in the pit in my stomach. "I told myself that when I got money, I would pay her back. Of course, I didn't."

"Stomach can control head," she said in broken Italian. "I have many regrets."

"Regrets hurt." I pressed my hand to my chest, and she nodded.

"Sienna," she tried to pronounce my name, and I

smiled, "I," she pointed to herself, "Anja."

"That's a pretty name, Anja."

She looked back at the house and twisted her sweater tighter around her body, which was odd as it was a very warm day.

"Anja, do you want to call your family? Talk to your mama or papa?"

"No," she shook her head, "no family. That's why I was chosen."

That caught my attention.

"Do you mean the man who took you?"

Her eyes widened, and I thought she caught on to who I was getting at.

"My Italian very bad. I grow tired. So tired."

I stepped in her way as she started to leave. "I think your Italian is very good." I studied her pink cheeks and saw fear flicker across her eyes. "You're safe here. No one will hurt you." Her gaze moved up to the house, and I followed her line of slight but couldn't see anyone. "I just want to be your friend, Anja. Everyone needs a friend."

"So tired." She moved past me and hurried toward the house, leaving me to wonder what in the world was going through her head.

I sank down to sit on a stump and tried to gather my thoughts. So many things were happening that I wasn't sure where to even begin. But my heart broke for Anja. She had no one and was now living in a place where she had to learn the language and live in a stranger's house. Not to mention one that was ruled by a crazy old lady.

I plucked a weed that was encroaching on a flower and scowled at it. *Why can't you leave good things be?*

"I told you to keep your head down and not talk to her," one of the workers snapped at someone else. I squinted through the garden, trying to see who it was.

"Remember what he said. Scared eyes bring big paychecks."

I froze and held my breath, terrified they might hear me. I was quickly jolted back to a memory of one of Jacob's men saying that very thing in New York.

Without a thought, I scrambled to my feet and raced to the open door and flung myself inside. I texted Vinni to come get me but stopped short when I heard Mariano's voice almost in a yell. Slowly, I moved toward the partially closed door and peeked inside.

"We had a deal, Anja. You listen and tell me what you know."

"She didn't say anything." Anja smacked her hand down on the back of the chair, and it wasn't lost on me that she spoke Italian very well. "She just wanted to make sure I was all right and said if I needed anything to come to her."

"And did you ask her about—"

"No! I didn't have the chance. Mariano, you need to back off, I know what I have to do, but breathing down my neck every few days isn't going to make it happen any faster."

"I just need to make one call to Stefano and your ass will be shipped back to that hell-hole life of yours. Understood?"

"Yeah."

"Pardon me?"

She glared at him. "Yes, boss."

I stepped back, shocked at what I was hearing. Had Anja been planted here by Stefano? And in what sick world did Mariano need to be called "boss?" My stomach rolled, but when I heard a chair scrape in the room, I snapped out of it and raced to the front door as Vinni pulled in the driveway.

"Hey, you!" He opened the door for me. He looked over my shoulder and smiled at someone. I didn't wait to find out who, and didn't want to know, so I slipped into the seat, not making eye contact with anyone.

"Have a good one, Nonna." He waved and joined me in the car. "How was the visit? Seemed short."

"Yes, but it was interesting." I started to open my mouth but stopped myself. Perhaps I needed to wait and just share this with Piero.

"I think it's a start." His eyes met mine in the mirror as he spoke.

"Mmm."

"The boss is back. I'm sure he'll be happy to see you."

Oh?

"See me or have another tantrum?" I chuckled darkly.

"Oh, yeah, you got him all twisted up." He grinned. "I've never heard about anyone speaking to the boss that way. I can't believe I missed it." He hit the steering wheel with a laugh.

"Something tells me we'll be at it again soon."

"I'll bring the refreshments." He chuckled, and we settled in for the drive home.

Once he parked, I shot out the door and caught Andrea in the study.

"Hi, have you seen Piero?"

"He's in his office."

"The door is closed." I sighed.

"Just knock. He'll tell you if it's a good time or not."

"Thanks." I hurried down the hallway, took a deep breath, and gently knocked.

"Come in."

I pushed the door open and found him reading something on the computer.

"Good afternoon, Piero. May I speak to you about something?"

"Now isn't the best time."

"Please." I stopped myself, nervous I was overstepping. "I wouldn't ask if it wasn't important."

He nodded and pointed to the chair across from him. He lowered the top of his laptop so I would have his full attention.

"I know everyone has been very busy with everything that's going on, and I understand that, but I still haven't had anyone teach me the mafia ropes." I took a deep breath, trying to find the right words. "So, when I hear or see things, I don't know who I go to about it or what the protocol is."

"That's fair, and it's something Elio and I have discussed a few times now." He removed his glasses and studied my face. "I take it you have some information for me?" I nodded. "Okay, why don't you tell me what it is, and we'll go from there."

"Noemi asked me to try to befriend Anja since she's all alone here, and when I went over today, we spent some time in the garden. Her Italian isn't great, but she could understand me, and I could her. She mentioned that she didn't have any family and that was probably why she was chosen."

"True, most girls who are picked up and trafficked are ones without any families to look out for them."

"Right, but after we talked, I overheard her speaking to Mariano in perfect Italian, and now I'm thinking her being found at the dockyard was what Stefano might have wanted all along."

His face twisted into a dark expression, and his jaw ticked exactly like Elio's did as he leaned forward. "Tell me everything."

He sat like stone as I told him everything I had heard, including the gardeners' conversation. I tried to remember every detail I could so he could make sense of it.

"I don't know if it counts for anything, but when I was speaking to Anja, she never once asked me anything about my life here or anything at all, for that matter. I was the one who asked all the questions. Maybe she's stuck in this situation for whatever reason and has no way out."

"You have a kind heart, Sienna." He sighed. "It's one of the main reasons we love you so much, but I do think it's time you knew some rules, especially since it's apparent you're good at discovering information." He gave me a half smile as he picked up his phone. "Francesco, I need to skip our meeting. Something's come up." He turned his phone off and brought his attention back to me. "All right, let's start from the bottom and work our way up."

I nodded and spent the next two hours learning how the Capri Syndicate operated.

"You look fried." Vinni found me out back sipping a glass of prosecco as I relaxed on a lounge chair.

"I had a meeting with Piero."

"Yeah, that'll do it." He chuckled. "Oh, by the way, this came for you. It was sent to the newspaper, and Wyatt had it sent on to you."

He handed me a big envelope, and I tore it open to find a letter inside. I examined the writing trying to place it.

"Oh, my God!" I cupped my mouth and sat up with excitement.

"Everything all right?"

"Yeah, um…" I wanted to be alone. "Would it be okay if I went for a walk? I'd really like to enjoy this alone."

"Sure, I don't see the harm." He smiled as I raced out the side gate.

I took the path and strolled through the sunflower field. I wanted to take my time. I savored the handwriting on the envelope as I walked. I stopped when I found just the right spot and settled in to open the precious letter.

Dearest Sienna,

I hope this letter finds you well and happy. It took me nearly a lifetime to find you. I read the article about your life journey, and I cried once I realized how well you're doing now. There are some people in this world who deserve happiness, and one of those is you. I often dream of meeting you again and us becoming lifelong sisters. I have to know, are you still in contact with the boy from the pond? Elio, I believe, right? I'm living in Florence now, and how I wish we could meet up. Please do reach out. We have a lifetime to catch up on! I have included my address and cell number.

Sincerely, your sister, Cara

P.S. I hope you finally got to run in that field full of sunflowers.

If she only knew! I looked around at the smiling yellow faces that surrounded me and dried the tears that had raced down my cheeks as I read. I threw back my head and laughed with pure happiness. How I'd missed Cara. I always wondered if our paths would link up again. I couldn't believe how many people the article had brought me. I snapped a photo of the letter and sent it to Wyatt with a crying emoji, and somehow my mother crept into my thoughts.

With my newfound high, I moved to the road and started to walk up the hill, only to be greeted by a car that slowed and lowered its window.

"Good afternoon, Ms. Sienna." Gain—an odd

name—was one of Elio's soldiers. He gave me a warm smile and a wave. "Do you need a ride?"

"I'm heading to the Hill House."

"So am I. Hop in."

"Thanks."

Within thirty seconds, we arrived in the driveway, and I hopped out, spotting Elio in the doorway. He looked at me oddly, then at Gain.

"Were you just in the car with Gain?"

"Hello, dear." I rolled my eyes at his lack of greeting. "Yes, your soldier spotted me coming up the hill and offered me a ride."

"But I thought Vinni got you."

"I've already been home, but then I went for a walk."

"Why?"

Seriously, I hadn't seen him in three days, and he was questioning me like I was up to no good.

"I was posing for my photoshoot." I smirked.

"Sienna," he growled in warning, and I was instantly turned on. He waved Gain to move on, and we were left alone in the driveway. "I will take you upstairs and prove to you just how wrong that comment was."

"Is that a promise, Mr. Capri?" I raised my eyebrow playfully. "Because if that's the case," I stepped closer, lowering my voice, "I was in a black lace corset with a red thong and matching heels." My fingers traveled down my beloved necklace, and I fingered the crow pendant between my breasts.

His hand cupped my jaw as he grinned his interest and lowered his head to mine. "The only one who's going to see you naked is me. If I find out you accepted that deal, we will have a problem. I will show you my darker side, and, *bella*," he paused, "you won't like it."

I shuddered under his hold. I was both terrified and equally turned on.

"Maybe if you were anyone else," I licked my lips as his hand dropped away from my chin, "I would behave and know better, but when you get like this," I ran my hand down his stomach and across his erection, "all I want to be is bad. Very, very bad."

He growled, grabbed my hand, and pulled me toward the garden shed. "You want to push my limits?" He slammed the door behind me and pressed me down, front first, across a stone table. He hiked up my dress as he dropped his pants, shifted my dripping panties aside, and plunged deep inside me. I shot forward in a moan, loving him inside me. I used my arms to prop myself up, but he took a fistful of hair and gently lifted my head to see out the window. Mariano had pulled in and was now in the driveway as he made a call. My phone rang, and Elio dumped out my purse and slid my phone over to me.

"Answer him," he commanded.

"No." I hated that idea.

"Sienna." He gave my bottom a swat, and I squeezed my eyes shut, trying not to come.

"Fine," I groaned and answered the call on speaker. "Hi, Mariano."

"Where are you?"

"I'm, ah…" I fought to keep my head straight. "Almost there, I mean home."

Elio slowly dragged out of me to the tip and plunged back inside with such force I was thankful for the strength of the table.

"Are you okay?"

"Mmhm."

Elio's hands moved to my hips under my belly and palmed my breasts.

"I want to take you to dinner."

"I'm pretty full at the moment." Elio chuckled quietly, and I rolled my eyes at my cheesy choice of words.

"You can eat. We have some things to discuss. I'm in the driveway. How long until you arrive?"

"Any moment now." I clicked the phone off and let out a much-needed moan. "Yes, Elio, I'm so close."

"Yeah?" He pounded harder, and I started to see black spots. I was racing so close to the finish line I could taste sweet victory. My body coiled, my toes curled, my mouth watered, and-and…

"My *bella*." Elio suddenly stopped. "I told you not to test me." He slid out, and I gasped. "Now," he moved my panties back into position, lifted me onto my feet, and finger brushed my hair to lay smooth, "if you want to come, you need to behave."

"That's messed up, Elio."

"What's messed up, my love, is that you want to test my limits for your enjoyment. When you're ready to be a good little lady, you know exactly where we are." He smirked and kissed my lips roughly.

"So, you're holding out on me? No sex until I

behave?”

“Sex yes, coming no.” He grinned in delight.

“Oh, Elio,” I matched his tone, feeling so much better than I did this morning, “game on.” I winked and thought how fun this would be.

I started to gather my belongings that he had so nicely dumped on the table when he snagged my letter.

“What’s this?”

“A letter.”

“From?” He didn’t enjoy my sarcasm.

“You remember my old friend Cara, from the DeVaio house?” His expression changed to a serious one. “I guess she found me. Found me at the newspaper, I mean, then Wyatt sent it to Vinni, who gave it to me. She wants to meet up.”

“Why?”

“Because she’s my friend.”

“I want to read it.”

My head snapped back, and I tried to understand where that tone was coming from. “Elio, is there something you want to ask me?”

“I just did.”

“No, you demanded.”

He shook his head like there was too much going on inside it. “Let’s talk tonight, our place, eight p.m.”

“Okay.” I tried to follow his spinny head then gave up and slid my letter from his hold. He left, and I waited a beat then approached Mariano, who was looking in the other direction as he lowered his phone. I came up behind him.

"Hey, Mariano. Sorry, but I can't make it tonight."

"Where is the car?" He looked at the driveway.

"I was walking."

"Sienna, do you just not want to be alone with me?"

"Like I've said countless times, I'm not looking to date. Honestly, Mariano, I think given recent events, going out for anything at all just isn't appealing."

"You know I'll protect you."

I internally rolled my eyes. "I know, but I need to pass."

His hands were in his hair pulling roughly. "You're a God damn tease, Sienna."

"What? How? I've been honest with you from the very start."

"Have you?" His eyes searched mine, and I took a step back. "Do you have the notebook?"

"What?"

"Don't play games with me!" he nearly yelled, and Francesco appeared at the top of the steps and cleared his throat. "Sorry." His face smoothed out, and the scary, intense lines that had just creased his forehead disappeared. "That's not what I meant to ask." He rubbed his face with both hands like he was coming down from a high. "I think I need some sleep."

"Agreed."

"I'm sorry." He took my hand and gave it a squeeze. "We can do dinner another night."

"That would be best." I stepped back and watched him get back into his car and peel out of the driveway.

"Are you okay?" Francesco asked as he joined me.

"Yes, thanks. Dealing with Mariano is always such fun." I grimaced.

"He's getting worse." He watched as Mariano took the corner hard. "We have someone tailing him, and I hope it's only a matter of time before he leads us to something worth all this. It's so frustrating."

"I think I want to see my mother. Can you take me?"

"Yeah," he smiled, "I can do that."

As we drove, I sat quietly. Francesco seemed to understand I needed that and did not break into my thoughts. There was so much racing through my mind I wasn't sure where to start.

"Again," I started to speak in the middle of a thought, "you're not blood related to the Capri family, correct?"

"No, just very good friends with Piero. He trusted me, and I became his right-hand man."

"Right-hand man, that's also known as his *consigliere*, right?" He nodded. "And you've been in love with my mother since forever."

"Yes."

"You're not my father, because my father was murdered."

"Correct."

"But you've been around the Capri family for nearly a lifetime."

"Yes…" He eyed me for a moment, trying to catch up to where I was.

"Which means you know his family like you would your own?"

"If not more."

"Is there anyone you don't particularly like?"

He pulled into the driveway of the hotel and left the car on for the cool air.

"Sienna, did someone do something?"

"I…" I paused, unsure I wanted to pull at the thread just yet. "I guess I'm just a little confused over a conversation I had with someone."

"What was said?"

"They told me I needed to leave. They acted like they knew me, but I had never met them." I flipped my hair out of my face, needing something to do. "It was their tone and anger toward me that was so confusing."

"Can you share with me who it was?"

I bit down on my lip and chewed the inside of my cheek. My nerves got the better of me, and I couldn't say it.

"All right." He held up a hand. "You don't have to say, but tell me, whoever is saying this, are they part of the Capri family?"

I held his gaze for a moment then reached for my purse and politely thanked him for the drive. Dashing across the parking lot, I headed inside. The maid was just coming out of the door, and I stepped around her.

"Mama?" I called. After a moment, I realized she wasn't there. I sat on a chair and waved the maid goodbye. She didn't question me as she closed the door behind her. If there was one thing I'd learned in all my years of chasing stories, it was to look like you belonged, and no one questioned you.

I went into her bedroom and sat at the vanity and

admired her makeup and perfumes. I removed the cap to one of them and breathed in the heavenly scent of roses. I liked being in her space. Like a child seeking comfort when they didn't feel good, I just wanted to feel her.

I held an earring up and watched it sparkle in the light. I loved her fashion sense. She was just an older version of me. I placed the earring with the other and knocked over a lipstick.

"Shoot," I muttered and reached under the chair for it. When I bent down, I saw a stack of papers under her suitcase. Curiosity got the best of me, and I pulled them free. A copy of *Fab Magazine* was on top. I felt something stiff between the pages, so I tipped it upside down and caught a card before it fell to the floor.

Scribbled in black marker was, *"You couldn't hide her forever."*

I blinked at the sentence and stood. I felt frozen and barely registered the door being opened and my mother's gasp.

"Sienna what are you doing here?"

"Who sent this?" I held up the card and watched her eyes close as she let out a long breath.

"I don't know."

"Why are there people after us—after me?"

"Because a bad thing happened, and we were part of it."

"What bad thing?" I shouted.

"The-the men who killed your father are after us too."

"Who are the men? No," I tossed my hands in the

air, "better yet, who was my father?"

"That's a lot for me to explain and a lot for you to understand."

"How do you know Noemi Capri?" Her face fell, and she took a step back. "I saw you at the party. I saw what passed between you both."

"That's complicated."

"No," I laughed lightly, "try being on my end, the end of not knowing a damn thing!" I grabbed my purse, stuffed the note inside, and headed for the door.

"Wait," she called after me, and Oscar blocked my path. "Okay, fine, just come back in the room and I'll tell you."

I glared at Oscar then turned on my heel and closed the door in his face.

"Noemi used to date my brother. She's a crazy, controlling woman who is only after money and the finer things in life. When she grew tired of my brother, she latched herself to someone else."

"Who?" I crossed my arms, refusing to play her Mad Libs game.

"Your father." That took the wind out of my lungs. "In fairness they were dating before I met him, but nonetheless, that's who she wanted. Only thing is, she wasn't part of the family agreement, I was. So, when it came time for us to marry, Noemi didn't take it very well."

"Hold on! You're telling that Noemi dated your brother, and Francesco never knew? I find that hard to believe."

"They dated for such a short period of time, and Francesco was working a lot, plus Noemi made it very clear she wanted nothing to do with the Capri syndicate. It was the one thing we ever agreed on." She scoffed. "But where there's money and power, Noemi will be there, and Theo kept her out of the public most of the time. She made my life hell for a good number of years. Meanwhile, my brother was suffering from a broken heart and tried to win her back. I know she pulled some strings and made him disappear."

"It wasn't the Capris who killed him."

"Believe what you want," she dismissed me. "All I know is that woman turned your father and his family against me, against us, and forced us to live in a horrible situation."

"She doesn't come across as someone who would do that."

"None of the Capris show their true colors until they need to." Her voice dripped hatred.

I wrung my hands as her words sank in. "But I've met Noemi countless times. Why is she so nice to me?"

"Because she doesn't know who you are. When I couldn't take it anymore, I grabbed what I could and left. I legally changed your name for your own protection. You weren't born as Sienna." She sank onto the vanity seat. "Your birth name was Alessia. Sienna was a name Francesco and I had chosen years before when we dreamed of having a baby girl together."

I wiped a tear away, feeling emotional all of a sudden.

"She only knew you up until we left. You were very young then, and now have a new name. She wouldn't put two and two together. And I'd really rather keep it that way, Sienna." She waited for my spinning brain to focus on her. "I know you and Elio are close, and I know I need to accept that, and I will," she let out a frustrated sigh, "but I need to ask you for a big favor."

"It depends."

"Elio's family doesn't know about Noemi's past, and that part of it is deeply connected with ours. Just for right now, could you keep what I share with you private until I know it's safe for it to come out?"

"Francesco is going to dig."

"I will deal with him."

I hated the idea of not telling Elio what I knew. That wasn't who I was, but it was my life, my past, so maybe I needed to think about it from a different angle. I needed answers, and she had them. If this promise was what it took to find out, maybe it wasn't such a bad thing.

"If I agree to this, will you promise to share more with me?"

"Yes."

"All of it?"

"Yes."

"All right." Everything in my gut told me it wasn't wise, but really, what choice did I have? "Now that's been settled, can you tell me anything else about who sent you this card?"

"I had Oscar look into the postmark, and it was sent from Venice. After a lot of digging, we found nothing."

I sank onto the bed, and we went back and forth wondering who in the world it could be, but we both came up empty.

Finally, after my head hurt, I checked the time on my phone and saw I needed to get home to Elio. "I need to get going."

"You can't stay a little longer?"

"I promised Elio I would be home for dinner." I threaded my purse over my shoulder and headed for the door.

"Teddy," she blurted, which made me turn around.

"Huh?"

She took a deep breath and held her stomach. "Your father's name was Teddy."

"Oh." I instantly reached for my teddy bear pendant and held it tightly. "Teddy," I whispered, testing out his name.

"Yeah." She caught a tear and turned to look away, making a show of fixing the belt on her dress.

"Thank you," I paused, "Mama."

I heard her breath catch in her throat as she tried to hold it together. Slowly, I left with a glare at Oscar, who quickly moved out of my way.

Vinni was waiting outside for me. I jumped in the car, and we drove away.

"How was your visit?"

"I'm still digesting it."

"Bad or good?"

"I'm still unsure."

"Sorry." He went back to driving while I stared at

the countryside, letting my tired head idle.

When I arrived at Elio's, I hopped out with Vinni behind me. Francesco stepped out of the house with a handful of files. I didn't break my step as I flung myself in Francesco's arms, holding him tightly.

"Hey, are you okay?"

I nodded. I just needed the moment. "Thank you."

"For what?"

"For my name." I felt him stiffen, but he bent down, holding my shoulder, and whispered, "Sienna you can't tell a soul about that. I mean, your mother should not have shared that."

"I made her a promise to keep it quiet," I assured him. "I will honor it, until I feel it's safe to share it."

"I hope you come to me before you ever make that call, because—"

"I know, people are looking for me."

"That and…" He stopped himself. "Just talk to me first."

"I will." He smiled and got into Vinni's car. Vinni looked at me strangely.

I gave him a wave and a smile, then I headed inside the house, where something smelled really good. Our earlier conversation suddenly hit me like a brick wall, so instead of heading to the kitchen, I decided to go upstairs, as I needed to go through a suitcase of my belongings. I had packed it the other day, and Vinni was kind enough to drop it off here without anyone noticing.

I found exactly what I was looking for and started to strip down.

Chapter
NINETEEN

Elio

"Okay." I had checked each pot and was pleased everything was cooking just right. Flipping the hand towel over my shoulder, I sliced the homemade bread Donte had made me this morning and drizzled a little olive oil over top then set it on the dinner table in the next room. I dimmed the lights and lit the candles, thinking how nice the table looked.

I dropped the lighter, and it rolled under a stool. I bent and retrieved the little contraption, and just as I was about to stand, a pair of sexy heels appeared next to me. The air in my lungs stayed put as I dragged my gaze from her come-fuck-me heels, to her toned legs, to a very short black skirt that sat just below her ass. Still without a breath, I took in her stomach and her plump breasts that were barely tucked into her plunging neckline and then allowed my eyes to go to her gorgeous face. Slowly, I sucked in a deep breath as I stood. I kept my body inches from hers until I was towering over Sienna.

"Where were you?" I tried to play it cool, but my hands twitched with the need to touch her.

"Out." She set her purse on the counter and broke eye contact with me.

"In that?"

"What smells so good?" She avoided my question and brushed by me to peek inside one of the pots. "I didn't know you cooked."

"Mama wouldn't have had it any other way."

"I love that woman." She chuckled as she leaned over, and her breasts almost fell out of her top.

"It'll be ready in just a few minutes." I moved close to her and poured us a glass of wine. Her perfume attacked my defenses, and I gave in and inhaled her fresh scent. "Thirsty?" I whispered, trying to rein in the fact that I wanted to toss her perfect ass up onto the counter and devour every inch of this perfect woman.

"I am." She took the glass from me and sipped, watching me. "How was your day?"

"Frustrating."

"Sorry to hear that." She played with her necklace.

"I heard what you brought to Papa today. That was a pretty big discovery."

"I'm just glad I heard what I did before anything more could happen."

I studied her face, wondering what the odds were that she would have overheard two big things, one after the other. "How was the rest of your day?"

She turned away and moved to look out the window. "It was interesting."

"How so?"

"I don't know." She shrugged, and I could tell something was bothering her.

The timer went off, so I filled our plates and motioned for her to move into the dining room.

"Filetto di maiale sott'olio," I announced, filling her in on what I had made. "It's one of my favorites."

"It looks really good." She tried a piece of the pork and moaned at the taste. "I'm impressed."

"Happy to hear it," I leaned back in my chair and started to eat. Although, ten minutes in, all I could hear was Nonna's conversation playing like a loop inside my head. It didn't help that she called just moments before Sienna arrived, asking me some questions. Ones I didn't have the answers to.

"I found you a new driver."

"Oh?"

"Yes, Abramo will be your new driver."

"Who is that?"

"Nonna's *consigliere*." She quickly turned to look at me and became still. "What? He's been in the family since before me. He's trustworthy, and he'd take a bullet for you. That's what I want for you."

"Why? Won't she still be needing him?"

"She doesn't go out often, if ever, and she said you

two can work it out. It'll be good. It will help you two get closer."

She started to protest. "I'm not sure."

I grew frustrated with her hesitation. After all, I had spent a lot of time and energy finding her the ideal driver.

"It will be perfect. What's not to like about it? I'm confident." I handed her a card with his number on it. "Enter it into your phone."

"So, that's it?" Her eyebrows drew together.

"No." With Nonna's voice in my head, I decided to ask. "I want to ask a couple questions. I'd like to know how many men you dated during the time we weren't together."

She lowered her fork and cleared her throat. "Is that really something you want to know?"

"Yes."

"Three. One lasted a while."

"Who was the one that lasted a while?"

"Martin. He was a decent guy, but we wanted different things, and eventually, well, that was what ended it."

"What things?"

She shifted uncomfortably, which piqued my interest even more.

"He wanted to get married, and I didn't. He wanted to have kids, and I didn't."

"You don't want those things?"

"I do, just not with him."

I nodded and took a sip of my wine. I couldn't help but watch her breasts. They were like magnets that pulled my mouth toward them.

"What else?" Her expression was unreadable.

"What was living on the streets like?"

"Very different than living in a mansion," she shot back, and I felt my temper spike.

"I was simply asking. Did you ever find yourself in any trouble or mixed up in something like drugs?"

"Drugs?" She shook her head at me like I was crazy. "What is this? When have you ever wondered if I was on drugs?"

"It's just a question, Sienna."

"Is it, though? Because somehow this feels more like an interrogation."

"It's not. I'm just doing what needs to be done to protect my family."

"To protect your family?" Her eyes widened. "Elio, really?"

"I don't see what the big deal is here." She looked away, and I could tell she was trying to control herself. "I'm just making sure I know everything before, you know, before we go any further." She suddenly stood, tossed her napkin on the table, and walked out the front door.

Anger coursed through me, fanned with a little guilt. I refused to go after her. I tossed my fork, sent a text to the guys that I wanted a family meeting, and started to clean up. I bent a lot of rules with Sienna, and it was time she learned who was in charge here. Still, I glanced at the window, hating that she left the way she did.

Just as I finished cleaning the counters, I heard the

guys arrive.

"Elio cooked?" Vinni looked at his brother over his shoulder. "Damn, I didn't have any time to prepare myself." He made a show of himself, studying his reflection in the microwave, fixing his hair.

"Where is the pretty little lady?" Harris, Niccola's good friend and one of our soldiers, smiled and set a box of beer on the counter.

"Out," I grunted, not wanting to talk about it.

"Oh, shit," Niccola eyed Harris, "sounds like things aren't going well."

I made myself a sidecar and motioned for them to follow me into the living room, where I had the game table all set up.

"Evening, all." Papa entered from the back door with Francesco. "Ready to lose some money?"

"Always," Vinni sighed shuffling the cards.

I couldn't get my head on straight, and I knew everyone sensed it. Twice I folded, even though I had great hands.

"I'd ask what's wrong," Papa cleared his throat, "but I only know of one person who can get you this out of sorts."

"Just a disagreement, that's all." I huffed as Vinni tossed down a nine of hearts and I finally was able to get rid of my ten. "She just needs some time to cool off."

"Is her mother harping in her ear again?" Niccola asked, which made me look over.

"I didn't know she was."

"The night of Vinni's party, I heard her mother

saying Sienna should be looking at us for answers about her past."

"What?" That was odd. "Why would she say that?"

"Elenora carries some old wounds from the Capri family." Francesco came to her defense. "However misinformed, she still has the scars. Those issues have since been cleared up, Niccola."

"Sometimes it's easier to hate." Niccola shrugged. "She's not happy about Sienna being with you, and I'm guessing she will work her way in between the two of you."

"Sienna knows better." Papa shook his head. "She's different."

"What if she's not?" slipped out of my mouth, surprising even myself. When Vinni's face suddenly froze, and Harris closed one eye, I knew someone was behind me.

Sienna came into view with an armful of books. Her face was pale, and her mouth was set in a tight line.

"Excuse the interruption." She set the books on the bar top and put her hands on her hips. She was still in her sexy black dress and heels, and I noticed Vinni was gawking, so I pinched the back of his knee, and he yelped and glared at me.

"What are those, dear?" Papa smiled warmly.

"I started to journal when I was younger, to help ease the chaos around me. Maybe it will help to clear up any concerns you might have about my past." She made a point to look directly at me. "These are the most important things I own, next to these." She grasped the pendants that hung from her neck. Then she rested her hand on the journals for a moment before she turned on her heel and marched from the house without looking back.

"What did you do?" Papa didn't miss a beat.

"What I had to do." I snatched my glass off the table and headed to the bar to fix another drink. I didn't really need it. My head already spun, but the rest of me was twisted in a giant knot.

"What does that mean?" He followed me.

"I'm just doing my job."

"Hurting Sienna is doing your job?" He let out a long sigh. "Oh, son, doing your job should never hurt the ones you love. I never taught you to do that."

"I have a duty to the family, to protect us. I mean, do we have any idea where she was for the past ten years?"

"Time to go." Niccola motioned for the guys to make a hasty exit while Francesco stayed put in his seat.

"How do we know that she didn't get tangled up into something that can blow back on the family? Think of the parties, the dinners, the lunches we had when we lived in Sicily. Everyone knew she and I were together. What if, after we left, they approached her asked her questions, offered her money to come find us?"

Francesco spoke up. "I knew where she was for most of the time after we left. I know she had ample opportunity to use the Capri name to get help or to exchange information, but she never did. And if she did know anything about who we really were, which I know she didn't, we'd know it by now. That girl took every hit in life and never once used her connection with your family for anything."

"And are you her father?" I shot back. I did wonder about that, but right now I was also just looking for a fight to rid myself of some of the anger.

"No," he made a sad face, "her father was killed."

Suddenly, her words, *can you mourn for someone you've never met,* came rushing back to me.

"Where is this coming from, Elio?" Francesco asked.

I wanted to explain, but something held me back. Maybe Nonna was right, maybe Papa was too soft with Sienna. He always had been right from when they met.

"Boss?" Donatello was in the doorway of the living room. He nodded out of respect to my family. "My apologies for the interruption."

"Out with it." I waved my hand, welcoming the change in topic.

"I just got word that Jacob Raine's been poking around the New York dockyard and talking to people he shouldn't be about you and yours."

I glanced at Papa, who gave me a nod. It was time to deal with Jacob Raine once and for all. I could feel my excitement brewing at the idea of a good hunt and the ensuing bloodshed. If I focused very carefully, I could feel Zazzero clawing his way back to the surface.

I packed my bag and waited long into the wee hours of the morning. I sipped a drink and tried to be patient, but Sienna didn't come back.

I eyed her journals and wondered which one held

the heartbreak of me leaving without a trace or perhaps which one held a secret. I pushed Nonna's words out of my head and leaned forward to slide out the third journal from the top and rested it on my leg. My thumb fiddled with the cover, wondering if I wanted to know the truth this way…

"Trust is everything, grandson." Nonna held my hand in hers. *"If there is the tiniest shred of doubt, there's something wrong."*

I opened the book and scanned the first page.

Wyatt left me another meal outside the bar tonight, covered in tinfoil. I'm glad he knew the rats and flies would attempt to feast before me and had made sure they couldn't. He's kind to me, but I couldn't help staying hidden in the shadows as I ate the bread. Food still has no taste, colors are still dull, and I'm still completely hollow. My heart beats lonely inside me.

I used to wonder where he was all the time, but it consumed me.

Was he okay? Had he moved on? Did he ever think of me?

Now I let my imagination paint me a better picture, one of a man looking for his lost love. But still, every night I say goodnight to the stars, and when I wake up and take a breath, feeling the sun on my face, I hope that somewhere, somehow, he is doing the same. That he can feel me.

I snapped the book closed, squeezed my eyes shut, and felt guilty that it had come to this. I would go through them more later, but right now her words cut deep. Yet, on some level, it made me feel a little better reading her words and knowing she'd felt the same way I'd felt at that time. Tossing the book aside, I leaned forward to stare out the window.

The light in her bedroom at the Hill House never turned on, and I wondered what she was up to. I could have gone to look for her, and maybe I should have, but I also wanted to let the darkness seep into my veins to be ready to deal with Jacob. I dwelled on every inch of the conversation we'd had and thought of him as he carved his initial into *my* woman's skin, touching and hurting what was *mine*.

Minute by minute, I sank back into my old self, the person I had become after I had left Sicily without her. The tunnel vision, the racing heartbeat, the manic thinking of one thing only—to kill. I was born into this life, and although we presented ourselves as reserved and classy to the outside world, beneath it all we had learned to be ruthless. Now, I would honor my roots with Raine's blood on my hands.

The next morning, I unfolded from the bedroom chair, grabbed my bag, and headed up to the Hill House where the guys were prepared to leave with me.

"Morning, boss." Vinni poured me a cup of coffee and tried to gauge my mood. There wasn't one; I was on autopilot.

"Good morning, boys." Mama floated around the kitchen making small talk with Donte. "Be sure to eat a good breakfast before you leave."

"Yes, ma'am." Niccola shoved a pastry in his mouth.

"When you see Sienna," Mama stirred her hot tea, "could you please send her to see me?"

I nodded once and went back to reading emails on my phone.

"Don't you three look sharp." Mariano strolled in. For once, he didn't look like he was up all night long. He made my eye twitch. "Whose funeral are we crashing today?" He looked around when no one bit at his tasteless humor. "Anyway, where's Sienna? I want to take her to the beach today. Her in a string bikini makes my mouth water."

I slammed my cup down and stood towering over the man I once considered my best friend. Mama caught my attention, and her eyes begged me to calm down.

"I need a moment, then we're leaving." I couldn't curb my murderous tone as I hurried down the hallway and up the stairs to my bedroom. "Sienna." The room was empty. I immediately tried her room, but the door was locked. Using my key, I opened the door to find Sienna packing a suitcase.

"Where are you going?" My voice made her jump and drop her shirt.

"I'm going home."

"The hell you are." I moved into the room, closing the door behind me.

"Elio, I just need a break."

"From me?"

"From everyone. You all forget that my life has stalled staying here, my job, my social life, my responsibilities. I did that because you asked me to, but now," she shook the emotion from her head, "I'm being questioned by you." Her voice cracked on the last word. "I know the risks, and I know how this might look to everyone, but I don't care. I'm taking some time because I need it."

"That's not how this works." She wasn't getting it.

"Maybe not in your world, but it does in mine."

I fought through darkness I'd purposely let in.

"What about your mother?"

"She'll understand."

"What about my mother? She loves you too."

"If only her son did."

"Sienna," I rubbed my head, not needing this right now, "you're not leaving."

"Elio, just stop. You may be the boss to many, but you're not to me."

What was happening? How was I losing control here?

She zipped the suitcase shut and let it fall to the floor. I toed it from her reach and sent it spinning on its wheels across the room. I swung her around and pushed her into the wall, using my knee between her legs to hold her still. Both of my hands slammed to the wall next to her head.

"I'm not in the right frame of mind to deal with this right now. I'm about to go hunting, so my mind is focused on ending someone's life." I spoke slowly, making sure she heard each word. "And the biggest part of this particular death is making sure that he experiences a lot of fucking pain." I was inches from her face; I could feel her heartbeat against mine. I closed my eyes and steadied my feverish temper. "I'm in a pretty dark place right now, so do me a favor and stay put." My hand snapped over her mouth when she went to speak. "If you need some time alone, take our house and seclude yourself there. No one will bother you. But for God's fucking sake, do it there and not somewhere Stefano can get to you. If you have any sense at all and want to live to see another day, stay home. Do you understand me?"

She held my intense gaze, and I wanted to shake her for even having a thought to leave.

"All right," she hissed and shoved my arm out of her way, but I shoved her back in place, grabbing her chin and kissing her hard. "Elio," she squeaked, and I took advantage of her open mouth and kissed her deeper, stroking her tongue and sucking on it just the way she loved. It was all I could do to make myself stay calm. If I was leaving her for a few days, she was going to let me have her.

She tried to shove me away, but I didn't budge. I was a brick wall that she'd never get by, so I snagged her wrists and lifted them above her head. With one hand, I parted her legs and skimmed my fingers over the silk fabric and nearly groaned at how turned on she was. I slowed the kiss and let her take a breath. Sienna was a sexy kisser. It was one of the main reasons I couldn't stop demanding them from her. In all the years we'd fought, she'd always kissed me back. Even when I pissed her off royally, she always made sure I knew we connected. Tonight, she kissed me back, so I knew, deep down inside, she was still with me.

"Be pissed at me," my chest heaved with the need to be inside her, "but don't ever deny me something that belongs to me," I warned as I rubbed my middle finger over her sensitive bud. For a single moment she slipped, but then I saw the fire back in her eyes.

"You're infuriating," she huffed, knocking my hand away.

"And you're turned on, so don't tell me you don't like it."

"So, what if I do?" she shot back, further pissing me off. "You're using sex as a way to make me submit."

"You've never claimed to have a problem with it before."

"That's different."

"How?"

"Elio, I'm really bothered by what's happening here. You tell me you love me, tell me the house is ours. You tell me you want me to sleep next to you every night, and the next minute you're questioning my history, seeing if I could be hiding something that could hurt your family. I have been nothing but honest with you. I've never lied to you, or ever did or said anything to hurt your family. I'm the one who takes all the hits in our relationship, and after everything—*everything* that has happened, I'm still here." She brushed a tear away.

My phone buzzed, and I glanced at a text from my nonna.

Nonna: Did you get some answers? Everyone has something they keep quiet.

My head spun harder.

"Elio, what's happening to us?" Her words hurt, and I wanted to explain, but I also needed to know more. I had too much respect for Nonna to ignore her warning. The doubt that had taken root inside me was confusing. It had never been there before with Sienna, ever.

I loved her. She was my everything, but I had to question if what I felt was important. If she couldn't see that for what it was, then she had some things to work out as well.

My phone buzzed again, and this time it was Niccola saying we needed to leave. I slipped back into dark mode and slowly let her go.

"Elio?"

"Don't question me, Sienna." I headed for the door before I heard her whisper.

"But yet you question me?"

A part of me cringed at her words, but I had a job to do.

Chapter
TWENTY

Sienna

"I'm saying it one last time." Piero closed the door to his office. "You don't have to do this."

"Yes, I do," I whispered, feeling lost. I turned to nod at Donatello, one of the *caporegimes* behind the machine. "Please start."

"State your name."

"Sienna Marie Giovanna." I locked eyes with Piero as the questions were asked. I was giving them bare, raw truth. It was painful, and this had never been asked of me, but I still felt like it was the only way to totally clear myself and prove I was no threat to anyone. When I first brought up the idea to Piero, he had said a definite no, but I finally got through to him that it was necessary, and he had grudgingly made the call. Now, here we were in his office, so I could prove my loyalty and regain the trust of the ones I had come to love.

"Have you told a secret about the Capri family to anyone?"

"No."

"Have you ever shot someone?"

"Yes."

"Have you ever killed someone?"

I hesitated as a flashback gnawed at the fragile edges of my memory.

"Pass." I didn't know for sure and certainly wasn't about to lie when I was here trying to prove myself to them. Donatello looked at Piero, who nodded for him to keep going. I knew we'd address that question again later.

"Have you ever…" As the questions continued, I shifted my brain to power down a few levels and relished the hurt that smothered my chest. I was answering the questions, but they didn't really register. They came to my consciousness, then I deleted them from my memory after each was answered. I wasn't sure how much time passed before my focus was pulled back to the room.

"Sienna," the man's tone suddenly changed, "is there something that you know that the Capri family should know?"

I blinked for a moment and thought about the story my mother told me about Noemi's past. I dismissed it, as it wasn't dangerous, and it was not my story to share.

"No."

"We're finished." Donatello stood and handed the printout to Piero, who scanned the report with check marks.

Slowly, I removed the sensors from my skin and stood with a heavy heart.

"Sweet Sienna," Andrea came up and took my hands, "why did you do that?"

"Because." I sniffed lightly, happy it was over. "He doubts me."

Both of their faces fell as I turned and left them standing in some discomfort.

I pulled my purse up over my arm and headed outside to see if I could find that bicycle Vinni had told me about a while back. As I stepped out the door, I found the man in the gray suit again, standing next to a beautifully polished and very old car.

"You've been watching me."

"It's my job." His face was set in its usual stone. "Ms. Sienna, I'm Abramo, your new driver." He opened the car door and stepped back. I hugged my purse tighter. "I'm under strict orders," he stood very straight as he spoke, "so, if you'd like to walk, I'll drive behind you. If you'd like to run, I'll drive behind you. However, given how hot the day will be, I'd think you might like to drive." He waved for me to get in.

"And if I don't?"

"There isn't an *and*."

"I'm meeting a friend in town." I decided not to push my luck today and just roll with it for now. I hopped inside, and he slammed the door a little harder than necessary then walked around to get into the driver's seat. He sat there quietly until I realized he was waiting for me to give him the address. I prattled it off, and he gave me a curt nod and put the lovely vehicle in gear.

The car might be old, and smelled it, but it had been carefully maintained, and it was very impressive. I couldn't help but admire my ride as we glided along the road. I caught sight of an old newspaper neatly tucked in the pocket behind the front seat and tugged it free. It was dated over a decade ago. Seriously? I wondered why they kept it there.

"Nice car." I tried to make a little conversation, as the quiet was awkward.

"It was time to work out the kinks. She's been sitting a while." He eyed me from the mirror.

His expression was odd, but what did I expect? He worked for psycho Nonna.

I settled into the soft, leather seat and looked out the window. The small talk made me uncomfortable. I really missed Vinni.

By the time we got to town and weeded through the traffic I felt myself get excited about seeing Cara after all these years.

"Please stay where I can see you," Abramo insisted as he held the door, and I tried not to poke him in the eye as I climbed out of the back seat. "Just signal that you're moving, and I will follow from a distance."

I didn't say anything and started my way down toward the park where I was to meet Cara. There were bright, colorful flowers for as far as I could see. I took a moment to admire the view. Oh, how I loved this part of the world. It was truly beautiful.

"Sienna!" Cara called, and I spotted her waving. Her hands flew to her mouth as she raced toward me and nearly jumped into my arms. "Hi, friend!"

"Hi!" I hugged her back, and all my childhood memories of her came rushing back, and I started to cry. "I thought I'd never see you again."

"Me too." She pulled away and dried her cheeks. "You look so good!"

"So do you."

She held up her hand and showed me her rings.

"You're married?"

"Five years last month, and I have two boys." She beamed and showed me a photo on her phone. "They are my everything, Sienna."

"They're so sweet." We continued talking as we took a seat at a little table under a tree for shade.

"Wow, it's so good to see your face." She reached for my hand and gave it a squeeze. "I was so scared when you left that day, but I just imagined that Elio had swept you away and you were living in a castle way up on a mountain where no one could touch you." I couldn't help the few tears that slipped out. "Oh, no," her face fell, "please tell me that's what happened."

"Not exactly." I cleared my throat. "It's a long story, but Elio had to leave Sicily suddenly, and so when I got to his place, he was gone."

"What?"

"I couldn't go back to the house, so I ran." I gave

her a quick rundown of what had happened in my life after I ran so many years ago. "Then I met a guy who became my best friend and slowly started to turn my life around."

"I can't believe that's what happened, but I get not wanting to come back to the house."

I gave her a terrified face as I shook my head.

"What about Elio?"

"The article that helped you find me was also how he found me." I skipped over everything else. "It wasn't all that long ago when we were reunited."

"And?"

"And things are…" I fiddled with my hands, "complicated but good." The words stung so hard I flinched at them. Elio and I weren't okay, not even close.

"Well, that's something. Was he married or have any kids?"

"No," I smiled a little, relieved that he didn't, "he's just a little different than I remembered, but we're trying to make it work, so we'll see."

"I'm glad." She smiled warmly. "You deserve it."

We sat and watched people walk by, we laughed at the ducks in the little pond, and chatted about her family. She seemed happy and content, and I envied her, but in all the right ways. We strolled arm in arm around the water to order lunch from a vendor.

"I have to ask," I fingered the paper from my sandwich, "what was it like after I left?"

"Oh," she made a face, "it was ugly. Andrew was pissed and made everyone's life even more miserable for a while, but Julie was just happy that there was one less mouth to feed. I do remember there was someone who came by a couple of times to ask about you, but I have no idea what Andrew said to him. Things settled down, and life went on pretty much the same."

"What about Renzo?"

"He flipped out, although when didn't he?" She rolled her eyes. "He left about a year after you did, and we didn't hear from him again until the cops dropped by one night."

"Oh, Lord, what did he do?"

"He was murdered," she said through a mouthful of sandwich.

"Oh." I forced my own bite of sandwich down my dry throat. "What happened?"

"They don't know, exactly. No one was charged, but he was apparently beaten to death with a pipe." She shrugged, and my stomach sank again.

"When was this?"

"Umm," she closed one eye as she thought, "maybe five-ish years ago."

I tried not to react, but that was right around the time Renzo had found me on the street.

I instantly slipped into a memory of that awful day.

I was huddled against the cold with a piece of cardboard under my bottom for some protection. My jeans had seen better days and were merely a thin layer between me and the outside elements. I was hungry and cold and totally miserable. I sipped some water and forced my brain to believe it was food.

I didn't know what it was that caused me to look up in his direction. I often wondered who or what was looking out for me in that moment, but I'd have known that walk anywhere. My stomach twisted, and sweat broke out, and all the little hairs on the back of my neck bristled. I was able to take a moment to pull myself together before he reached me and formed a quick plan.

"Sienna!" Renzo barked, curling his fingers into a fist as he grew closer. "You think you can just leave? You think I can't find you?"

I jumped to my feet, fueled by his words, and lunged toward the trash can where I knew Mad Red kept his weapons for moments just like this.

I held up a pipe and fixed my stance, ready for a fight. I was thankful Mad Red had taught me a few things.

"Oh, that's cute," he chuckled down at me. "Nice to know the streets kept you scrappy."

I kept quiet, again something Red had told me to do. If you spoke, you'd lose your concentration, and that was the key in these situations. You had to be calm and watch for weaknesses and seize any opportunity you could.

"Come on, it's time to go home." He reached for my arm, and I swung hard, clipping him in the elbow. He yelped, and I saw his temper flare. "Listen here, you little bitch," he snarled. "You belong to me! I was willing to look past this minor separation, but now I think I'll just have to remind you of who's in charge. Starting with me inside of you..."

I snapped.

Years and years of putting up with his abuse coursed

through me, and I saw red.

I let loose and swung at his kneecap and felt a satisfying crunch as he dropped to the ground. I hit an ankle hard to ensure he couldn't get back up, and then swung again with everything I had right into his stomach. The wind went straight out of him, and he didn't make a sound.

He lay there curled in a ball as he tried to fight through the pain. I watched and could hear my teen self begging for him to leave me alone.

"I was a child with no family, no friends, and no real life, and you tried to rob me of even that," I shouted as my grip tightened on the pipe. Tears of hate fell down my cheeks, "I was a helpless kid, and you were nothing but a predator that fed off my fear and helplessness." He rolled onto his side and laughed like the nut job he was as he clutched his stomach.

"I still am." He swiped out at my ankle and knocked me off my feet, and I landed hard on my back.

"No!" I screamed. This was my turn, this was my moment to stand up, not just for me but for all those kids who needed a voice, who wanted to take back what was ours. Our freedom.

I kicked out wildly, flipped onto my belly, and snatched up the pipe that had rolled just out of reach.

"Come here!" He clawed at my legs, trying to pull me down to him, but I held it high in the air and lost myself.

Moments later, I shimmied away from his unconscious body and stood in sudden fear that rocked my core.

What had I done? His face was battered and covered in blood. I tried to convince myself to check his pulse, but my heart was in my throat. "Come on, Si!" I coached myself as I inched over to touch his neck. If there was a heartbeat, it was barely there.

A sudden sound behind me made me whirl around. A man slowly approached us. I immediately dropped the pipe, grabbed my bookbag, and got out of there.

I often wondered about the man who had interrupted us, did he try and get help for Renzo, or was it too late? Maybe he would have tried to kill me too. The streets were a tough place, and I sure wouldn't have stayed around to find out.

"If you ask me, the world did us all a favor." Cara's voice pulled me back from my memory.

"Sounds like it."

"It did." She lowered her tone. "Imagine if Renzo was alive and saw your article. He would have hunted you down."

"Don't say that." I folded up the rest of my sandwich, unable to take another bite.

"Did you ever find your mother?"

"Oh," I wasn't sure if I should say yes or not, "we did make contact. We plan on meeting up at some point."

"That's really good."

"What does Elio do for a living?"

Again, I stumbled and figured I really should have a blanket statement rehearsed for times like these.

"Import-export stuff."

"Sounds broad," she laughed.

"It's really not that interesting."

"Seems it." She brushed the crumbs from her palms. "I hate to go, but I have to get back to the boys."

"Of course." I gathered my things, and she walked with me back toward where Abramo had parked the car.

"Yikes, who is that guy?" she asked as we approached.

"That would be my driver."

"Driver?" She looked at me, confused. "Fancy."

"Yeah, not really."

"He looks a little scary."

"I think that's just his normal expression." I chuckled. We had spent over two hours at our lunch, and I wondered if he had just stood there the whole time.

"Well, on that note," she chuckled as she shot Abramo a quick glance, "promise me you'll keep in touch."

"You have my word."

She wrapped me up in a hug. "God, I missed you."

"Me too."

We said our goodbyes, then Abramo, with his face like stone, escorted me back into the car.

"Abramo, would you happen to have a phone charger?" I held up my nearly dead phone.

"I don't, but I'll get one." He waited for me to climb in.

We started down the road, and I leaned back and let my head soak in all Cara had told me, particularly the bit about Renzo. Over the years, I had replayed that day so many times in my head that it was like a mini movie trailer set on loop. Had I really rid the world of one more villain? There was a part of me that hoped he had rotted away in that alley. I wondered how I was never charged. My prints were all over that pipe, and I knew they were in the police database from a breaking and entering I'd done a few years before. I'd gotten off scot-free, but still I had been processed. I wasn't complaining. My freedom and his death were well deserved, but it was the one secret I'd kept locked up tight. I never told a soul about it, not even Wyatt. Maybe Mad Red had witnessed my crazy moment and had stashed the weapon before anyone found it. Either way, I felt justice was served, and now I knew he was truly gone from my life forever.

I was so lost in my thoughts that it startled me when the car came to an abrupt stop. I blinked and looked around, seeing that we had stopped between two buildings. My heart started to pound as Abramo turned the engine off.

"I need to talk to someone. Stay here."

"Where are we?"

"Stay here," he repeated before he jumped out of the car and locked the doors.

I unclipped my seatbelt and dug around in my purse for my phone but discovered it was on its last leg, and after two taps on the home screen, it died.

Dammit.

I rummaged some more and found a pen but no paper, not even a gum wrapper. Where did the newspaper from earlier go? Mr. Friendly must have tossed it. I leaned forward and dug around on the front seat and in the glovebox, but I came up empty. With a huff, I sat back down and searched the back pocket of the seat in front of me. I cringed at the thought of what I might be touching, but at the very bottom I was rewarded.

"Yes," I mumbled at the little piece of cardstock. It had some writing on one side, so I flipped it over and wrote down the numbers above the door Abramo had disappeared through. I glanced back and wrote down the street name I could see. Maybe it was nothing, but Elio said rules were rules, and Abramo had officially broken the number one rule of a driver. He left me alone, and second, he left me alone in a car in a strange area. Normally, I wouldn't rat someone out, but I hadn't wanted Abramo as my driver in the first place.

I tucked the paper in my purse, scrunched down in the seat, and waited for him to return. He didn't return for another ten minutes. When he did, he slipped behind the wheel and glared at me in the mirror without an explanation. I didn't give him the pleasure of asking him anything as he pulled away. I didn't say a word the entire way home, and his little glances in my direction gave me the creeps. I would not be going anywhere with this man again.

He parked out front of the Hill House, and he didn't get out of the car to open the door. He just sat. I reached for the doorhandle to get out of the car, and he turned around in the driver's seat.

"I want to apologize for leaving you alone in the car today. I needed to pick up something for my niece, and it was the only opportunity I had before her birthday tomorrow. If it counts, I could see you the entire time."

Something told me not to trust him, but maybe he was telling the truth.

"Okay." I wasn't sure what to say, so I jumped out and hurried inside. I did catch his intense stare as I closed the door.

I found Donte in the kitchen elbows deep in dinner.

"Hey, are you okay?" He stopped what he was doing and eyed me.

"Is there any wine?" I felt my nerves tingling. "Better yet, is there anything stronger?"

He handed me a bottle of whiskey and a glass.

I poured a small amount and took the shot. My eyes watered at the taste, but I poured another.

"Donte," I grunted through the burn, "what can you tell me about Abramo?"

His mouth dropped, and he looked around before he moved closer.

"Why are you asking me this?"

"Because I just spent the day with him as my driver, and I will never do it again."

"He's not good, Sienna," he warned with such intensity that I wanted to shiver. "How did he become your driver?"

"Elio arranged it."

His eyes closed and he cursed. "The family thinks he's great, but they don't see him for who he is. He does all the dirty work for Mrs. Greta. That's Elio's nonna," he clarified, and I bit my tongue to not share my own feelings on her. "No one touches or speaks badly of Mrs.

Greta. You'll soon learn that the older generation holds tremendous power within any syndicate. Anyway," he shook his head to get back on track, "I've heard stories about Abramo that make some nightmares look like a child's show." He suddenly stopped talking and went back to work as footsteps became louder. "Shh," he warned.

"Why didn't I get an invite to the party?" Mariano came in and snatched the bottle from my hand then poured himself a double shot.

"I just got home." I downed another drink, not needing him right now.

"So, are we going out or not?" Anna snickered as she came in, half in the bag.

"Yes, yes." Mariano brushed her off and gave me a look. "Why don't you join us?"

"No," Anna spoke for me, "no tagalongs. I refuse to babysit a prissy little uptight girl who wants to pretend she's the princess in the castle, when she's anything but..." She flipped her pin-straight hair over her bony shoulder. When I didn't react, she went on. "Elio was supposed to marry me. That was the deal after what my father did for their family."

I felt rage burn through my veins at that. It was the first I'd heard of it.

"It was all supposed to happen, and then you came along. Little orphan girl, with the big blue eyes, and the big fake boobs."

I licked the inside of my mouth, leaned over the island, grabbed her hand, and yanked her straight down onto the marble countertop. I moved my face inches from hers and smiled like the crazy person I was becoming.

"Elio wants a real woman, not some skinny drunk who can't keep the bottle from her jacked-up lip job. Nor would he even want to entertain visiting your eight-men-a-day, stretched out, trailer trash vag." She blinked at my crass words. "Come at me again, and I promise I will show you what I learned on the streets."

I let go and leaned back, snatching the bottle from Mariano, who stared at me with a gaping mouth. "Oh, Anna, these are far from fake." I took another shot, high-fived Donte behind the counter, and left.

A while later and after the whiskey dulled the pain, I made a plan. I needed this for me. I sent a text and headed downstairs.

"Donte?" He looked up at me and smiled, but it fell when he looked at the bag I carried. "Can you give this to Elio?" I handed him a piece of paper. "I'm not leaving the country. I'm just going to the hotel where my mother is staying. I need a break."

"Of course. May I?" He took my phone from me and entered his number. "I might be crossing a line here, but friends are supposed to exchange numbers." I gave him a hug.

I retrieved my luggage from the entryway of the Hill House and once again felt like I didn't belong as Cousin Ugo opened the car door for me.

"I was shocked when you called."

"That makes two of us." Happy Abramo had gone back to his lair at Nonna's, I climbed inside the black town car and was glad to hide behind its tinted windows.

By the time we arrived at the hotel, it was dark, and I checked into a room a few doors down from my mother's. I could barely hold it together. I sat on the edge of the bed, clutched my necklace, and felt my sides burn.

What was happening with Elio?

I leaned back, closed my eyes, and fell into a restless sleep.

Elio

New York was hot and muggy when we landed at JFK, and I was more than ready to climb in the back of the limo when it arrived on the tarmac.

"He's in town," Niccola said as he climbed inside the car and removed his suit jacket.

"Good." I knocked on the partition for the driver to take the detour. I pointed the air vent at me and tried to focus. The heatwave that was smothering the west coast had now reached us.

"I'll wait in the car." Vinni tapped his knee, nervous as always whenever we met up with this particular man. "The guy gives me the creeps."

"You killed for the mafia this morning, you have

friends in the Mexican Cartel, but yet *this* guy gives you the creeps?" Niccola rolled his eyes, and I smirked behind my hand.

"Yeah, he does." Vinni's heel started to tap rapidly. "I get you've known him since you were young, and I know there's some crazy story about you two fighting and then flipping the tables on some event, but at the end of the day, there's the mafia and there's him. Plus, he has a stare that goes right through me. It's like he can see your soul."

"Deal with this, then." I dropped a file on his lap and watched his computer brain tackle the latest numbers on our last oil shipment. Papa wanted me to see if I spotted anything, but, of course I didn't, since I now knew Stefano was only using the trafficking as a ploy. However, an extra pair of eyes on it never hurt, and Vinni needed the distraction.

We parked under an overpass, and when I stepped out and buttoned my jacket, the doors to a warehouse opened and out came the Devil's Reach. To anyone else they were ruthless, but to us they were an ally. Trigger and I did have a history, one that dated back to our youth. We fought in the same underground competitions. The first fight he won, and the second I won. The only difference was I didn't get a beating if I lost. After I met Trigger's soulless father, we made a deal never to set foot in the same ring together. Instead, we worked together to weed out any scum that crossed our paths—that was, until I stopped fighting. Since then, we kept our friendship quiet and our working relationship a secret.

The best allies were the ones you never saw coming.

"Heard you found your girl," Trigger said through a joint that dangled from his mouth.

"And I heard you got married."

"Yeah," he smirked, "who'da thought?" I'd normally give a handshake, but I knew better with Trigger.

"Shit." Rail, one of Trigger's men, pulled at the crotch of his jeans. "Damn humidity. It's makin' my balls stick to my leg."

"Really?" Brick rolled his eyes. "Then maybe you need to start wearing fucking panties."

"Fuck you, you know I love being commando."

Trigger cleared his throat, making the guys shut up.

"So?" I didn't have a lot of time. "Anything?"

"Yeah." Trigger glanced back at Brick, who came forward holding some paperwork. He handed it to me. "It took some digging, and Brick pulled an unusual favor, but we got a little info on Stefano."

I flipped through the photos and scanned the research. Stefano *was* working with Jacob. In fact, he had bought a house in northern Italy. On my land. The notes indicated that he blew through women quickly then beat them when he was finished with them. There were no police records of any of them coming forward with complaints. That didn't surprise me. I kept scanning until I found a location of where he and Jacob had been seen together. There were also some credit card numbers that I could run later. It would help me study his habits.

"No mention of a Mikey?"

"Dead end." Brick shrugged at me. "No one in the

Coppola syndicate or affiliated with them came up with that name."

"All right." I held up the papers. "I appreciate this."

"We have some shit to deal with ourselves." Trigger nodded over his shoulder to a guy who hung from chains. He looked to have a dislocated shoulder, and his head was a bloody mess. "But if you need help."

"Oh, yes," Rail flicked his tongue like a snake, "say the word, and we'll be there."

"Thanks, but this one is all me." I smiled then pulled out an envelope and handed it to Trigger.

"I said no payment. This was no trouble."

"It's not a payment," I motioned for my guys to prepare to leave, "it's a wedding present."

Trigger chuckled as we slipped in behind the tinted glass of the limo, and Vinni let out a deep breath.

"Did he know I was here?"

"You know, he didn't ask." Niccola snickered at Vinni. "Some people can be so rude."

"What did you hand him at the end?" Vinni ignored his brother.

"A wedding gift."

"Which was?" He looked panicked while I let my smile stretch across my lips. "No. Oh, fuck no. I won't be there when he arrives. Why the beach villa? That's my favorite spot."

"Because," I watched Trigger glance inside the envelope and nod, "he deserves it."

After a quick trip to the hotel, we met up with some people to prepare for the evening. We headed out for dinner at the Flatiron Room to pay some respect to Maxon, the owner.

I wanted to show him my gratitude for letting my men know that Jacob Raine was running his mouth all over the city by gifting him one of his favorite bottles of whiskey, a twenty-one-year- old Suntory Hibiki. A bottle normally ran around fifteen hundred US dollars. I also would do us both a big favor. I would get rid of Raine once and for all.

He was blown away by the whiskey and was relieved to hear that the little shit was not long for this world. The truth was Jacob Raine was becoming a problem for a good number of people in the city, and if I didn't act fast, I just might miss the moment to kill him myself.

"Anything they want, it's theirs," Maxon told the waitress. She nodded as she took out the key to the whiskey cage on the wall.

"I'll be right back, gentlemen." She winked at me, and I nodded but turned away to indicate I wasn't interested in anything but the whiskey.

"Seriously," Niccola shook his head, "Antonio Gattani still hasn't paid his bill for that wine."

"Don't you mean *Cavaliere Bianco*?" Vinni rolled his eyes at the asshole's lame last name. He was a shit wanna-be bigshot that had a reputation for stalking young women. As far as I was concerned, he had dug his grave and now just needed to be in it.

"Kill him." I shrugged.

"Or can we give him a warning?" Francesco eyed me and tread carefully.

"I already did. His time has already started."

"All right, if he doesn't pay, then we kill him."

"Yup, I'll pass that along." Niccola started typing while I remained quiet waiting for the green light that one of my men had found Jacob.

"You okay, Elio?" Francesco leaned over.

I turned to look at him dead-on and waited a beat. "Never better."

"Have you spoken to Sienna since you landed?"

"No." I had a moment of clarity and wondered if I should reach out. I pulled my phone from the breast pocket of my suit jacket and sent her a quick text.

Elio: Are you at our place?

I stared at the screen and wondered if I should say anything else. Part of me wanted to call, but before I could think, another message popped up with a street address.

"It's time." I stood, buttoned my jacket, dropped a hundred on the table, and we headed out into the night. We handed our phones to one of my men who would attend a Broadway show tonight and made sure he would buy a few drinks on my credit card. We went over the plan one more time then loaded into another car that was waiting for us.

Niccola watched the mirrors while I played my part.

I moved into position outside his door, holding a bag and a soda cup which was full of gasoline. They had ordered food and were waiting for their order. I was only too pleased to deliver it.

"Knock, knock." I used my best American accent

and pounded low on the door. "Chinese delivery."

"It's about fucking time, son," Jacob yelled than barked at one of his guys to answer the door. I heard a sound and knew Francesco and Vinni had done their part to take out his guys in the back. I knocked again loudly to draw Jacob to the door.

"Food delivery!"

"Shit, I'm comin'!"

Jacob swung open the door, and I tossed the gasoline in his eyes. He bent down and screamed as it burned his eyeballs and stung his skin.

"Ahh! What the hell?" he screamed and rammed into a table. For a guy with his money, he had a nasty-ass shoebox of a house. I stepped inside, closed the door, pulled out a handful of zip ties, and pushed him into a chair. I snapped the ties tight around his legs and wrists. "Who are you? I'm gonna kill you!" His eyes squeezed tight against the sting of the gasoline, and his head shook back and forth.

My mind was on one thing, blood. I didn't say a word.

Vinni quickly cleared the other rooms and signaled to me the place was clear.

I hauled Jacob to his feet and pushed him out the back door into the waiting SUV.

"What the hell happened?" Vinni pointed to Niccola's busted lip.

"The bitch chucked his gun at me." He kicked the man in the back of the knee, making him fall to the ground so he could snap a tie around his wrists. "I mean, who throws a gun?"

"Toss him in," Vinni said as he shoved the other man in the shoulder to make space for his friend. Jacob started to yell, so I sucker punched him in the gut.

I slammed the door closed, hopped in the back, and tapped Francesco on the shoulder to get moving.

Vinni kept a gun pointed at the men while I had my eyes peeled for the police. Unlike Italy, we couldn't pay off the officers here. A few might look the other way for some cash, but chances were, we'd get a rookie trying to make a name for himself, and that would blow the whole situation to shit.

Finally, we pulled into the dockyard and parked behind the offices. Niccola had a buddy who had supplied us with IDs that gave us full access to the entire yard. He'd also set us up with the crane we'd need at the end.

Niccola and Vinni pulled the zip-tied men from the vehicle while more of my men arrived. Francesco and I hurried them along through the gates and over to where the propellor blades for a ship were being repaired and stopped at the griding wheel.

"Drop them here," I ordered my cousins. "Remove the duct tape." Niccola ripped the tape from their eyelids, and they both yelped in pain. Their eyes bugged trying to focus while I lit a joint and stared down at them. "Tell me about your involvement with Stefano Coppola."

"We have no involvement—"

"He wants what's yours," the other man interrupted, looking desperately at Elio, "your business, your land, your girl, everything."

"You're dead." Jacob laughed through his own pain as he eyed his traitor. "You flipped like a pancake, for what?"

"I flipped because I don't want to die."

"Well," sweet smoke wafted from my mouth, "you'll die with less pain, anyway."

"I'll take that." He nodded, and I respected his wish to go out easier.

"What else do you know?"

"All I know is he isn't moving girls. That was just a front."

"Shut up, you fool!" Jacob hissed as he tried to breathe through his agony.

"He's always smoke and mirrors." the man went on. "Nothing is ever what it seems."

"Who's Mikey?"

"Ah," he closed his eyes while he thought, "I don't know, but there was a Mari or something."

"Mariano?"

"Yes! That's it." My blood burned white hot.

"How long have they been working together?"

"Maybe eight-nine years?"

I glanced at Francesco then at my cousins, who all now wore the same expression. The son of a bitch had been playing our family since the start.

His buddy next to him shoved off his knees to ram him, but I grabbed him by the collar and belt and kicked him off the ledge into the ocean. His bound legs and arms would prevent him from swimming.

"Where were we?" I paused to dab the seawater from

my face with my silk handkerchief. "Oh, yes, anything else?"

"Just that Stefano paid Mariano a lot of money to find your girl. He was supposed to deliver her to him but didn't. I guess he wasn't ready to give her up just yet."

I cleared my throat and tugged on my suit jacket, trying to focus on the fact that she was still with me, and that Mariano would be taken care of very soon.

"Stupid coward," Jacob hissed like the reptile he was. "You betrayed your oath to me and to the Coppola name!"

"Since you still have your eyes, you can watch this." I directed my comment to the guy who had given me the info.

I dragged Jacob by his shirt over to a grinding wheel and signaled for Vinni to turn on the machine and watched as the coarse stone spun.

"I don't care. Do what you want." He moved his head around as though looking for some sort of escape even as he said it. His eyes were still red from the gasoline. I was tempted to put a match to his shirt which was still soaked with it but held off for now.

I grabbed his hand and pushed it against the wheel and watched the splatter of blood and flesh as it instantly ate away to the bone.

"You like to inflict pain?" Sienna's terrified expression popped in my head, that of her face when she jumped into my arms, covered in her own blood that night in the hotel room. Blood this man had shed. Hatred coursed through me, and I held his other arm to the wheel. He screamed and bucked as the blood and sparks shot around like fiery-eye spinning fireworks. His screams, however, were far from the ones you would hear at a holiday event.

His face went white, and saliva pooled at the corners of his mouth. He moaned and jolted as his brain tried to process the damage and pain.

"Sweet Jesus." The man who had offered the information looked away in horror.

"Did you enjoy carving your initial into my girl's skin as she screamed and begged you to stop?"

"She's," he cried out and attempted to act as though the shock didn't consume him, "she's lucky that was all I did!"

Pure white rage took over me, and images of previous killings flickered in front of me. Nothing else mattered but finding ways to inflict pain on this man. I lifted Jacob and let the wheel tear into one of his arms until it fell to the floor. He became a rag doll as I removed the other arm, then both legs. Only the sound of the wheel could be heard now. I dropped the battered torso on the ground with a scream of my own. It ripped from my core as the darkness inside me was finally free.

"Please." The other man looked up at me and begged for his life to be spared. Then, as I turned my murderous gaze on him, he sighed. "Just make it quick."

Niccola handed me his gun, and I shot him between the eyes.

I huffed as the adrenaline started to wear off, and I looked around at the remains that surrounded me. Vinni and Francesco just stood there with stony faces while Niccola started to collect Jacob's limbs to throw them in a crate.

"He got off easy." I sniffed and rubbed my arm over my face to clear the blood from my eyes. "I should have dragged it out more."

When I got back to the hotel room, I removed my clothes and tucked them into a garbage bag, along with the burner phone I'd used to alert my men to clean up the dockyard. I scrubbed myself clean, then did it again, and then texted Niccola how great the live show of Hamilton had been. He responded, saying he'd had a little too much to drink and was heading to bed. We knew our phones had pinged the correct towers all night on the off chance we ever had to prove where we were.

Once in bed, I checked my texts. The last one I'd sent to Sienna still had no reply. I wondered what was going on with her. I knew she was upset with me, so perhaps I shouldn't expect a reply. I would call in the morning and make sure she was all right. I slipped off to a restless sleep.

Our flight was early, and once we were in the air, I rubbed my eyes and wished I had another few hours of sleep.

Niccola and Vinni were on their phones checking to make sure our arrival would go smoothly without any unwelcome visitors, and Francesco was talking away updating Papa on what happened. When Vinni suddenly hit Niccola's arm, I looked up, knowing something was off.

"What?" I grunted as I sprinkled some pepper on my eggs.

"It's nothing." Vinni cleared his throat.

"It's not nothing, so out with it."

"Sienna has decided to spend a little time at the hotel where her mother is staying." Niccola took over for his brother. I dropped my fork and cursed.

"Is that so?"

Francesco butted in. "I think that's a good idea. They could use some time together."

"The last I heard, her mother wasn't exactly a fan of our family," I reminded him. "All I need is that woman getting inside Sienna's head."

"Sienna is a smart girl, Elio. Give her a little credit," he said softly, but I eyed him a warning not to push me too far. "You were gone. I bet she was feeling lonely."

I pushed my plate away, closed my eyes, and tried to control my temper.

When we landed, I was shocked to be greeted by my nonna and Abramo, who wanted to take me for a ride to discuss a few things. I just wanted to get home, but I would never disrespect my nonna. So, I handed my bag to Francesco, who gave me an uneasy look before he disappeared into Vinni's car.

"How was your trip?" she asked as I sat next to her.

"Productive."

"That's good to hear." She kept her eyes on her window as she absently worked over her ever-present rosary. "Have you questioned Sienna any more on the ten years she was away?"

"A little. I really don't see anything that stands out."

"Perhaps you need to dig a little deeper."

"Nonna, I'm really not sure why I need to question her further. She's been nothing but—"

"Did you know that she met up with her old friend, Cara, from the Di Vaio house yesterday?"

"No, I—"

"Did you know that Cara drilled her on questions about you, what you do for a living…?"

"No, I didn't, but—"

"These are the things you need to know, Elio. This Cara woman has ties to some very high-level detectives. Sienna told her that you worked in import-export. Perhaps you should ask what else she said. One slip on Sienna's part could take down everything that we've all worked so hard for. Your papa barely missed one hit on him, and chances are that another just might find its mark. Love can be blinding, and at the worst of times, Elio." She took my hand and gave me a sweet smile. "I see so much potential in you, my sweet grandson. It would be a shame to see our empire crumble because of a woman."

She was right. I needed to keep my eyes open.

"Now, tell me about your trip, and leave nothing out."

I laughed and filled her in on all the details. Nonna was very proud of the work I had done years ago as a Santoro brother. In fact, it was she who had helped me spin the story about how we were brothers and out for blood.

When I got home, I searched the house, but it was empty. It sat just like I had left it, and I started to get angry. I had told her to stay put. Why didn't she? I tossed my bag on the bed, changed, and hurried up to the Hill House.

"Mama," I called as I burst through the door and headed down the hallway, checking the rooms as I went. "Mama!"

"Boss," Donte flew out of the kitchen and held up a letter, "Ms. Sienna wanted me to give you this."

"Why didn't she just call me?"

"I'm not sure."

"How did she seem when she gave it to you?" He pressed his lips together and hesitated. "I know you two are friends, so out with it."

"She seemed a little rattled yesterday. She also snapped at Anna when she tried to push her buttons again."

"Explain." I folded my arms to calm my nerves. Anna really needed to leave the house.

"Anna told her that you were supposed to marry her." The rest of what he said faded away as the blood rushed to my ears and my temper started to boil over. "Sienna put her in her place, but shortly afterward, she left."

"Who picked her up?"

"I'm not sure."

"Not Abramo?"

"No, boss."

"Okay." I nodded at him. I appreciated that he'd been honest and had shared what had happened.

"There you are." Mama found me in the hallway. "I heard your trip was successful."

"It was. When were you going to tell me about Sienna leaving?"

"I only found out this morning. I thought she was at your house. She called to tell me she wanted to spend a little time with Elenora." She looked at me strangely. "I'm not sure what is going on inside of that head of yours, but you're pushing her away."

"It's complicated."

"When is love not?" she countered and stared into my eyes a beat longer. "I know that look." She paused, and I saw the spark in her eyes when it suddenly hit her. "Oh, no, Elio. Oh, sweetheart, why are you spinning back into the darkness?"

"I'm not."

"Then why are you questioning Sienna on her past?"

"Because it's my job."

"What do you think she's hiding from you? She gave you her journals, she's answered any question you've asked her, and she even did a polygraph test."

"When?"

"Yesterday."

"And what were the results?"

Mama's face fell, and she stepped back like I had just stung her.

"Elio," she shook her head, "really? You think your

father and I didn't vet her way back when you were kids or again when she arrived here?" She let out a long breath. "You have never disappointed me before, until now." She turned on her heel and headed outside.

"You're slipping." Papa stood at the other side of the hallway with some papers in his hand. "You promised this family that your alter ego Zazzero was finished."

"What are you talking about?" I grew instantly annoyed. I hated to openly talk about the time Tieri and I went dark.

"We let it slide at the time because you were grieving from a broken heart, and what you did benefitted the family, even though I didn't always agree with your tactics." He came closer. "But now, you have her back, and here you are pushing her away, questioning her. You actually have the gall to ask what her results were? Do you really think I'd still have her here if she lied?"

"You do have a reputation for trusting the ones you love."

His expression flared then turned to stone. "And what's wrong with that?" He nearly vibrated, and I knew I pushed him too far. "What's wrong with loving that sweet young woman, who I know loves my son? Who put everything she's built over the last ten years on hold to be with you? We raised you better than this, Elio, so whoever or whatever is causing you to behave this way, it needs to stop. The family has too many things to deal with right now for you to be this goddamn selfish."

"It's not just for me, Papa. I'm only trying to do my duty as an underboss."

"This is not part of that. And she's clean, Elio." He sighed, shoving the paperwork at my chest. "But the damage is done, and only you can clean this mess up."

Chapter
TWENTY-TWO

"Sienna?" Elenora tried to get my attention, but I was lost in thought about Elio.

I stared at his text all night long, wondering if I should answer, but the truth was I didn't want to fight. He was on a business trip, and I didn't need to be distracting him.

"Sienna?" This time her hand squeezed mine, and I blinked back to the present. "You have been distracted since you arrived here. I may not have been there for most of your childhood, but I know when something is bothering you."

"Sorry," I forced a smile, "I just have a few things going on."

She eyed me then nodded for Oscar and Ugo to leave us. We were sitting on her private patio. They were her ever-present shadows, and I was getting used to having them nearby. It surprised me a little that she sent them away.

She pushed her empty lunch plate aside and smiled warmly. "Let's pretend for a moment that we've had a lifetime together of happiness and love. That we're mother and daughter having a weekend together because we both need it. This would be the time, as we sit here on this patio enjoying a lunch, that I would say, 'There seems to be something bothering you. Would you like to talk about it?'"

"I've pretended this moment for years, so you'd think I'd be better at it." I chuckled darkly.

"Can you try, for me?"

"Under one condition."

"Name it?"

"You don't judge or flip out."

"You have my word." She folded her napkin and waited for me to start.

I wanted to blurt everything, but it was hard when I knew how she felt about the Capris. I felt so twisted and jagged inside maybe it would help to get it off my chest and get some motherly advice.

"Elio is," I reached for my glass and took a few sips of water, "acting differently all of a sudden, and I'm not sure how to navigate it."

Her lips twisted as she thought.

"How is he acting different?"

"Elio and I pretty much grew up together, we knew each other inside out, and when I first arrived here, after all those years apart, it was like we just picked up where we left off." I skipped over the part where I had finally gotten over him after he left me all those years ago. "We were great, and now, out of the blue, he's questioning me on my past like I'm hiding something." I let out a long breath. "I'm not hiding anything, and I've gone over and above to prove it."

"When did this start?"

"It's been brewing for a few weeks."

"So, since I've arrived?" She gave a little shrug, but when she saw my weary face, she lifted a hand. "I'm not going there," she assured me. "However," she made a hand gesture to someone behind me, and a few moments later Oscar handed her something, "I would like to defend myself on something, if you're all right with it?" I nodded out of starved curiosity. "Remember when we were in the sunflower field, and I told you that maybe you should be looking at the people you call family a little closer?"

"Yes."

"Have you ever asked Piero about me?" I sat perfectly still, unsure I wanted to know what was coming my way. "Because," she placed a photograph in front of me with an orange-highlighted date from back in the seventies, "that's me, Francesco, and Piero." Her gaze moved up to meet mine. "It was taken before you were born but, nonetheless, he can't say he didn't know me when clearly he does."

I held the photo between my fingers and tried to make sense of what I was seeing.

"That was the day my parents met Francesco," her voice changed, "and the day they told me I could never be with someone who associates with criminals. They recognized Piero. The Capris may be handsome, but they certainly have a reputation across Italy as ruthless men. Even though it is well known they are classy and reserved about it, they still murder."

"So, you and Piero knew one another?"

"Francesco is his *consigliere*, Sienna, so needless to say, we didn't have much alone time."

"But Piero seemed so confused on who you were, and Andrea too."

She shrugged and handed me another photo of Piero, Andrea, Francesco, and Elenora, along with three other people, and I recognized, a young-looking Elio. The air from my lungs emptied, and I found it hard to breathe.

"He was sixteen at the time, old enough to remember this day." She raised an eyebrow at me. "I know this is confusing, Sienna," she sounded a million miles away, "but his family sank their claws into you many years ago and have you so tangled up that you can't see the truth."

"But why?" I felt like crying and yelling all at the same time. "Why lie about knowing you?"

"Because they killed my brother and know I can prove it. They got their claws into Francesco and now you." She quickly brushed a tear away. "What better way for them to keep me from coming forward when they have control over the two people I love most in this life?"

I broke.

Tears streamed down my face, and my chest heaved in pain. How could this be? How could I have been so used by those I had come to love? By the only man I had ever loved? There had to be some kind of explanation. Then Elio's words from Vinni's party came screaming back me.

"Wait, what do you know?"

"I know enough that you shouldn't have seen what you just did, so keep your eyes on Vinni until whatever you saw is finished."

No. It couldn't be. There must be some mistake.

"Hey," she rubbed my back as my world tilted around me, "this is why I'm so careful with what I share with you. You're a strong woman, Sienna, but sometimes life can be even stronger with its hits."

"But I love him." I sobbed uncontrollably. "How could he lie to me?"

"It's the world of crime, my sweet daughter." She kissed my head lovingly. "Trust me, I've been living in that pain for years, grieving my brother and grieving for the man who would never leave that life for me."

She pulled me to my feet and took me inside to rest on her bed. I thought I had hit the lowest of lows before, but this was something else. My eyes grew tired, and my head needed to rest before it could process any more.

I wasn't sure what time it was when I crawled out of her bed to find the room empty. I squinted with sore eyes at the clock and saw it was six at night. Did I really sleep through the afternoon? I looked around and found my purse, wanting to be in my own room to digest everything. I swiped the photos from the desk, tucked them away, and made it to the door where Oscar was standing guard. He gave me a concerned expression but didn't move out of the way.

"Can I pass?"

"Ms. Elenora would prefer you to stay in her room." I was tired of people telling me what they'd prefer I did.

"Where is she?"

"She stepped out."

"Without you?" I called bullshit.

"She downstairs with a visitor."

A visitor? Who would that be?

"Well, I want to pass, so let me go."

"I can't do that."

"Oscar," I huffed, so tired my bones hurt, "I want to go to my room, have a shower, and be left the hell alone. Surely there's a part of you that understands that?"

He closed his eyes and thought.

"Just to your room."

Pardon me? Who the hell was this man to tell me what I was allowed to do?

He stepped back, and I marched out into the hallway and into my room, slamming the door behind me.

I stripped, hopped in the shower, and let the cool water soothe my aching eyes. After what seemed like forever, I washed and toweled off then brushed my teeth. I slipped into my pajamas and crawled under the foreign hotel sheets, cringing at how they didn't feel like Elio's Egyptian cotton ones. I turned my head into the pillow and sobbed, hating that I broke for the second time today.

***

My body felt like I'd been hit by a train by the time I made it downstairs to eat the next morning. I texted Elenora when it came time to order, but she told me she had a meeting to attend and couldn't join me. I had yet to figure out what she did for a living to have the kind of wealth she seemed to have.

I opened my book and tried like hell to retain what I was reading.

"I owe Niccola sixty euros," Vinni snickered as he sat down across from me and took a menu from the waitress who trailed behind him. He gave his order of a glass of water then looked at me with a question, as if I'd asked him to join me for breakfast at my hotel.

"Um, good morning?" I tried for a smile.

"Is it? Because I'm out money, and you look hungover."

"I wish." I rubbed my aching head. "What did you bet?"

"That you were doing just fine."

"Far from it, I can assure you."

"I can see that now."

"I do appreciate you hoping I was fine." I felt my eyes water and tried like crazy to hold back the levy. "Did he send you?"

"He didn't." He pulled out his phone and set it on the table. "But the family is worried about you, and Elio is spinning dark pretty hard, so I just wanted to make sure you were okay."

"Spinning dark?"

"He's got a lot going on and, with this last trip, his mind is in a dark place."

"We all have a lot going on," I reminded him.

"He took care of Jacob Raine."

"Took care?" I shifted in my seat, remembering how terrified I was of him.

"I can safely assure you he won't ever bother you again." He made a face, and my stomach rolled. "Look, he loves you, and while we have no idea what is going on in his head right now and why he's behaving the way he is, it would really do him some good to see you."

"I'm not sure I can do that, Vinni."

"Why?"

"Because while he was dealing with Jacob Raine, I was dealing with some things that I'm not sure I can deal with just yet."

"Meaning?"

"Meaning Piero, Andrea, and Elio have some explaining to do." I folded my arms to hold myself together.

"I won't pry, but I will give you this." He reached into his breast pocket and handed me a Sunflower Fields Wine Festival brochure. "It's being held in town, but we host the event. It gives us and other Italian vineyards a place to showcase their own wine. It's been a tradition for some time now, and Elio will be there." I stared at him for a moment and wondered what the catch was. "No catch, Sienna. I just think it would be good for him to see you."

"I'll think about it."

"That's all I ask. Just call Abramo to pick you up and take you there."

"No," I said quickly and shook my head. "I'll call a cab or ask Ugo to drive me."

"But Elio hired Abramo to drive you."

"And while I appreciate the offer, I decline."

"Why? What happened?"

"It's not important." My voice was firm. "I just won't be needing his services anymore."

He studied my face for a moment, sipped his water, and decided to back off. He stood and removed some money from a clip then dropped it on the table. "If you could at least text me, I can come and get you, but either way, let one of us know if you're coming."

"I will."

"Oh, and Sienna?" He pointed at my chest. "Do me a favor and wear something that will keep his focus on you and not on wanting to kill everyone else around him. One day without bloodshed would be nice." I waved him off and stared at the brochure. Maybe we should clear the air.

That afternoon, I changed into a red floral ruffle-trimmed mini dress. It tied in the front at the bust. I felt it fulfilled Vinni's request to make sure I drew Elio's eye. Nothing like some good cleavage. I hoped that maybe I could get Elio to talk to me rather than shut down.

Ugo handed me my purse and made a face at the crowd. "I feel like I shouldn't leave you alone here."

"Really I'm fine." I wasn't anywhere close to fine,

but I hated having to have a hovering bodyguard all the time.

"Maybe you should have brought a sweater."

I smirked at his sudden concern and was pleased the two of us were at least getting along some. He wouldn't answer any of my questions about my past, but he did share his interest in things, and I appreciated that he was trying.

"I'm fine." I patted his arm. "Besides, Vinni should be joining me soon."

"Are you sure?"

"Very."

"Call me if you need anything."

"Thanks."

I took a breath after he left and decided to do a little exploring on my own before Vinni knew I was there. One by one, I sampled the wine at each table and made small talk with the owners. Everyone was nice and very welcoming. One table in particular was my favorite. Her twin boys were a riot and spouted off endless knowledge on how the grapes were grown and later made into wine.

"So, Sienna," Kep, one of the boys, beamed up at me, "are you married?"

"No." I laughed as he batted his eyes at me.

"Boyfriend?"

"Yes."

"Oh, so close." He snapped his fingers in disappointment.

"Sienna Giovanna, correct?" A man in a business suit joined me. He took a glass from the center of the table. His bald head shone in the sunlight as he took a sip of the flavorful wine.

"Yes." I tried to place him. "I'm sorry, have we met before?"

"No," he flashed me a smile, "I'm a friend of Elio's."

"Oh, how nice." I let my guard down a little. This place was packed full of Capri friends and associates. Plus, I spotted Tieri across the way watching me continually.

"Have you seen him? I've been waiting to talk to him all day."

"I just arrived, so I'm not sure where he is." I started to look around. "I could call him if you'd like?"

"No need." He placed his hand on my purse to stop me. "I think you can help me."

Elio

I wasn't in the mood for small talk, but I knew how important this event was to everyone. I also knew that if someone was going to show up, chances were it would be here.

Mariano came out of one of the tents, rubbing his nose like he just took a hit. He'd been in a mood all morning until one of his friends showed up.

"What?" he snarled at me, instantly irritated.

I grabbed him by his suit jacket and yanked him toward my face. I towered over him and made sure he knew just how finished I was.

"Either get your shit together or get the hell out of here."

"Seriously?" He wiggled free and looked around, embarrassed. "What do you think I'm doing here?"

"Doing a line in the tent." I tapped my nose. "This is your last warning before I toss you, your tramp of a mother, and your heart attack father out on your asses."

"You might be untouchable, Elio," he squeezed his eyes, trying to seem clear-minded, "but she's not."

"What?" I hated to play dumb, but I did. "Who, Sienna?"

"They're everywhere, just waiting."

"Who are?"

"Your kingdom is falling," he seethed, "and just when you think you have it under control…" He snapped his fingers. I knew the drug was coursing through his system at that point because his eyes were mere slits and his words slowed. "Just wait." He let out a wild laugh. "You have no idea."

Everything inside me went still. I tossed a punch at his face and another to his chest. It happened quickly, and I held back from doing anything more. As he heaved over, I reached out to hold him up as the pain burst through his body. To anyone else, I was coming to his aid, and as I held him up, I chuckled darkly.

"I know…" I paused as he tried to draw in a breath. I knew every intake of air into his bruised lungs would hurt like a bitch. I spoke slowly because, drug or not, I knew this would get through to him. "Whatever the hell is happening with you and the drugs needs to end, or I will end it for you." I shoved him down into a seat and ran a frustrated hand through my hair. "Watch him," I ordered one of my soldiers.

"Vinni," I called as he looked at Mariano with a sour expression.

"Yeah, boss."

"Have you spoken to Sienna? Is she still at the hotel?"

"Ah," he hesitated, and I felt my sixth sense kick in, "I went to visit her today and invited her to come here, but that was hours ago, and if she was coming, she was supposed to call me, and hasn't yet."

"And why did you do that?" I couldn't believe what I was hearing. I had not authorized that.

"Boss," he waved me away from Mariano, "you're pushing her away. She literally left you, and you haven't gone after her." He made a face, knowing he was crossing over lines by being this blunt. "Your mama, papa, Francesco, we're all trying to figure out what's going on, and I don't want you to lose her. She's the best thing that's happened to you in years."

He was right.

I hated that he was right.

Nonna's warnings were so deeply rooted in my head they were confusing me. It was easier to try to keep a step back from her than to try to process what I might be doing to our relationship.

"How was she?"

His shoulders dropped in relief that I wasn't going to rip him a new one.

"Not good."

I closed my eyes and wished I could pull myself

from this state.

"I think there's something more going on with her than just you two."

"Why do you think that?"

"She was different. I really think you should talk to her before it's too late."

"Yeah."

"Good, because she's right over there."

I whirled to find Sienna talking to Tieri, who had told me he was going to be out of town. I hadn't forgiven him for talking to her behind my back with The Finder and Mariano.

I was jolted into a memory.

"You look like you need another." A guy sat down at the table next to me. We both faced the pool tables, and I didn't turn to look at him. I had found this dive of a bar when I first moved here six months ago. I liked it, as no one paid attention to me, and I got to be left alone with my rum and twisted head.

"What can I get you?" the waitress asked him, and I looked down as my phone vibrated on the table. It was Mariano. Not right now.

"Whatever he's having, and get him another too."

"Ahh," she hesitated, and I felt her indecision as she glanced back at me. "Sure."

"Bad day?" he asked.

"Yeah," I huffed, letting the glass dangle from my fingers as my elbow rested on the wooden table.

The waitress returned. "Here you go, sir. And for you, Mr. Capri." She didn't wait around for a tip. She knew I had a running tab, and I always made sure the bar was well compensated.

"That's why you look so familiar." He chuckled into his glass. "We met a while ago back in Sicily. My family's in the export business, too."

I nodded, not giving a flying shit. My head was elsewhere.

"I heard your family moved up north." I nodded, and he turned to face me. "You look like you're in a real dark place." He paused. "Maybe I can help with that."

That piqued my interest, and he smirked, leaning back.

"Are you okay?" Vinni pulled me back to the present, and I shook the memory away.

"Yeah." I moved past him and headed in her direction.

Sienna must have felt me coming because she said goodbye and met me halfway.

I drank in her outfit then pulled my eyes higher. I couldn't keep my gaze off her as she came toward me.

"You look nice." God, I loved those deep blue eyes of hers. I didn't know where to start. "When did you arrive?"

"Over an hour ago."

An hour ago? Be calm.

"What did Tieri have to say?"

"He asked if I wanted to go to dinner."

Did he, now?

"And what did you say?"

"That I had one Santoro brother in my life," she

held up a coaster with a phone number written on it and tossed it on a nearby table, "and I didn't have room for another."

Good answer.

I could tell she was uncomfortable with me, and I hated it, but now wasn't the time to try to fix things. She finished off her wine and licked her lips, which made my erection twitch. I could have her under me night after night and never tire of being inside her. Every inch of me wanted to find a quiet room and let loose. Yes, we both used sex as a weapon, but it also helped ease the unspoken tension we had toward each other. I admired her dress, the way it emphasized her breasts, hugged her curves, and stopped entirely too short on her thighs.

Focus.

"Where's Abramo?" I asked as I looked about, unable to spot him in the crowd.

"No clue." Her voice had an edge to it.

Before I could ask what she meant, Vinni came running up with Niccola right behind him.

"Boss, he's here." Niccola had his phone to his ear. "He was just spotted over there."

"Who?" Sienna glanced around.

"Caio."

"Oh, is he a tall, wiry, bald guy?"

"Yeah?" I glanced a question at Niccola, who pulled his phone away from his ear. "How do you know what he looks like?"

"We just had a drink together. He knew me by name and said he was a friend of yours."

"What?"

"Ah, yeah." She glanced around at the three of us. "He seemed nice. Why?"

Vinni filled her in. "Caio is one of Stefano's *capos*. He works directly for the Coppola family."

"He didn't mention that." She turned a little pale. "Oh, my God."

I rubbed my mouth with both hands and felt the tick in my jaw start. She could have been taken, or…I stopped my train of thought.

"Sienna," I lowered to look at her straight on, "what exactly did he say to you?"

"He wanted to know how I was enjoying the festival, what I thought of the wine, would I be interested in writing an article for the local newspaper, nothing that sent any red flags. Trust me, if he said anything that was out of the norm, I would have come directly to you and not stopped to talk to Tieri."

"Maybe he was testing her out?" Vinni tried to make sense of it all. "Or maybe he was trying to see how much she'd say?"

"No," my chest tightened, "he was sending a message that he could get to her in broad daylight at a family event."

"You need to leave, Sienna," Vinni hissed.

"No," she held up her hands, "they had their chance and didn't take it. If I leave, it means they got to you."

"She's right," I cut in, scanning every face in the crowd. "If she leaves, it shows weakness."

"Boss?" Vinni looked at me in shock, clearly

thinking I wasn't in my right mind, but I was.

"Hey," I pulled her closer and spoke quietly into her hair, "I know we have things to work out, but give me today to prove to these snakes that we're not backing down. Tomorrow we can fight." I couldn't help but rub my thumb over her arm as I held her close.

"Okay."

"But you need to stay close to me, understood?" She nodded, but I shook my head. "I really need you to say it."

"I understand and will, but, Elio," she tilted her head to look up at me, "just today."

I squinted at her. "What does that mean?"

"Sir," a waiter came up, "your table is ready for you and your party. If you would just follow me."

I nodded curtly and tried to stifle my temper. Reaching for her hand, I kept her close as we began to follow the man across the park to the restaurant.

"Ah." She held up our linked hands to question my public display of affection.

"He's out of it, and I don't care anymore." I helped her through the crowd of happy people enjoying their day, most totally ignorant of the dangerous people among them.

"Only you would wear heels to a grassy park," Vinni joked, trying to lighten the mood once we got to the pavement.

"Think of it as aeration," she scoffed and glanced at me.

I smirked, remembering when I'd said that to her

not long ago and what happened afterward. I will never look at a mausoleum the same again.

Once inside, I spotted my parents at a table in the corner with the DeSimones, my uncle Bosco, Aunt Noemi, and Francesco. Mama stood and looked like she was about to come over, but I held up a hand to stop her, knowing that she'd make Sienna emotional. Papa understood and encouraged her to sit back down.

My *capo*, Donatello, and soldier, Gain, joined the four of us at our table while my other three soldiers, Ernesto, Brando, and Niccola's good friend, Harris, covered both entrances.

"Niccola," Sienna nodded over his head, "why does that woman look so familiar?"

"Vinni's birthday present." He winked, and I was impressed with how calm she was being, given the situation at hand. "She was a solid eight."

"Seven," Vinni corrected him.

"No way. She does yoga and can fit her legs like a pretzel over her head."

"True, but she also does this thing to your balls— wait, how did you know that?"

"How do you think I chose her?" He chuckled.

"You test drove my birthday present?" Vinni looked like he might be sick.

"Seriously? I had to get you back!" Niccola tossed his hands up. "Does the summer of 2018 ring any bells?"

"I thought he was a girl!" Vinni yelled, which caused Donatello to burst out laughing and brought Sienna nearly to tears. "*She* looked perfect for you."

"Did his stubble not give him away?"

"His eyes were very deceiving."

"But the bulge between his legs wasn't?"

"He tucked it!" He slammed his hands down on the table, trying to defend himself. A few people around us looked over, and I rolled my eyes. They never stopped. Ever.

"So, tell me this," Sienna piped up, "how are you ranking the girls? Like, what makes you a solid ten? Or is there even such a thing?"

"You know what I like about you?" Gain leaned back in his chair while he scanned the room. "That you didn't take offense to that."

"You are men, you rank. We do, too, just in a different way." She stopped to think. "We're just a little less crass about it."

"I respect that." Gain nodded.

"There's a few steps to the ranking," Vinni explained like he was in a business meeting. "Is she a good kisser? How flexible is she? Does she talk too much? Her sex sounds—"

"Oh, yeah, that's an important one," Niccola added. "Remember the winter we spent in the cabin and that girl with the big lips?"

"Yeah!" Vinni pointed to him, looking at Gain then Sienna. "She was the soundtrack to a perfect sexual experience."

"Well, wait, what's a good sex sound?" Sienna seemed to be enjoying herself as the waiter poured our wine.

"Some women can be too throaty when they moan, so it can feel like you're with a man," Vinni quivered, "or they can be too dominating with their words. I like a woman with some fire outside of the bedroom, but I need a submissive one inside the bedroom."

"So, that runs in the family," she muttered under her breath as she looked up at me, and I gave an unapologetic shrug. It was true, and I'd never denied it.

"Then there's the physical part, how she looks." Vinni held up a hand to silence the chatter. "Every man has their own scoring card for this one, and it's where it gets really personal. I'm an ass man, while Niccola here is all about a woman's neck. Donatello is ass as well. Gain is eyes, and the boss is all about—" He stopped himself when he realized what he was saying.

She looked up at me, and I dropped my gaze to her breasts.

"Hang on, hang on," Donatello waved his arms, "help us men out, Sienna, and give us a few secrets on how females rank guys."

"That's only fair." She dragged her gaze from me. "Let's see." She cleared her throat and sipped her wine, which drew my eyes to her wet lips. I had been watching the doors while enjoying their banter. Even though we had our *capos* and soldiers and most of northern Italy's police force, I was the underboss to our family, and I needed to be alert. "Like your scoring chart, it can be based on an individual, but some things are across the board. How good is he at foreplay? Does he go right for the goods or warm you up first? Is he a sloppy kisser?

How adventurous is he?"

"Adventurous?" Niccola stopped her.

"Like does he have to be in a bedroom, or is he willing to do it anywhere? Missionary, or does any position go?"

"I see." He waved her on as our food arrived.

"We all have acquired tastes." She swallowed hard as though remembering something. "It's finding the right man who can meet them, that's the trick."

"What's a must requirement for you?" Vinni was lost in her storytelling.

"A must would be anywhere, anytime. If you want me, take me, don't think about it. Be confident because that's sexy as hell."

I slid my hand under the table to land heavily on her upper thigh. I pulled up her dress and cupped her, feeling the warmth from her arousal. A reminder that I'd heard her, and knew we ticked off all of each other boxes. She didn't push me away, but she didn't acknowledge me either.

My eyes were drawn to Papa and Mama, who were being escorted out of the restaurant. They were followed by the DeSimones. I kept still and didn't draw any attention to what I was seeing.

Francesco leaned down and whispered, "Tent straight out the window has eyes on you, and there's a man out back near a vendor truck. I'll deal with the one in front of you. Your parents will return to the house, but I suggest everything else stay normal." I nodded, understanding what needed to be done.

When I turned back, I found Sienna watching me closely, and her hand landed on top of mine on her leg.

"Elio," she whispered, "what's going on?" I squeezed her thigh before I removed it and handed her my Glock 48, sliding it over her warm skin under the table. "What?" She froze. "No."

"Put it your purse," I ordered, and shockingly, she did as she was told.

"Just tell me what's going on." I could see she needed this, and for some reason, my head cleared a little and I understood. This was who we were, and she could handle it.

"We're being watched. It's being handled, but I need to step out back."

"Hey." She grabbed my arm and paused.

I leaned over and kissed her collarbone, not caring about anyone else and what we were supposed to hide. "Just act normal until I come back." I glanced at Niccola, who nodded at me then disappeared out back.

The hired staff didn't bat an eye when I came whipping through the kitchen or when I grabbed the cleaver from one of the cooks. I kicked the back door open and stumbled upon two men who were wailing on one of the waiters. Gain and Brando were right on my heels but stayed back, knowing they were to step in if needed. I didn't want to risk a panic by using my 9mm, and didn't have my silencer handy, so I fixed my grip on the bone handle and charged the men. They both jumped into fighting positions. The waiter ran toward the door with blood streaming from his nose.

"Elio Capri," the taller man who looked to have at least a hundred pounds on me laughed, "if this is how easy it is to get you alone, we should have paid a visit a long time ago."

"Agreed." I entertained him, and we circled each other. From the corner of my eye, I saw the smaller man go for his gun, and I launched myself at him and jammed the cleaver in his neck, then kicked his gun over to Gain, who wiped it down and tossed it in the trash bin.

The big guy took a millisecond to digest what happened as my foot landed in his stomach, but he didn't go down and smoked me in the shoulder. I took the hit and let myself twist to the ground to land near the smaller guy. I yanked the cleaver out of the man's neck as arterial spray pumped from the wound over my shirt. I lunged and sliced the big man across the stomach. He chopped down hard on my shoulder as I slipped on the bleeding corpse and fell again. I heard the material on his cheap suit strain as he fought to keep his own footing. He raised his arm to shoot me, so I flipped over and used the half second I had left to live to slice him from asshole to junk. His eyes bugged out and his body stilled while he registered what I had done. I jolted out of the way as he fell straight down. I rolled to my knees and tossed his gun toward Brando. I wasn't proud of that kill. It was messy and desperate, but I wanted to live more than I needed a clean kill.

A kitchen grunt burst through the door with a pair of earphones on, and when he spotted me, he dropped the bag of trash he was holding and lifted his hands, noticing

Gain and Brando.

"Sorry!"

I moved to my feet and followed his line of sight and realized my white dress shirt and suit jacket were covered in blood.

"Shit."

Beyond caring, we rushed past the kid and over to our table where I pulled Sienna quickly to her feet, keeping her in front of me. Everyone stood and gathered their belongings.

"Time to go," I told her as she gasped, and I knew she had seen my bloody chest. "It's not mine," I whispered. "Stay in front of me.

"Donatello and Gain, you go out front, Niccola, and Vinni with me, Brando up top," I ordered, knowing we needed to get moving.

With a good grip on Sienna, I pushed her through the kitchen and out the back.

"Oh!" She cringed at the two dead men in a heap.

"Come on." We headed toward the main street and then down another side street. I kept an eye on Brando's shadow as it raced along the rooftops above us in case he signaled for us to stop. I almost lost track at how many turns we made before I came to a screaming halt.

"What?" she huffed, trying to catch her breath.

"Police." I whirled and spotted more, seeing that both of our exits were now blocked.

"I thought you paid them to look the other way."

"We do," Niccola spoke for me while I tried to figure out our next move, "but Elio is covered in blood, and there's only so much they can overlook."

"Besides," Vinni said, "many of these officers are new."

One of the officers spotted us and spoke to his friend, who lifted a radio. He called out to us to stop, and I knew this was going to be bad. Even by his walk I could see he knew he had us.

"Shit, we don't need this right now." Niccola nodded in agreement.

Sienna pulled her hand from mine and dove into her purse. She pulled out a bottle of wine, wrapped it in her sweater and pretended to sag against the brick wall as she smashed it.

"What are you doing?" She pulled a piece of jagged glass free and held it up before she closed her eyes and quickly sliced into her upper arm. I lunged forward, but I was too late. She started to bleed, then smeared it all over her arms and dress.

"It's not deep, but I've had a bit of wine, so it should be pretty messy."

I stared at her, stunned she just did that, but my shock would have to wait because the officer was gaining on us fast.

"Officer." Vinni took two steps forward to address him first.

"Hands up." He pointed his gun at me and, with a glare, I did as I was told. The way his weapon bounced around in his hand told me he was fresh out of the academy. "Same with the rest of you." Vinni and Niccola slowly did the same. "What's happening here? Whose blood is that?"

"It's mine." Sienna stepped out from behind me holding her bloody arm. "I'm not sure how deep it is, but they were only trying to get me some help, officer."

The officer spoke into his radio, calling for some backup and an ambulance.

"Apply pressure." His lack of confidence was almost comical. "Do you know them, miss?" His gun wavered, and he blinked hard. He was so nervous I knew if I so much as flinched, he'd fire his weapon—into the air, no doubt—but I wasn't going to risk it.

"Yes," she pointed at me, "he's my boyfriend, and the other two are his cousins." She did a stellar job of dramatically holding her arm. "He was only trying to help, but I can see how this looks." She spoke calmly and added a few comments about how much it hurt. "It all happened so fast. One moment I was holding the bottle of wine, and the next it hit the table, the bottle broke, and the glass cut right through me." She held up her arm, and the officer cringed, clearly affected by the sight of blood, because the cut wasn't all that bad. "Do you think I'll need stitches?"

"Just-just stay put until my partner shows up." We could hear the footsteps approaching as he spoke.

An officer came running up and quickly assessed the situation. He looked at me. "Oh, Mr. Capri." He reached out and lowered his partner's weapon and shot him a nasty glare. "Forgive my partner for the misunderstanding." It took me a moment to place this officer, but then I remembered he was the one who stopped us on the way to the church function a few weeks ago. He knew the agreement we had with the local police. "I told you to leave the Capri family alone."

"I didn't recognize him, and he was covered in blood!" the rookie officer shot back, clearly annoyed that his partner didn't have his back. "Who wouldn't stop them?"

"Remember," he lowered his voice, "who they are."

"It's still not right." The rookie pointed a finger at me, and I gave a pointed look at Niccola, who immediately took out his phone and called for a ride home.

"Hi, miss. I'm Officer Hector." He gently examined Sienna's arm. "I think maybe you'll only need one stitch. It doesn't look too bad. Would you like me to get someone to look at that?"

"I'll take her to get checked out," I assured him. "I appreciate you showing up when you did, Officer Hector."

"No problem, sir. Sorry for the misunderstanding." He winked at me, and I tried not to laugh at him trying to be cool. "Are you sure you don't need a ride anywhere?"

"No, our car will be just up the road any moment."

We headed in the opposite direction toward the open road. I pulled my handkerchief from my breast pocket.

"It's not that deep." Sienna brushed me off as I wrapped her arm. "It's a clean cut, and it doesn't even hurt."

"Why did you do it?"

"Because, you stupid ass, we were in trouble!"

"Did you just call me an ass?"

"Yeah, and I was being kind." She batted my hands away from fussing with her arm. She was right. It wasn't that deep, but it was still nasty, and she needed it tended to.

Niccola and Vinni turned away, but I knew they were laughing. I never let anyone speak to me that way, so they were thoroughly entertained.

Two cars pulled up and parked by the curb. My cousins hopped in the first one, and I turned to help Sienna inside the other. She suddenly had a gun pointed at me, stopping me dead in my tracks. Nonna's words blew into my head. *"Can you really trust her?"*

A tear streamed down her face as her chin quivered.

"Sienna?" What the hell was happening?

"Don't make me do this!" she screamed, and my heart broke into a million pieces. "Stop!" Her eyes widened, and her finger squeezed the trigger, and I waited for the impact of the bullet. A sudden irrational thought hit me that if I was going to die I would rather it be her than any Coppola. Only it zipped over my shoulder and clipped the neck of Caio. He went flying back, and his gun that had been aimed at me went spinning into the air from the momentum.

Her terrified expression moved to mine as she lowered the gun. I removed it from her hand, tossed it at Vinni, who was now at my side, and I jumped into the car with her. Where there was one rat, another was never far away.

Once the door closed and we were behind the protection of the thick tinted glass, I grabbed her

shoulders to face me.
"Are you all right?"

Sienna

My hands shook as I tried to process that I just killed someone on an open street in the middle of the day.

"Hey." Elio grabbed me and made me look at him, but I was so far away from reality that it was almost overwhelming. "You're okay. Take a breath." He made quick work of fixing my arm with the first aid kit that came out of nowhere and assured me I didn't need a stitch after all.

I was pleased the partition was up and we were in a limo instead of a town car. I needed to be grounded because I felt like I was being pulled in a hundred different directions at max speed.

I swiveled, dropped to my knees in front of him, and

desperately grabbed for his belt to release it. His hands came down and covered mine to stop me.

"As much as I understand your need to feel something, let's just get home, because chances are we'll have company." He kissed my hands, and I tried hard to pull myself together to see his point. "When I'm inside you, Sienna," he purred as he pulled me up onto his lap, "everything else just fades away. I can't protect you when we're like that."

I nodded my understanding, but the need for a release was consuming. I could also see by his eyes that he was in a battle to calm his own inner fire.

"What you did back there was impressive but incredibly reckless. I appreciate what you did and why you did it, but these are not your average criminals. These men are highly trained and have a shoot first, ask questions later type of mentality."

"So, you're saying I should have let him shoot you," I shot back, feeling edgy about everything that had happened and about what was not going to happen right now.

"What I'm saying," he grabbed my arm when I went to pull away, "is thank you." His gaze dropped to my lips, and I could see his battle with what he wanted to do and what he should do.

"Kiss me," he whispered.

It was as if something hit the center of my heart, and an all too familiar pain spread through my chest like paint oozing out of a can. It filled the gaps and grooves of my battered heart. The photos flashed in front of me, and

I didn't know how to deal with it. I loved Elio, there was no question, but things were strange and different now.

When his grip loosened on my arm, I slid from his lap and took a seat across from him, crossing my legs and my arms.

He glared at me in confusion and was about to speak when a phone call came through and he quickly took it. Once he hung up, he seemed deep in thought, and in those moments of silence, my brain ping-ponged from all that had happened. I had ended a man's life. It was a terrible thing to try to get my head around. Elio's hands came down firmly on both my knees.

"There's a place in your head where you can put what happened tonight to rest. You just need to find it," he whispered. I nodded once, understanding what he was referring to because I'd had to utilize that place before. He leaned back, and we returned to our silence.

Once we were outside the town, I lowered the partition. "Please drop me off at the Il Giglio hotel."

"No," Elio hissed.

"You don't get a say in this."

"The hell I don't," he snapped back, and we skipped by the turnoff completely. I should have known the driver would side with Elio.

I slipped back in the seat and crossed my legs. "What about my stuff?"

"I had it returned to our house after I saw you at the festival."

"What?" How could he?

"It's not where you belong." He looked out the

window, calm as ever.

"And where is it that I belong, Elio? Because you're doing a stellar job of making sure it's not with you."

His head slowly turned, and his jaw started to tick as he stared at me. He was pissed, but so was I. We sat in silence for a few more minutes until we passed through the Capri gates, and I let go of the breath I was holding. When we arrived at his house, I hopped out, needing space away from him.

I unlocked the door, dropped my purse, and went for the stairs, only to have him snag my arm. As he spun me around, I pushed him down on the stairs. He lost his footing and went down with a hiss. With quick hands, I undid his pants and freed his semi-erection and shifted quickly onto his lap.

"Sienna?" He tried to get my attention, but I couldn't do it. I was spinning and had no way to stop. He took pity on me and hiked up my dress, slid my panties over, while he quickly grew hard.

I didn't wait, I just lined him up and slid down and only focused on him inside of me.

"Jesus." His head snapped backward, and his neck strained.

I gripped the railing, turned my mind off, and lived in the moment. His hands slid around and cupped my ass before they took hold of my hips, helping me ride out my tension.

"Kiss me," he ordered, but I couldn't. I was still so hurt by him doubting me, by the photos, by all that we had between us. "Sienna!" he barked, but again I just took what I wanted and didn't care. He smacked my ass, and the sting only fueled my fire. "Dammit!" He grunted, and I knew he was close, because so was I. The sweet taste of bliss was near and drew my sensitive nerves to high alert. He grabbed my head and slammed his lips to mine, but I cried out as pain and anger ripped through my chest. "Fuck," he cursed when he didn't get his way. He knew how I felt. I wasn't trying to punish him, but he took me when he wanted, so shouldn't I be able to do the same?

Three more thrusts, and we both jumped off the deep end together. He buried his face in my chest, and I held on while I rode out a long much-needed orgasm. Bliss and pain were a dangerous mix during an orgasm, and my mind spun into a dark web, and I wasn't sure if I should relish it or fight it…it felt better to give in.

Once I was done and my lungs could take in air again, I slipped off his lap, fixed my dress, and rushed by him, wanting a shower. I ignored his command to come back. Elio might have a big bark, but tonight I wasn't listening.

To my surprise, he let me be, and I was grateful. I needed time to get my thoughts in order. The hot water pounded down on my head. Its white noise filled the air around me, blocking out everything else. I wished I could stay there and just live under the spray.

Stealing one of his white dress shirts, I fastened a few buttons and pulled on some lace panties, then I went to look for my phone. I felt I should let Elenora know where I was.

I took the stairs quickly, grabbed my purse, and as I dug for my phone, I walked into the kitchen where I knew he had chargers.

"Yes, Papa knows everything that happened today. I just got off the phone with him." There was a pause, and his shoulders flexed as he rolled his neck, holding the phone to his ear. "Because she doesn't belong there," Elio said quietly. He stood by the window with his bare back to me. I could see his frustration in the reflection of the glass and by how rigidly he stood. He had showered, and his hair was wet. He'd pulled on a pair of workout pants. It was an interesting look for him. I'd never seen him in anything but suits and on a rare occasion a pair of jeans. "No, I didn't ask her." There was a pause. "Fine. I will ask her."

I felt sick. Who was he talking to, and what more did he want to accuse me of?

He suddenly sensed me and turned to find me staring at him. I shook my head slowly, plugged in my phone, and made the decision to text Elenora later.

"I have to go." He hung up and followed me out of the kitchen and into the living room, where a specular storm was rolling in. His huge windows gave a panoramic view of acres and acres of land, and it made me feel like I was in a cinema in front of those massive screens.

"I want to talk to you about your visit with Cara." He didn't waste any time jumping right in. "Did she ask you about me?"

"Of course she did! She was the one who would help me sneak away to visit you."

"And what else did she ask?"

"What you did for a living, were we still together. That type of thing."

"What did you tell her about my job?"

"Nothing, I kept it vague." I felt my back rise. "What? Did you think I sat there with a family chart and explained how you're the underboss to one of the biggest syndicates in Italy?" He lifted a shoulder, and I covered my face, wanting to lose my shit. "If you have something to ask me, ask me, Elio!"

He disappeared through a door I hadn't been through before and returned with the polygraph test printout. "What is this?" He pointed to a high line that was circled. "What do I not know about my family but you do?"

"What?" I snatched the paper and read the questions next to it. *Is there something you know that the Capri family should know?*

I opened my mouth to be honest, to tell him the truth, but something stopped me. Maybe because I knew it wasn't my secret, but I also knew it wasn't that bad of a situation. Suddenly, something came over me. I folded my arms and popped out my hip, feeling a new sense of confidence.

"It's not fun, is it?" I waited to watch his eyebrows draw up. "Not knowing something about your family when others do."

"This is different."

"I see." I sighed, hating that he couldn't see the hurt he was causing me. "I've been honest from day one. Have you?"

"Of course."

"Really?" I reached inside my purse and handed him the photo of Piero, Francesco, and Elenora. "Have your parents been?" He studied the picture and shook his head in confusion. "I'm going to ask you again. Have you and your parents been honest with me?"

"I won't repeat myself." His tone told me that dicky Elio had returned. I then handed him the photo he was in. "I don't remember this."

"But I'm supposed to take your word on that? That you didn't know my mother at sixteen?"

"Yes."

"Right." I turned my back to him as I moved closer to the window. "So, when were you going to tell me you were supposed to marry Anna, before I arrived and messed it up?"

"There's a difference between being told to marry someone and loving that person enough to marry them. I didn't love her, so it didn't happen." He rubbed his head in frustration, and I turned back to face him.

"And you claim to love me, but you suddenly don't trust me." I tossed my hands in the air. "You want me to take your word, but you won't take mine."

"I have more to lose than you do," he snapped, and I felt a fire ignite inside me. "I mean," he paused, "I have many lives that I have to protect and many plates spinning that can't fall. You showed up, and suddenly the Coppolas are on my territory sniffing around, meddling in my business. My closest friend turned out to be playing my family, and then your long-lost mother surfaces, tilting my entire life on its axis. So, yeah, Sienna, I have to look at the common dominator right now, because that's all I've got." My mouth dropped open at the thought that he might think I had anything at all to do with any of it.

"And yet, after all of you have assured me that you never knew my mother, I have photos of you and your parents with her, and your *consigliere*, your right-hand man, knows my life story, but I'm the villain here." I shook my head, unbelievably hurt. "We're not getting anywhere. It's pointless for me to be here."

"What happened with Abramo?" he barked behind me.

"What happened?" I repeated as I grabbed my purse and dumped it upside down on the table, sending my stuff everywhere. Once I found the little piece of paper, I tossed it at him. "Unlike the first guy, your professional driver decided to take a detour after my visit with Cara. He broke the number one rule, leaving me alone. That's the address of where he took me. He gives me the creeps, and I will not be driven by him anymore."

Elio's face fell, and he went silent.

"Where did you get this paper?"

"What?" I huffed. "I needed paper to write on, it was tucked down in the cubby on the back of the seat. Why?" He lowered onto a chair and studied it, then turned it over a couple times. He looked at the address I had written.

"Was this the reason your heartrate spiked on the polygraph test?"

"What? No." I wasn't following him.

"What spiked it?" His voice was eerie.

"It's nothing bad. It's just not my secret to share."

"I've killed people for withholding information from me."

I chewed the inside of my cheek a moment then let his words wash over me. He had no idea the damage he was creating inside me. Again, that dangerous web began to form inside my head as it spun its sticky darkness around all of our happy moments and drew them deep within its hold. I headed to the bar, pulled his handgun from behind the stacked glasses, and knelt in front of him. I placed it in his hand, wrapped his fingers around the handle, and pointed it at my heart.

"Rules are rules, right?" I barely recognized my own voice.

He jolted his hand away and set the gun on the table with a curse. His hands went to his head like there was a lot going on inside.

"I can't do this." He abruptly stood and stepped away from me like I might have stung him. "I need to figure some things out."

"Right." I stood too and gathered my belongings and the photos, holding them up to him. "Of all the things that you're questioning me on, do you have photos to back them up?" I made a point of waving at the photos. "I also find it interesting that while you continue to vet and question me, you've failed to notice my real hesitation during that polygraph."

He closed his eyes and tried to calm himself. I knew his signs well enough to know we weren't going to get anywhere tonight.

"I just want to know what you're hiding from me."

"Me too…" I dropped my arms, suddenly feeling so heavy.

An uncomfortable silence fell between us.

"I think our boomerang effect just officially broke." I waited a beat, then I left him there and headed upstairs.

It wasn't until much later that night when I was curled up in the seat in the guest room that I heard his car engine turn over and he peeled out of the driveway. I reached for my phone and called the one person who would cry with me into the night.

"Who do I need to kill, because my week has been shit?" I broke down, unbelievably happy he answered.

"I need you, Wyatt."

"That's a damn good thing because I'm five minutes from you and I need my Sienna."

My heart surged with happiness as I wiggled into some comfy clothes and raced downstairs. I nearly tackled him as he got out of the car.

"If that's not a greeting." He hugged me back just as hard.

"How did you know I needed you tonight?" I sobbed.

"Elio called me."

"What?" I pulled back, confused.

"He doesn't sound good either, but I think he's more concerned about you right now." I dried my tears, trying to make sense of what he was telling me.

"I need to know more." I took his suitcase, and we headed inside where we were soon curled up on the couch with a bottle of wine and some cheese.

"Wait, so he told you to come and told you he needed to deal with something but didn't want me to be alone?"

"Yeah, when I asked him what was wrong, he just said the gate had my name and license plate and that I would be escorted here by those two guys who follow me everywhere."

"Nothing else?"

"Not from him, no."

"Meaning?"

"I called Vinni on my way here and asked what was going on." He nibbled at some cheese. "Apparently, Elio told the guys he was going out and not to follow him. What the hell happened, anyway? Because when I left, you two were all Fifty Shades of Elio, so what gives?"

"I don't know." I sighed, feeling the weight of our mess on my chest. "So many secrets are surfacing, and I just feel that someone is working against us."

"How so?"

"You saw how we are together. I mean, we have a history that's built on a solid foundation, we fit, we work, and suddenly he went all dark and doubting. He's questioning me about my history and how he needs to understand my past in case I've done something that can hurt the family." I brushed a tear away.

"Could it be he's nervous of your mother showing up?"

"I think we're all a little nervous of Elenora, only because she comes with her own bag of secrets. I still have no idea what she even does for a living. Francesco assures us we are safe from whatever she was afraid of, so there's that, at least."

"And you trust him?"

"I do." I nodded without a doubt. "He was there for me when she wasn't."

"I think I'm missing some story holes."

"Okay, here's what I know."

Wyatt stared blankly at me while he digested my family update. It was a lot, which only led to more questions, but at least he spent time trying to figure it all out.

"That's a lot."

"Yup." I shimmied down on the couch with a yawn.

"Then he called me and left with the paper that had the address you wrote on it."

"Yup."

"He's so sexy!" He leaned back and covered his face.

"What?"

"He's all dark and brooding. Come on, Sienna, isn't there a part of you that finds it a little hot?" I rolled my eyes and screamed into a pillow. "Oh, my God, you two are having brooding sex, aren't you?" He ripped the pillow from my hold and saw my flushed face. "You bitch!" He laughed. "I've never been more jealous."

"Jealous? Weren't you in a sea of army men a bit ago?"

"Oh, yes, every gay man's wet dream." He flopped backward with a sigh. "Thank you for reminding me."

"While you relive your memories, tell me about the case, because I'm going to lose my job and will have to live through you from now on."

"Lose your job?" He reached for his bag and pulled out his laptop. "As far as Georgio is concerned, you're still working." He pointed to my name under his on the last article he submitted.

"Really?" I beamed and felt a little weight leave my shoulders. "You did that for me? Thank you! But if this is how it's going to be, I want—no," I stopped myself, "need to do something. I'll take over writing the articles while you do all the fun stuff."

"Well, I mean, if you insist!" He leaned over and hugged me, and I wiggled to snuggle in. "I've missed you."

"You have no idea how much I needed this."

TWENTY-FIVE

The night was warm as Oscar filled me in about Sienna. He told me one of Elio's men had come and gathered up her belongings. I only hoped our chat had been enough and that she was going to pull away from him.

"What, exactly, did you gain by telling her about those photos?" Ugo took a seat on the patio railing while I watched a family unload their suitcase from their minivan.

"Everything." I tapped my lips as I slipped into a memory.

Mama handed me two bags then collected the rest from the store counter. Papa paid the bill, and we headed out to the sidewalk to discuss our weekend plans.

"I'm thinking a barbeque with sweet potatoes and corn smothered in Papa's special honey sauce," I said as I rubbed my grumbling stomach at the idea of a homecooked meal.

"I think that can be arranged, but I will need to stop in at the office to make some calls first."

"Papa, you know when you get to work, you—"

He stopped walking as he remembered something. "Darn it, I forgot my wallet in the store."

"Of course, you did." Mama laughed and motioned for me to wait. I turned and walked a few steps as I heard my name called.

"Elenora?" Francesco had rounded the corner and stopped short as he saw my parents, and his eyes widened. It took a hair of a second to understand why.

"Oh." I nearly jumped as Piero Capri came up behind him. I'd never met him before, but I knew who he was and knew enough to be polite. I glanced over my shoulder to see my parents' backs were turned as Papa patted his pockets.

"E," Francesco used my nickname, I was sure to keep a little distance between his personal life and work life, "this is Piero Capri. Piero, this is E, a friend of mine."

"Nice to meet you." He extended a hand, and I took it feeling a little ill. He was powerful looking in his expensive black and white suit. Even his cufflinks had an engraved C in the center. He seemed preoccupied and held back a moment as one of his men whispered

something in his ear. Then he turned with a smile and made an effort to be nice. "How are you enjoying your day?"

"Fine, thanks. I was just," I scrambled for something to say, "taking pictures."

"She's got an eye for photography." Francesco beamed at me. "She's making a book about the people in the town and all the beautiful places here."

"Is that so?" Piero held up a finger to the man behind him then took the grocery bag from my arms and handed it to him. The other men who surrounded us looked like they were on edge. It made me anxious and unsure of my surroundings. "Well, then, let's not let an opportunity such as this be wasted on only a pleasant conversation. It is obvious to me that my Francesco has a good eye for a beautiful woman. Let's see what your camera can capture." He snapped his fingers at one of his men, who took my beloved camera from my arm then waved at me to stand next to Francesco. Then he joined us in the shot, the underboss of one of the scariest syndicates there was. I couldn't help but notice his men created a protective horseshoe around us as the cars went by. "Smile." I swallowed but played my part well. I knew Francesco would never let anything happen to me. The shutter went off a few times, and then my bag was handed back to me and so was my camera. "It was lovely meeting you, E." Piero smiled absently then stepped a few feet back as his man once again was in his ear. I could tell his mind was already in another place.

Francesco's eyes widened as they moved over my

shoulder, and I knew what was about to happen.

No, please not now.

"Sweetheart, what is going on?" My mama glared at Piero as she and my father approached. Thank goodness he didn't seem to notice her expression as his bodyguard was still whispering in his ear about something.

"Papa." I paused, curbing my nervousness. This was not how I wanted them to meet Francesco. "Mama, this is Francesco, my boyfriend." I lowered my voice at the last part.

Both of their faces dropped, and Mama became pale as she soaked up Francesco's appearance and clear connection to Piero. It didn't help that Francesco's gun was visible under his open jacket.

"Nice to meet you both." He tried to smile, but it fizzled out quickly. We both knew there was nothing in the moment to smile about.

"No." Papa's stern voice left no argument, and I flushed. "No way. This is over right now. I forbid it."

I didn't get to say anything before I was yanked by my parents down the street, leaving the rest of them behind.

My mind came back to the present for a moment, and I thought about Francesco and me and our lives after that. We had managed to date in secret after that awful meeting—for a while, anyway—but I wouldn't see Piero Capri until many years later. Once again, I slipped away into a memory of the other photo and how it came to be.

Francesco hadn't returned my calls, and I was going crazy wondering if something happened to him. I hadn't had an update on Sienna for nearly two months, and I needed to know they were both all right.

"Ms. Elenora?" Oscar held up an invitation to a party that was being held in the city for a visiting artist. "I checked the guest list as you asked, and he'll be there."

"Excellent, then I will go after all." I plucked the card from his hand and headed to my room to get ready. I knew I should stay hidden. After all, I had spotted Mikey at the art exhibit when I went to spy on my father. I was still unsure if Mikey knew it was me or not. I pushed that thought out of my head with a bigger agenda in mind. The party theme was Midsummer Night, so I made sure I dressed accordingly, using lots of white powder and sparkle to create a stunning eye mask.

When we arrived, Oscar escorted me inside. He was dressed to play his part as well. To the average person, we looked like a couple that was anticipating a night of expensive champagne and rubbing elbows with the artsy crowd.

"Right corner," he whispered in my ear, and I scanned the crowd until I spotted Francesco next to Piero, who had his arm around a stunning woman. Slowly, I made my way over and did a double take at a boy that looked to be Piero's twin. It must be his son.

I softly cleared my throat as I stepped up to the table and turned to look at Francesco straight in the eyes. His face blanched as he took me in, and his mouth dropped like he'd seen a ghost.

"So, you can attend a party, but not return my phone calls?"

"*You can't be here.*" *He glanced around nervously.*

"*You think I wanted to risk everything by coming here with these snakes?*" *I hissed.* "*You promised me you'd check in about Sienna, and you didn't.*"

"*I'm sorry.*" *He closed his eyes.* "*There's just been so much going on. There have been threats to the family, and we're trying to get to the bottom of them. We are only here to see who we can flush out.*"

"*It takes two seconds to pick up the phone and leave a message.*"

"*You're right.*" *He shook his head.* "*I'm sorry. I assure you, she's fine, and I'm fine, and you have my word that I will call you tomorrow and fill you in on everything.*"

That was all I wanted.

"*All right.*" *I took a breath and let myself calm down a little.*

His gaze raked down my dress, and he let out a long breath.

"*God, you're still as gorgeous as the last time I saw you.*"

I smiled, falling for his charm. I was hopelessly in love with a man I could never have because he chose to be with my enemy.

"*Francesco.*" *Piero was suddenly next to us, and I stood straight, feeling the hate smother my soul.* "*Oh, hello, excuse me.*" *He smiled. Clearly, he didn't recognize me, but why would he? It had been at least eighteen years since we'd met, and I was wearing a heap of makeup.*

"*Hello, I'm Violetta.*" *I used my fake name before Francesco could introduce us.* "*Nice to meet you.*" *My tongue burned at the words.*

"*You as well.*" *A photographer came up and held up his camera.* "*Photo?*"

I wanted to protest, I wanted to smash my champagne flute and ram the jagged glass into his cold, black heart for killing my little brother, but instead I waited for him, his wife, and his son to gather around while a fake photo of happiness was snapped. I glanced at Oscar, who stepped in behind the photographer and snapped a photo for me. Who knew, I might just need it someday.

Chapter
TWENTY-SIX

I pointed my camera at the dome of the church and snapped a few photos as we walked around the outside of it.

"It's nice." Ugo followed me.

"The temple took twenty-seven years to build, finishing up in 1545." I motioned for him to follow me inside the Tempio di San Biagio.

"That's a long time."

"It was built by Antonio da Sangallo." I snapped some more photos of the artwork on the wall, careful not to use a flash. "They say that two maidservants, Antilia and Camilla, and a peasant named Toto were passing in front of a fresco that depicted the Madonna and Child, and St. Francis saw the Virgin open and close her eyes." I waited for a woman to leave, then I leaned way back to admire a particularly beautiful painting on the ceiling. "Lord bless the world, give health to bodies and comfort to hearts. Do not leave us at the mercy of the storm."

"I know that…" He trailed off while he thought.

"It's Pope Francis's prayer."

"How do you know this stuff?"

"It's part of my job to dig, and I retain a lot of stuff, plus I find it fascinating."

"Our ideas of fascinating are very different." He laughed, and I forced a smile. "So, did you drag me here to look at this church or to escape what's happening back at the house?" I lowered my camera and looked at the floor, hating that he could see right through me. "Don't get me wrong, I've been waiting to spend some time with you for a while now. I feel a kind of sadness about you. You want to talk about it, maybe? You'll feel better."

"Doubtful." I turned and snapped some more photos, needing something to do. Something caught my eye, and I zoomed in on the photo I had just taken.

What the hell!

When I locked eyes with him, he motioned for me to meet him outside. I pulled out my phone and held it up to Ugo.

"I need to take this. I'm going to step out for a moment."

"Okay, I'll be here." He shrugged.

I tucked my camera back in its bag as I made my way outside. I looked about and spotted him. He had his back to me.

"Why does it feel like you're following me?" The Finder turned, and by the way his face twisted, I knew I wasn't going to like what he had to say.

"Because I needed to talk to you."

"Well, here I am."

"I heard your mother found you." My mouth suddenly went dry. How in the world would he know that? "It's my job to know these things."

"No," I shook my head at this sudden invasion of privacy, "it's not."

"Look," he stepped closer, "I know you don't know me, and I want to keep it that way, but the truth is you are caught up in a very dangerous game of tug of war. You can't see the wolves that are circling you, pawing at the sidelines, waiting in the mist for their turn to pounce." The skin around his eyes deepened. "You need to be very careful, Sienna. Your mother is a very dangerous woman, and the secrets she carries are not in your best interest."

"Rather dramatically stated, don't you think?" I was rattled by what he said but didn't want to show it. "And how do you know all of this?" I tried to speak matter-of-factly, even as I felt a chill spread to my fingertips.

"Because it's what I do."

"Anything else?" I lifted my chin, trying to look confident while I absorbed what he was telling me.

"Yes." He paused when Ugo called out my name. "You need to be careful with the Santoro brother."

"Which one?"

"Sienna!" Ugo drew my attention to him, and he was

suddenly at my side and tugging on my arm. I looked at him, then when I went to turn back to The Finder, he was gone. "Who were you talking to?"

"No one." I searched the few faces on the property, but it was as if he had evaporated into thin air. Ugo looked at me but didn't push it.

"Come on. We should leave."

I didn't protest because I needed to be alone with my thoughts. Once again life had tossed a fork in the road and left me with a missing puzzle piece to try to solve.

By the time he dropped me off, my stomach was a ball of nerves. Why couldn't I go one day where life was normal, light, and free? Ugo wanted me to return to the hotel to see my mother, but I couldn't do it. I needed to think first. I could see her later. The fact The Finder went out of his way to hunt me down to warn me only made things much more confusing.

"Hey, Sienna," Donte greeted me as I eased down on the bar stool. "You look like you've got something on your mind." I laughed darkly. "Anything you wish to share?"

"You're not the first person to ask me that today, and although I appreciate the offer, I wouldn't even know where to start."

"Fair enough. Just know the offer stands." I smiled and dropped my head into my hands, feeling lost inside.

"There you are." I lifted my heavy head to see Aunt Noemi coming into the kitchen with a warm smile. She placed a riding helmet on the island. "I hate to seem needy, but I could really use some girl time. Are you up for a ride at my place? I grabbed this from Andrea. I think it will fit you."

Fresh air, speed, and a wide-open space sounded divine.

"That actually sounds perfect right now."

"Great. Get changed out of those heels, and we can head out."

Forty minutes later, I had my legs around the second strongest male in my life. I smirked at that thought as Elio's face popped up in my head. I hated that at the same time a ping of confusion and hurt mingled with the joy of the ride.

"I love riding." Noemi came up next to me as we followed a trail through the woods. The shade provided cool spots from the sun, and the sound of the birds helped soothe my aching head. "There's something freeing about knowing you can disappear into the woods whenever you want for as long as you want. Especially when you can feel the strength and spirit of these animals along with it."

"I agree, it's wonderful. Does your husband Bosco ride with you at all?"

"No," she laughed, "that would require him to stop working for five minutes. Now, if I was to suggest going to a football match, that would be different. Anything can be stopped for that sport."

I knew I shouldn't tug at the thread, but I couldn't help myself. We were a few miles from the house, and I figured it was now or never. "What about Nonna Greta? Has she ever gone riding with you?"

"No," she let out a long breath, "she doesn't leave the house, and I'm pretty sure it's God's way of punishing me." I let a chuckle go but tried to hide it. She smiled and gave me a worn-out expression. "I knew what I was getting into when I met Bosco, but Lord, no one could prepare me for that tough-as-nails old bat." She laughed loudly. "Wow, that felt amazing to say out loud." I laughed along with her and felt a little better that I wasn't the only one who saw psycho Nonna for who she really was.

"I don't think she's too fond of me either."

"She doesn't like anyone who might come between her and her grandsons." She rolled her eyes. "I love my sons more than anything, but she tries to control their lives to a point where she suffocates them. I've tried to step in a few times, but it only makes things worse." She paused for a moment then looked over at me. "I take it by now you know about the family business."

"Yeah," I nodded, "thanks to Mariano."

"You need to watch out for him. He's nothing but trouble."

"I've noticed."

"If I can give you any advice about being a woman in the Capri family, it's this." She ducked as we rode under some weeping trees. "Stay off Greta's radar. That woman is old school mafia and, though Piero is the boss, it's Greta who holds much of the power and influence over him. She's looked at as the most experienced in the family, and since her husband died, they all have her on a pedestal."

"And if you're already on her radar?" Panic washed over me.

"You might as well dig your own grave now." She gave me a weary smile.

"Must be scary living with someone like that." I tried to push back the haunting feeling in my bones.

"It was at first, but now I just dodge her at all costs. It's the perk of living in such a big house, plus her stones on her rosary beads click together and give a warning when she's nearby. My ear is trained to hear them a mile away." She laughed as I shivered, remembering the sound of them. "All right, enough of this. Let's have some fun." She tapped her horse and shot off into an open field, and I happily let loose behind her and let the wind clear my mind for the next few hours.

When we returned to the barn, Noemi handed me a bottle of water from the barn fridge. "That was a long ride. Thanks for coming." She walked her horse over to the side of the stall, and I followed, leading mine.

"I had a great time. Thanks for the invitation."

"Anytime." She smiled over her shoulder. "Would you like to stay for a drink?"

"Sure. Nothing like a good ride to make you crave a prosecco."

Her hand dropped away from the reins like I reminded her of something, and she slowly turned to look at me.

"What?"

"Nothing." She shook her head, and whatever it was that she was thinking, she let it go. We handed our horses off to their groom and began to walk toward the house. "Let's go into the garden for those drinks."

Elio

"Wait." Niccola shifted on his bar stool, clearly eavesdropping on my conversation with Mama. "Even I could see that train wreck coming."

"It's not that big of a deal."

"How can you not see this for what it is, Elio?" Mama looked surprised. "Your life can't be filled with lies and deception. Not sharing that you were supposed to marry Anna with the woman you want to be with was a terrible decision. You men are so clueless."

I rubbed my eyes, hating all the voices in my head.

"I can't believe you couldn't see that coming." Mama shook her head.

"I can't either," Niccola chimed in, and I gave him

the middle finger.

"Listen," Mama swatted my hand away, "go talk to your father about this stuff."

"No," Papa yelled from another room, "I'd be zero help. Take notes from your mother."

I pushed the conversation aside. It wasn't the reason I started talking.

"Mama," I stopped her as she went to leave, "have you ever met Elenora before?"

"No. Why do you ask?"

"There's this photo with you, Papa, Francesco, me, and her." Her head snapped back, clearly confused. "It was taken years ago at some event."

"We meet so many people and take so many photos at those functions, I guess it could be possible, but that doesn't mean I knew her in any way. Maybe you should speak to Francesco about it?"

"Yeah, maybe." I started to pull out Sienna's note but shoved it back down as I saw my mother stand a little straighter.

"Anna, dear, how are you today?"

"Fine." Her annoying voice was like nails on a chalkboard. "Elio, can I speak with you for a moment?"

"I'll leave you two be. I have to go check on the staff."

"I'll help!" Niccola hastily abandoned me and ignored my death glare.

I kept my back to her but heard the scuffle of her flat shoes on the marble floor.

"I was wondering if we could talk for a few minutes."

"I have three." I had no time for her anymore.

"I know you're mad at me," she whispered. "I could apologize, but I won't."

"Good chat." I turned to leave, but she blocked my path.

"I won't because when you love someone as much I do you, you shouldn't have to apologize for your actions."

I dipped my head back and tried to calm the monster that begged me to rip her head off.

"Normally, I'd agree with you. Love can make you do crazy things, but I'm not in love with you, Anna. I've told you that before. I'm in love with someone else, and what you're doing is just plain hurtful."

"You never even gave us a chance!"

"There never was a chance!" My voice boomed throughout the room. "There was never a chance because my heart was taken when I was child. I can't keep playing this game with you. I've tried to be nice, I've tried to be a friend, but you're toxic to my life and to Sienna's." I waved my hand at her, wishing she'd leave my life forever.

"Toxic?" A pissy smirk raced across her lips, and I wanted to lash out harder. "Okay."

"I found my person, and you need to find yours."

"Got it." She turned on her heel, arms straight at her sides, and left. I knew there would probably be more repercussions from her family, but I was done caring. I headed in the opposite direction to speak with my papa.

"Papa?" I knocked on the door and pulled the note

out of my pocket. Roberto, Mariano's father, glared at me. He was downing a cookie like it was the last one on Earth.

Yes, eat up, fat man. Eat until you explode.

"I'm sorry, Elio," he held the phone away from his ear, "but whatever it is, it needs to wait."

"The manners on you." Roberto snickered then started to cough on the cookie. He turned red and gasped for air.

I stepped up to his side and whispered. "Does it hurt?" His fat face turned to look at me. "Maybe you should keep eating until you can't catch your breath anymore." I tossed another cookie at him and walked out, hoping to hell he choked to death.

"Where's Sienna, Vinni?" I barked, entering the kitchen.

"No clue. I know she told me she was working on a project with Wyatt, but her purse is gone, so I'm not sure."

I noticed Donte was working in the pantry, and chances were he'd know where she was.

"Have you seen Sienna?"

"She was with Ugo for the morning, then your aunt arrived and invited her to go horseback riding. I believe she's still there."

Shit.

Music pumped from my car speakers in hopes it would calm the rage that tore at my core. I had no idea what I was going to say, I just knew I wanted Sienna as far away from there as possible.

I hugged the corners of the twisted road. The trees and fields were a blur of color. I saw the lights of a patrol car in my rearview mirror, but with a shift of the stick, I lost him within seconds.

The rear of my car spun when I turned down the long road and came to a halt in the driveway. Dust rose in clouds behind me as I hopped out and raced up the stone stairs.

"Noemi!" I boomed as I entered the house, not caring in the least that I would terrify the house staff.

"In the kitchen, dear." She came out holding a bottle of prosecco. "What's the matter?"

"Where's Sienna?"

"In the back garden. We're just back from our ride."

I flew out the back door, down the stone stairs, and found her deep in thought, staring off at the flowers.

"*Bella*!" I called, not wanting her to spend another second in this place until I understood what the hell was going on.

"Elio?"

"Time to go." I took her hand and started to pull her behind me.

"Wait, what's going on?"

"You shouldn't be here. You don't belong here."

She didn't protest, but I could tell she was bothered by my words. I would explain things later, but right now the murderous feeling I had inside had me desperate to get us both away from the villa.

Sienna kept her head down, using her hair as a curtain between us. I wasn't sure what to say to her. I just knew I wanted to get her back behind the Capri family gates. Once again, evil had found its way to her, and the *what-ifs* crowded my head.

Nonna's words looped over and over in my head about not trusting Sienna, but now with this new discovery, I didn't know what to think. Once we were inside the car, my anger took over, and I slammed the steering wheel, needing to hurt someone as I waited for the main gates to open. Once there was enough space, I gunned it up the hill and into my driveway.

"I'm sorry," I finally muttered as I squeezed the leather steering wheel. "My temper is out of control lately."

"I'll survive." She unclipped her safely belt, and I grabbed her arm to still her.

"I don't like that you wouldn't kiss me back." I was referring to the last time we had sex. "You've never not kissed me."

"We're not in a good place, Elio." She shifted uncomfortably. "We've never been like this before. It doesn't feel right to kiss when I'm unsure what we even *are* anymore."

I felt split down the middle. I wanted to grab and kiss her and pull her on my lap and bury myself deep inside the only woman I'd ever loved, but another part of me kept sending a warning to guard my heart and my family from all the unknowns that came with her arrival.

"I guess things just got complicated quickly."

"You say that, but I'm over here trying to understand what I did wrong."

Her eyes grew glossy, and I saw the hurt from the last few weeks flash across her face. I wanted to give in, but…

"Stay here until I get back." I winced through the pain in my chest.

"Where are you going?" Hearing the nervousness in her voice, I ran my thumb down her cheek, and after a moment, she pulled away like it was too intimate for her. She was right. We were not okay, and I needed to figure this out before it was too late or too much damage had been done.

"I need to deal with something. Promise me you'll stay."

"All right." She slowly slipped her arm from my grasp and stepped out. "Where else would I go?" She gently closed the door and stepped back.

I tossed the car in reverse, pointed it back toward the road, and gunned it. I wasn't sure where I was going, but I needed to be alone to figure it out.

Elio

I went to the only other place, besides my special sunflower garden, where I knew I could be alone. It was where I'd escape when I needed to get away from everyone at the house, space to be with my thoughts of Sienna.

It wasn't far from home, maybe a mile or so. I randomly found it when I was hunting down a man who had stolen from us. It was a dome of trees that you could drive into, and it completely hid my car from the street. It was as if a camouflage blanket was suddenly draped over the vehicle and it disappeared suddenly from the world.

With a sick stomach, I dialed her number, knowing she'd answer.

She picked up after the first ring. "Hello, dear."

"I need to ask you something, and I need you to answer me truthfully."

"When have I ever lied to you, Elio?" Nonna's voice was soft, the same tone she always used when speaking to me. The same one she used when she read me bedtime stories or when we were having lunch in the garden. I squeezed my eyes tight, feeling the confusion and hurt of questioning a loved one.

"Sienna," I blurted, "found something, and I'm trying to make sense of it."

"And what was it that she found?"

"A piece of paper, the same type as the one that I found the day I went to go back after Sienna. It had a photo printed on it and a warning telling me not to go after her."

"I think I'm confused."

"Nonna, the paper I found years ago was a thick paper with a thin border pressed into it, the same type of paper that Sienna found in the back of your old car."

"I'm choosing not to address the fact that you are accusing me of something so outrageous and completely out of line, Elio. Think for a moment about just how many people rode in that car with and without me." She paused to let out an audible breath, and I stared straight ahead, trying to connect invisible dots to this story. "Why would I leave a note warning you not to go after someone you loved?"

"You're the only one who's been questioning her loyalty to the family."

"That may be so, but, dear, I've only questioned things about what she was doing when she was gone for those ten years. Why would I leave a note on your windshield years ago, when I'm only questioning her on her whereabouts now?"

"This is too much." I rubbed my head like it was going to explode.

"Elio, you're spinning out of control because you are blinded by love. Think about all that's happened since she arrived. She brought this storm to your doorstep. Who is trying to help you out of it in one piece? Me. It's my job to help guide you to be the best boss there is, and part of that is seeing things you don't want to. It's not just about you anymore, it's about our syndicate. Until you accept that, you'll be spinning until you crash."

"I know," I said through a clenched jaw.

"Just take a breath and remember who is important and who isn't. She needs to go."

"I'll call you later." I hung up and slammed my fist into the steering wheel, needing to find anything that would relieve the twisted knot that had its ugly claws in my gut.

I had lost ten years with the woman I loved, ten years I would never get back. And now look what was happening! When did life take a turn and make everything shatter in one giant heap? The damage tore through me like a tidal wave crashing and pulling me down. I felt as though I was drowning. The ripple effect of it all needed to stop, now.

I rubbed my face and took a breath. I needed to deal

with Sienna. I needed to fix this and make it right, no matter what the cost.

In a fog, I headed back out onto the open road and tried to get my head on straight.

As I got to the steps, I scooped up her sunglasses. She must have dropped them. I unlocked the door to find the house quiet.

"Sienna?" I called as I tossed my keys in the bowl and headed into the kitchen. "Sienna?" I hurried up the stairs, checking every room, but they were all empty. "Sienna, we have to talk." Nothing. I called her number, but it went straight to voicemail. I tried another number.

"Dammit." I hung up on Ugo after four rings, then Vinni pushed his call through.

"Hey, boss, I'm running behind for our meeting, but I'll—"

"Vin, is Sienna with you?" He went quiet, and I checked to see if the phone was still connected.

"No, why?"

"Because I dropped her off at my place a few hours ago, and she's not here."

"Did you try Ugo?"

"I did, but he didn't answer. Hang on." I headed downstairs to my office and clicked on the iPad to check the outside cameras. "What the hell?" I hissed as I watched my front door camera suddenly go black. The rest of them were still working.

"What?"

"Someone messed with my front door camera."

A slow, cold prickle crept up my spine, and my

temperature rose.

"I'll call you back."

I took a breath as I called her phone.

"Elio," Nonna was calm as can be, "calling to apologize?"

"Where is she?"

"Who?"

"Don't." I stopped myself from flipping off the rails. "Don't play coy with me, Nonna. Please just tell me you have nothing to do with her being gone."

"That's the second time today you've accused me of something outrageous. That was your last time. Forgiveness only goes so far."

"I know things too," I whispered, not hearing anything but my rapid heartbeat. "Two can play at this game." I hung up and tossed the photo of Sienna from my windshield across the room with a roar.

The walls closed in, the air felt heavy, and just when I was about to lose my shit for good, my phone vibrated in my hand.

Donatello: Boss, you need to get down to the dockyard now. We found another girl. Bring the notebook. I think there's a connection here.

I raced up the stairs, grabbed my keys, and retrieved the notebook from the safe. I stopped short when I saw Wyatt's ball hat on the table. Once I was back in my car and on the main road, I called Wyatt. Maybe she left with him?

"Not that I don't appreciate a call from you, but..." He cleared his throat. "Is everything okay?"

"Is Sienna with you?"

"No. Why?"

"Shit!" I closed my eyes as I came to a stop at the traffic light.

"She's not there?"

"No." I couldn't handle being still, so I slammed my foot down on the pedal and ran the red light. "Did she say anything about going somewhere today?" I tossed my finger at the guy I cut off.

"She called this morning and said your aunt had invited her over to go riding again. I must say, she did sound hesitant about it. I know she wanted to stay home and wait for you because you guys needed to clear the air. She's in a dark place, Elio, but I know she loves you very much."

I pulled up to the curb of the dockyard and looked around, not seeing anyone. I punched in the passcode.

"Where are you?"

"The dockyard," I muttered, annoyed that Donatello needed me.

"If you hear from her, tell I'm looking for her, okay? And Wyatt, I'm concerned that my nonna might have something to do with her being gone."

"Why?" His words sounded a million miles away as I focused on a sound behind me. I whirled to find Anna stepping off the office stairs. She tossed Donatello's phone on the ground and crushed it into the concrete with the heel of her boot. "Elio, are you still there?" Wyatt's voice came across the line.

"I think it's time we had a little chat." Anna smirked

as she took a step back and looked over her shoulder. I followed her line of sight and saw Stefano with a baseball bat in his hand.

Oh, shit.

Like water trickling through the cracks of a seam, at least thirty of his soldiers emerged from all around me.

"Wyatt?" I whispered, slipping back into the dark corners of my mind. "Call Vinni."

Chapter
TWENTY-NINE

Thirty minutes ago…

I sniffed, happy to be alone for a moment to gather my feelings on what just happened. I pulled out my phone and called Ugo, but he didn't answer, so I hung up. I had hoped maybe Ugo was up for another visit tonight. I could have used a little family time because, chances were Elio wouldn't return tonight. I dropped my phone in the pocket of my dress as I dug around for my house key. I turned the key, pushed the door open, and stopped short.

"Since when do you have a key to Elio's house?" Mariano's voice was calm. He sat on the stairs, arms resting on his knees, hands folded together, but his red-dilated eyes told me he had recently taken something.

"They're his," I lied, and a warning passed through me to leave.

"Where is Elio?"

"He," I paused, trying to find my voice, "left."

"I see." He unfolded from the stairs. "Well, that was a bad call on his part."

"What does that mean?"

He jerked me to his chest, and his big arms wrapped around me. I was lifted off my feet and carried outside and up behind the garage to a blacked-out town car.

"Ah!" I screamed. "No! Help me, someone, please!" I kicked at the door when Mariano opened it, which sent us both backward, and I landed on his chest. It took me a half a second to snap out of the stunned state I was in. Just as I scrambled to my knees, he rose above me with a curse and backhanded me across the face. His family ring caught the flesh of my cheek, and I instantly felt the pain as the blood ran.

"Piero! Francesco!" I screamed, begging anyone to hear my cries for help.

"Shut up! Help me get her in." Another pair of arms helped shove me inside the car, and from behind my wild hair I caught sight of the rosary beads and went ice cold.

Abramo glared at me as he slammed the door and hopped in the front seat.

"What? What's going on?" I cried as Mariano ripped my purse away from me.

"I told you, you were my little ace." He snickered with enjoyment.

Fire lined my veins and my temper rose quickly as I twisted and drove my heel into his mouth, hearing a crack. I repeated the action, driving my boot into the top of his shoulder. He grabbed my legs and yanked me to the floor of the car, clawing at my skin in fury, trying to inflict pain wherever he could. I was too amped up on adrenaline to feel much and fought back with everything I had.

"Enough!" Nonna ordered.

Mariano let me go and pressed a hand to his face, furiously cursing, but stopped suddenly when Nonna cleared her throat. Jesus, she really did have power over these people. His watery gaze swung over to mine and glared. He spat out a tooth into his hand and studied it as blood trickled out of his mouth. If I wasn't as scared as I was, I would have grinned at my handiwork, but instead my muscles locked in place with terror as I wondered what was in store for me.

"She's all yours," he hissed through his new gap, then chucked his bloody tooth into the car. Suddenly, Piero's words about the family business came rushing back to me. *"Proof of a hit is everything. Without proof, it's just one man's word against another."*

"Thank you, Mariano." Nonna carefully dropped a baggie of drugs into his bloody hand, and my mouth dropped open. She moved her gaze down to me as she pulled out a gun.

"If you try to escape, I won't think twice about pulling the trigger. Now, sit up in the seat."

Cringing, I tucked Mariano's tooth into my pocket

as I moved to sit back on the seat.

"Do you know the things that man's been up to?" I squinted at her. I needed to know if she had any inkling of what the rest of the family knew about that snake of a man. I couldn't imagine she'd let someone like him walk freely through the family.

"I know enough." Her wording made me wonder. I shook in my seat as the car peeled off down the hill. Several possible scenarios of what was going on passed through me, but none had a happy ending. "Men with habits are easier to control." She tugged at her blazer. "Mariano is nothing more than a stupid boy with a big ego."

"Ego?" I echoed, thinking just how far off the mark she was.

My phone vibrated in my pocket, and I tried not to react.

Carefully, I acted like my ankle hurt and leaned forward to rub it while I swiped the screen to answer it with the other hand. I had no idea who it was, but anyone was better than no one.

"Now," she moved to get more comfortable, "here's how this will go. I will drop you off, well away from town, and you will take this bus ticket and leave and never return." She tossed it next to me. "If you do, I will kill you. If you contact Elio, Vinni, or Niccola, I will kill you. If you even so much as look in our direction again, I will kill you."

"Can you just tell me why?" I begged, desperately trying to understand what she thought I'd done.

"I could," she started to run her white rosary beads through her fingers, "but if you really don't know, then I'm thinking it might just be best for us all if you stayed ignorant."

I closed my eyes and let some frustrated tears fall. I pretended to slump in defeat and glanced down at the phone and saw it was still connected. Whoever it was hadn't hung up.

Think.

"Why are we passing the old mill?" I blurted, and she stared at me. "Are we heading away from the ocean?"

"Be quiet." She rubbed her head.

"Please just tell me where we are going." I started to freak out. I had never been in this direction before, and I hoped the person on the phone would hear where we were.

"Shhh."

When the car started to slow about an hour later, I felt numb and defeated. I couldn't risk her seeing the phone and prayed whoever had been on the line was still there.

The car pulled over, and I saw a small sign. "What's the Greenery Gates?"

"Get out."

"No." I shook my head Dand gripped the seat.

She tapped on the window, and Abramo opened the door and pulled me out, tossing me on the ground. I hit hard, and when I tried to get up, he pulled his gun and fired a shot at the ground next to me. I froze in terror, waiting for the next one to end me.

"You should have listened." He shrugged then got back in the car. I watched as they sped away, leaving me in the middle of nowhere.

I stood on shaky legs and pulled my phone from my pocket. The screen was shattered. I tried to use it, but it was broken.

The hot sun beat down on me, so I found a tree and sat against its trunk, trying to process what the hell had just happened. I pulled myself together with a reminder that I had survived a bombing, I had killed a man, and I had Elio, and I knew he would find me. He always found me.

I lowered my head to my knees, closed my eyes, and tried to hatch a plan. Tears fell, but I stayed strong and worked out some possible solutions, but all required me to walk too far in the heat. Thankfully, I still had my boots on, and the sun was starting to set. At least I could walk in the dark and it would be cooler.

I must have been exhausted, because I woke up at the sound of tires on dirt. I jolted awake.

"Sienna?" I blinked to see Ugo racing toward me in the headlights. The sun was just going down. "Are you okay?"

"Yes." I nodded as I jumped up. I'd never been happier to see him than I was right then.

"Is she okay?" Elenora came racing up behind him, swallowing me up in her arms. "Oh, my god, Sienna, did they hurt you?"

"I'm fine." I let a wave of relief wash over me, pushing the pain from my cheek away. "How did you find me?"

"I tracked your phone when I heard your conversation in the car." Ugo gave my arm a warm pat. "I lost track of you at one point, but we weren't too far behind. I'm just glad we got to you before it was too dark."

"Can you drive me to the bus station? I want to go back to my apartment." I'd had enough of all of this for one lifetime. Elio could come there to find me, and we could work stuff out from the safely of my own place.

"You can't." Elenora sighed. "If you do, they'll find you."

"Save it." I held up a hand. "I don't want to hear that anymore. I'm not safe anywhere, so I'll take my chances."

"No." She took my hand and placed something in it. "You don't understand. This goes deeper than you think."

I eyed the red velvet bag and knew another secret lay inside. Slowly, I released the strings and opened the bag, and a wave of nausea and confusion washed over me. The headlights caught its grooves, and I felt my entire world tilt.

"Sienna, I couldn't share this until now…"

"No." I held it up between my fingertips as the soft fabric dropped to the ground. I wanted nothing to do with it. I knew exactly what it was. "Take it back."

"Sweetheart," she leaned forward and held my face in her hands, "it's yours. You had the truth all along, but you just didn't realize what it meant."

"How would I?" I muttered.

I glanced at Ugo, who looked upset for me, and then over at Oscar, who looked away, obviously uncomfortable.

I pushed her away and ran into the field, feeling like I was about to explode. When I couldn't handle it anymore, I grabbed my head, leaned back, and let out an Earth-shattering cry.

"Hey," Ugo came closer with his hands in his pockets, "I'm sorry it was presented to you this way, but you have to know it's not something easy to just bring up."

I held up a hand for him to stop. I couldn't handle any more tonight.

"Will you take me back to Elio's?"

"Sure." He nodded for me to follow him back to the car.

My mama watched me from the corner of her eye, no doubt wondering how lost I felt right now. I thought I had felt the lowest of lows, but I was wrong once again. It was a sick joke that life was playing with me. It fed off my pain and heartache and tested my will to keep going. The only thing that kept me from running into the woods and never looking back was the tiny hope that perhaps now Elio and I could be okay. Yes, there would be a ton to work out, but we could do it because at the end of the day we loved one another. Surely that would be enough. It had to be.

"I would like you to come back to the hotel." Mama placed her soft hand over my tight fist as we approached the turnoff to the Capris' estate, "I would feel a little better if you were with me rather than with them." Her tone was back to its old way, dripping hate for the Capris. I wanted to snap at her gall for being so insensitive at a time like this. Besides, The Finder had already planted doubt about her within me, and also about one of the Santoro bothers. I covered my face to stop from screaming and wondering which way was up and which way was down. I cleared my head and listened to my heart, listening to where it wanted to be.

"I want to be with Elio tonight."

"Sienna, I really think you should—"

"Ugo, pull over," I hissed, cutting her off, and Ugo immediately stopped the car. I opened my door then turned to her. "I'm tired of people telling me what I should do. Thank you for finding me tonight, but if it's all the same to you, I want to forget about the rest." I slammed the door and headed toward the gates that were just around the bend.

"Sienna!" Ugo got out of the car and chased after me.

"Please, Ugo, I just need some—"

"No, I understand. I just…" He paused as he stopped in front of me. "For what it's worth, I'm sorry for all of this. It's all very confusing and messy."

"Understatement of the year."

"Look, I can't even begin to understand all that you're going through, but—"

"No, you can't." I cut him off, both mentally and physically exhausted.

"I know, but I don't have much family, and neither

do you, so just call me if you need something, okay?" I could see the sincerity in his face.

"Okay, thanks." I nodded and turned my tired body away from them. I was thankful he didn't follow or let my mama come after me. Every step was hard, but my determination to get to Elio drove me forward.

"Good evening, Miss Giovanna." One of the guards eyed me. I was sure he wondered just where the hell I'd appeared from. "Shall I call you a ride?"

"No, thanks. I need the time to think."

"Very well." He hesitated but opened the gates to let me pass.

My pace was slow, and my legs were as heavy as my heart. I felt broken and dull and wasn't sure how I was going to share my news with Elio. I certainly would never keep anything like this from him, but I needed to know he would listen and not flip out. We just needed to lock ourselves in a room and air everything out.

The moon was full and provided soft light for my walk up the hill. Its light also allowed me to see the string of cars that lined the road up to his parents' house. As I passed by them, I wondered what it was about. I hoped it wasn't something I'd have to attend. I certainly wasn't in any mood to socialize and hoped I could sneak quietly up to my bedroom. I opened the door and heard voices.

"And where are Anna and the notebook now?" Andrea asked quietly.

"No clue." Elio's strained voice had me slowly walking into the living room to find Vinni, Niccola, Donatello, and Elio, who looked as if they had been to battle. Andrea and Piero looked worried, and Francesco was in the corner with his head down. Slowly, I drew my hand back behind me, feeling like they could see through me.

"What happened?" I whispered, trying to absorb the scene that lay in front of me.

"Sienna," Andrea carefully stepped away from her son toward me, "where have you been?"

"I…" I paused, remembering they didn't know about psycho Nonna. "I was out."

She took a deep breath and placed a hand on her chest like my words hurt her.

"Show me what's in your hand."

I squeezed my fist around the piece of steel and started to panic.

"Sienna, sweetheart, please show me what's in your hand."

I broke out in a sweat and wanted to cry all over again. This wasn't how this was supposed to go.

"Sienna," Piero said softly from behind her, "please do as she says."

As I slowly lifted my hand, my chin quivered, and my heartbeat pounded against my breastbone. One by one, my fingers uncurled until it rested in the center of my palm.

Andera covered her mouth as she inspected the engravings on the inside.

"Oh," she cried and turned her back to me. I glanced at Elio, my lifeline, who looked pale and ever so slowly turned his gaze away from me and turned to sink into a chair with his back to me, leaving me raw and exposed in front of his family.

"Elio?" The words had barely escaped my lips when I spotted her. Her evil eyes darkened, and a single brow rose as her hand landed on Elio's shoulder.

"Proof is proof," Nonna said in a strong, confident voice, reminding me this was her family and she held all the power.

My fingers almost burned as they squeezed around the hated metal, and I raced up to the guest room and slammed the door, locking it behind me. I sank to the floor like stone.

I thought this was what I wanted, to know my family, to learn about my past, but nothing could have prepared me for this.

Nothing.

I pushed my hand into my pocket and felt the crinkle of paper. It reminded me I still had one move left. I pulled out the bus ticket Nonna had tossed at me and eyed the final destination.

Rome.

At five a.m. I jolted awake. I could hear voices from down below. With a great effort, I moved across the room and stepped out onto the balcony.

"I want an army of soldiers protecting this property by daylight." Nonna's commanding voice came to me as she ordered Abramo. He held her car door open as she continued to speak. "I want to know Elio's every move. I can't have him slipping back to that woman!"

I pulled myself back against the doorframe and

folded my arms tight to hold myself together as I watched her get inside the car. The engine roared to life a moment later, and they were gone. I knew that was my cue to leave. Just as I was about to step back inside, I caught sight of Elio's shoulder as he stood under the balcony.

"Son, you can't leave," Andrea pleaded with him. "We need to figure this out."

"Mama, I need you—" He stopped abruptly and cleared his throat as a warning that someone had come up on them. "Mama, give me until mid-morning, and we can discuss things then, all right?"

"What about—"

"Don't," he warned and stepped away. Then he, Niccola, Vinni, and Francesco headed to the town car and flew out of the driveway and down the hill.

With a deep breath, I made my way over to the desk, found some paper, and started to write.

Dearest Elio and Capris,

As a little girl, I dreamt of having a place I could call home, a room that was just for me, and parents who would tuck me in, kiss me goodnight, and chase the monsters away.

Then one day I met you by the pond. You earned my trust and slowly became my friend. You taught me what it meant to share life experiences, and I eagerly awaited each note you would leave for me tucked in the trunk of a tree. As the years went on, I fell totally in love with you and let my guard down enough to finally meet your family.

I never thought I would ever be so accepted by anyone, let alone complete strangers, and to feel their warmth and love was overpowering. I'll admit I was nervous at first. Who could blame me? It was my first interaction with people who were so obviously happy and wanted to share it with me. You brought me that.

Then just as I became comfortable and felt a sense of belonging, my entire world disappeared. Nothing was left of you but a picture and a broken heart.

The only way I could cope with my loss was to put you in a box and seal it up tight in the fear that, over the years, if I slipped in a moment of weakness and thought of you, I wouldn't be damaged.

Moving on was the hardest thing I'd ever done.

Then life brought you back into my world.

I was tested, and I failed.

You chewed me up, swallowed me down, and spat me back out.

I thought I was doing everything right.

I thought my loyalty was enough.

I thought I was enough.

I never asked for this. I am not this.

But I know as I'm sitting here writing these words that this is it for us.

This is where we are supposed to say goodbye.

I can't—won't go through that again.

Instead, I will go.

Thank you for my memories. They will always

remind me of what family should mean.
I'll be all right and will do what I do best—survive.
Because I've put you back in the box.
Because some dreams are just not meant to be.

Once yours,
Sienna Giovanna
Formally known as
Alessia Coppola

Once I was done, I packed what belongings I had left at the Hill House and placed the envelope on the kitchen island and reached for the jar on the counter. I dumped out some flour on the counter and drew my finger through the fine powder.

I grabbed the handle of my suitcase and brushed a tear away as I headed outside.

"Ready?" Ugo opened the door to the town car.

"Yes." I lowered my head and took one last glance at the Hill House, and the oh-so-familiar feeling of being let go drained from my body.

"Where to?" He started to drive. "Your mother's hotel?"

"No." I stared out the window, mentally filing away every little aspect of this place. "I booked myself a room by the water just outside of town." I handed him the address, and he glanced at me in the mirror.

"That's near the train station. Sienna, are you thinking of leaving? Because despite what happened, you're still at a huge risk."

"I'm thinking I need some time alone, and that's the perfect place." I tugged at my thin sweater, feeling a cold touch brush over my sensitive skin. "I promise I won't leave without a word."

I wouldn't do that, not when I knew the risks.

"Very well."

I settled into the seat and let my tears fall, not caring that I wasn't alone. I hurt, and I was tired of hiding it. I plucked the tiny velvet bag from the corner pocket of my purse, and with two fingers wiggled out the ring and glared at my own birth date that was imprinted there next to my father's. I let it drop onto my lap as if it burned. How could such a tiny thing change my entire life?

La Fine

Acknowledgments

To Elizabeth Clark and Jamie Johnson for spinning with me for hours and for letting me ask endless mafia questions at all hours of the day.

To Christina DeTori for beta reading and helping me keep my dark side at the surface.

To Rachel Womack for all her help with Italian foods.

To my mother for once again being my person while I write my beloved stories.

To Kim Kelchner and Veronica Lane Nelson for always being there and for being such a huge part of the Blackstone Reader Group.

To Cody Hale and Lori Rossi for the Italian research, videos, and photos.

To editor Lori Whitwam for rocking another book with me.

To my street team for reading and reviewing my work early, helping me catch mistakes, and for your endless support.

To my reader group for always being a safe, fun, wild place to hang out.

And of course, to my readers. Without you, where would
I be?

I thank you!

A peek at what's to come in

Sienna

Ugo gripped the top of my arm as I swayed in fear in front of a sign that read Dager's Den.

"Why here?" I couldn't look at him.

"Because," I heard him rub his face, annoyed with my questions, "she's like clockwork. She'd never miss a day to flaunt her power to the other men."

Sweet Lord.

"I think I might faint."

He cut me a quick glance then shook his head and cursed.

My entire body froze with fear, and my eyes went wide at the sound of the handle being pulled. The door opened to reveal a woman with eyes as black as coal in a face with skin so white it almost glowed. Her dark hair was pulled tightly back into a bun, and a pair of glasses hung from the collar of her blue blouse. Her perfectly ironed gray slacks stopped at her ankles just above her small-heeled boots. Both hands rested on a glass ball that sat on the top of her black cane. I felt like I had been transported directly into a nasty scene from a Disney movie.

"Ugo." She only spoke his name then closed her eyes slowly, and when they opened again, they were on me. I stepped back, but Ugo pressed me forward, rooting me back in place. She was like a cobra only inches from my face. It made me want to run and scream at the same time, but my brain seemed to have shorted out at the simultaneous commands.

So, I just stared.

"Nonna Michele," Ugo addressed her, and I felt him look down at me, "I want you to meet someone."

A cold chill passed through my body, and I became lightheaded as my heartbeat pulsed in my ears. "This is Theo's Alessia, your granddaughter."

She lifted her eyes to stare at him for a brief moment then turned those black pools back to me. Her colorless lips pressed into a hard line as she tried to see inside my soul.

"Prove it."

I stood frozen, completely unable to respond. She had awakened such a deep fear inside of me I was completely at her mercy.

Ugo reached for my hand and held it up to show her

the ring.

She grabbed my hand between her icy fingers and held it close to her face. She closed one eye and twisted the band around and gave a low gasp.

"Impossible."

Coming March 2022

About the Author

J.L. Drake was born and raised in Nova Scotia, Canada, later moving to southern California. Though she loves the weather in Cali, she would sell her left kidney for a good rainstorm. Jodi's love of the seasons back home in Canada definitely appear in her books.

When she's not writing, you can often find her sitting somewhere along the coast of Huntington Beach, reading, or at home curled up on a couch with her two children and husband, binge watching Marvel movies.

Authorjldrake.com

Books by J.L. Drake

Broken
Shattered
Mended
Honor
Escape
Trigger
Demons
Unleashed
Freedom
Omertà
Courage
Darkness Lurks
Darkness Follows
Darkness Falls
Behind My Words
Christmas at the Cabin
All In
Quiet Wealth
Quiet Secrets
Quiet Power
Quiet Empire
Shadows
Whiskey
Tango
Alpha

When Two Worlds Collide

When two authors become so close, their fictional stories sometimes cross over, making their worlds collide.

Wide-release author J.L. Drake crosses worlds with KU author Vivian Fiano, merging a mafia boss with an obsessive stalker.

You just met Cavaliere Bianco, the obsessive stalker who will stop at nothing to get the woman he wants. To read more about his story and those who are caught in his crossfire, check out Seductive Prey, book 1 of The Relentless Trilogy.

Seductive Prey
Graceful Abduction
Delicate Recovery